Cat Got
Your Tongs

Books by Victoria Hamilton

Lady Anne Addison Mysteries

Lady Anne and the Howl in the Dark
Revenge of the Barbary Ghost
Curse of the Gypsy
Lady Anne and the Menacing Mystic
Lady Anne and the Haunted Schoolgirl

Vintage Kitchen Mysteries

A Deadly Grind
Bowled Over
Freezer I'll Shoot
No Mallets Intended
White Colander Crime
Leave It to Cleaver
No Grater Danger
Breaking the Mould
Cast Iron Alibi
A Calculated Whisk
Sieve and Let Die
Cat Got Your Tongs

Merry Muffin Mysteries

Bran New Death
Muffin But Murder
Death of an English Muffin
Much Ado About Muffin
Muffin to Fear
Muffin But Trouble
Double or Muffin

A Gentlewoman's Guide to Murder Mysteries

A Gentlewoman's Guide to Murder
Some Touch of Madness

Cat Got
Your Tongs

Victoria Hamilton

BEYOND THE PAGE
PUBLISHING

Got Your Tongs
Victoria Hamilton
Beyond the Page Books
are published by
Beyond the Page Publishing
www.beyondthepagepub.com

ISBN: 978-1-966322-04-7

This book is dedicated to the memory of my beloved late sister, Mickey Simpson, and the cats we shared/co-owned over the years. Here's to Puttin and Morris, Noël and Mats, Benny and BooBoo, and the current pair, Poodle and Jimmy. Mick and I shared many things — a love of music and writing and books, and yes, cats — and I miss her more than I can express in flimsy words.

She burned bright, but her luminous flame flickered out too soon.

Cast of Characters

in the Vintage Kitchen Mystery Series:

Jaymie Leighton Müller: wife, stepmom and collector of all things vintage kitchen-y!

Jakob Müller: her husband, dad to Jocie, Christmas tree farmer and junk store owner

Jocie Müller: *little* little person (as she says!) and happy daughter to Jakob and Jaymie

Becca Brevard: Jaymie's bossy older sister and co-owner of QFA (Queensville Fine Antiques)

Valetta Nibley: pharmacist and Jaymie's best friend

Brock Nibley: Valetta's older brother

Mrs. Martha Stubbs: Jaymie's elderly friend and confidante

Heidi Lockland: Jaymie's friend

Bernie Jenkins: Jaymie's friend and a police officer

Lois and Morgan Perry: Aunt and niece, friends of Jaymie's; Lois has been supporting a feral cat colony

Hoppy: Jaymie's Yorkie-Poo

Lilibet: Jocie's tabby

Cast of Characters

in *Cat Got Your Tongs*:

Bog and Duckie Brewer: aging British rocker and his wife, newly transplanted to Queensville
George Hellman: caretaker for the Winding Woods feral cat colony
Parker Hellman: George's ne'er-do-well nephew
Quinley "Quin" Gustafson: Morgan Perry's new friend
Dr. Dak Kasimo: veterinarian looking after the cat colony residents
Ethan Zarcone: Morgan Perry's love interest
Gabriella Zarcone: Ethan's mother
Olivia, Matt and Luke Zarcone: Ethan's siblings
Tolly and Judy Jones: aging British rocker and his wife
Fitzroy "Fitz" Jones: Tolly's brother
Detective Rodriguez: police detective
Rachel Kimball: Jaymie's college friend who now runs Tansy's Tarts on Heartbreak Island
Chief Ledbetter: Former chief of local police and Jaymie's friend

∅ Prologue ∅

WORST JANUARY ON RECORD, SO FRICKIN' COLD! Anxious and tired, Parker Hellman paced back and forth on the shore of the American side of Heartbreak Island, huddled in his parka, blowing on his hands to warm them as his footsteps crunched through a thin crust of ice on the gravel. The island was divided in half by a canal, the eastern side officially part of Johnsonville, Ontario, Canada, the western half part of Queensville, Michigan. Another few days of this frigid weather and the St. Clair River might ice up completely, and then business would be done until it thawed. It was almost pitch dark at midnight, but lights along the empty patio of the Ice House restaurant illuminated the icy beach with a pale glow. The restaurant's inside lights were dim, as befit a bar, obscured too by the drawn blinds. Still, Parker could hear the muffled voices of the patrons, alcohol making the party peppier.

His date was there, waiting for him to show. He said he'd meet her at midnight for a drink, and it was almost that now. Damn! He was gonna be late, and she was an on-time kind of girl. Would she wait for him? He hoped so.

The faint sound of stealthy footsteps crunching across frozen beach gravel reached him. His senses tingled; trouble or money?

A faint hoot, the agreed-upon signal, was given as the guy came closer, uneven footsteps slow and uncertain. Money; good thing, at least in the short term. He had a feeling in his gut that this dude was bad news, a sign that something hinky was going on. The others who had arrived in Wolverhampton earlier in January showed up on their choppers, but this guy? He didn't want anyone to know he was coming, which was why he was slipping over the border in secret.

Uneasy, Parker wondered why the mystery, but he couldn't pass up the extravagant amount of money he'd been offered. He might need it if he had to go into hiding, as those tingling senses insisted. His buddy was trying to get them involved in what he referred to as a business opportunity, but it felt shady. He was in too deep. *They* were in too deep. But he'd never let a pal down. If he had any code in life, that was it.

He paused and listened, calming his breathing. Was the guy coming? Yes, he could still hear the tentative crunch of feet approaching, but man, was he *slow*. Parker shifted from foot to foot and gave that soft hoot again, an affirmation that he was there and waiting for his client.

Pfft. *Client!* Another human to be smuggled across the border. This was his last ferry trip for a while, Parker vowed, though he had made similar promises to himself in the past and always broke them. His stomach churned constantly with worry about the guys they were dealing with. Buckets of money wouldn't help him if he was in jail.

Or at the bottom of the St. Clair River.

He was getting too old for this crap and he'd made promises. Why did those promises matter to him now? He'd never met a woman like the one who awaited him in the Ice House. He had an uneasy sense that his lifelong passion for doing whatever he wanted whenever he wanted to was waning. He was rethinking his dedication to what she called *hedonism*.

Hedonism. He'd looked it up. It meant the unchecked pursuit of pleasure for pleasure's sake. She was against it. She had goals that went beyond herself to community, she said. Life was about more than what we got out of it; it was about what we gave. He had nodded and made vague noises, but it made him think. That's what you got for dating smart women; they made you think about things, serious things.

Things like looking out for others, for the community. Uneasily he was aware that smuggling bad dudes over the border was the opposite of looking out for others, but he had committed to this and had to go through with it. Saying no now would be suicide.

However, he and his business partner-slash-friend were gonna have a conversation after this deal was over. What would he do if he didn't do this, though? What had following rules ever got him but crappy jobs literally cleaning up other people's crap?

He hooted again, and the answer came, sounding ragged and winded. Waiting was getting as old as his passenger. His nerves jangled. He sure hoped this wasn't a trap. He paced and peered into the gloom, staying in the shadows. Was there a hammer coming down on him?

Nah, not this time. He'd know if that was happening. He'd feel it in his bones. "Come *on*," he muttered impatiently. Old people like this guy and his uncle George were the worst. Their generation had it easy. They had forgotten what it was like to be young and trying to get somewhere. His heart thudded. He wasn't *that* young anymore, though.

Jittery, he decided it might be time to take off for a few days, or maybe a week. Something was up, and he didn't quite know what it was. He wished his buddy would tell him more about their plans. He was too closemouthed, like he didn't trust one to keep their trap shut, even Parker, who was in the awkward position, right now, of doing what he was told, like bringing this passenger over to Queensville.

Ah, finally! Here he came, an old man trudging along the poorly lit beach, the scarlet of his coat barely visible. "You got the money?" Parker asked the approaching form.

His passenger, who had slipped around the shore from the Canadian side of the island, handed him a packet.

"American cash? The whole amount?"

The old dude grunted in assent, his face gaunt, expression weary, long hair whipping in the stiff breeze. "Can we get a move on?" he hissed. "I'm freezing me arse off."

Parker opened the envelope and counted the cash. It was all there. "Okay, get in," he muttered, pointing to the small twelve-foot Sun Dolphin boat that was pulled up on the icy shore. His passenger clambered in awkwardly, almost taking a spill. Geez! Last thing he needed was the old guy breaking a hip. Once his passenger was on board, Parker pushed into the water and hopped into the boat as it skidded forward. He engaged the almost silent trolling motor into position and turned it on. They were heading toward the American shore, but first he turned upstream, the soft purr of the motor taking them away from Heartbreak Island.

The guy's cell phone jangled. He answered it, and a tense, muttered conversation followed. Whoever he was talking to, that guy better get his butt in gear and do as he was told because Old Dude was salty to the max. He hung up and looked around, frowning.

"Where we goin'? This ain't the right way," his passenger bleated, shivering in the icy breeze. He clutched on to the edge of the boat, his quivering not all from the cold, having finally figured out they were not heading to the lights of the marina, but away from them. Dimly lit by Parker's flashlight, his expression was fearful. Maybe he was afraid of boats. "Are you barmy? Yer s'posed ta take me ta Queensville."

"I can't take you straight to the marina or every security camera will catch me delivering you. We're going to a little spot I know upstream where you can go ashore."

"I ain't illegal, y'know, just don't like anyone knowin' my business."

"Taking you across the border this way *is* illegal. I'm not taking chances."

"How far is it from town, where yer droppin' me?"

"Walking distance," Parker assured him, but then wondered, *was* it walking distance, in the bitter cold, for this dude? He stole a look at him but could only see a skinny shadow. "You'll make it. Don't worry."

"But I don't know me bloody way!"

"It's easy, I told you. Everything you need is in a locked bin at the top of the path, including a map."

"Bloody Yank wanker," he raged. "You never said you were delivering me to the middle of bleedin' nowhere."

Parker rolled his eyes. His passenger could call a car service if he was too tired. "About the locked bin; I'll give you the key, but remember to leave it on the little ledge inside the bin—I'll get it later—and then lock the padlock again before you go."

"This weren't the bleedin' agreement," the passenger grumbled again.

"Too bad. You're in my boat now, and you'll get out when I say."

"You oughter watch 'ow you talk to me, you cow-brained clot."

Parker shuddered but kept up the bravado. "Do you want to get to shore?"

His passenger, hanging on to the side of the small boat, which chugged and rocked as it wove past a clump of drifting ice, growled but said, "All right, all right. Anythin' else I oughter know?"

"Ignore the cats."

"Cats?"

"Cats," Parker said. "This time of night they'll probably be sleeping, but the damn things are always there. I hate the little sneaks. Those eyes glowing in the dark freak me out. I feel like they're watching me." He eyed the shore, spotting a particular house on the rise above that had a constant light in the uppermost story. He turned the boat and revved the trolling motor as they headed to the riverbank. He killed it at the last minute, letting the boat glide forward and make a *shush* sound on the gravelly bank.

"Get me offa this effin' boat," his passenger grunted.

Parker helped his unsteady passenger ashore and tossed him his duffel bag, then handed him a flashlight. "There's a trail. Use the flashlight to find it, but don't keep shining it around, okay? You'll attract attention. Climb up that slope. That's where you'll find the locked wooden bin. Remember to lock it after, okay? If you see me around town, pretend you don't know me."

"Same."

"I've forgotten your face already. I gotta go. I'm expected back on the island."

⚥ **One** ⚥

TONGS FOR THE MEMORIES . . .

Why could she only think in puns lately? Jaymie Müller wondered as she snapped a set of pretty silver Georgian tongs with one flat side and one with finger-like claws. *Silly Love Tongs.* Argh! Maybe it was because she had a ten-year-old stepdaughter, Jocie, and puns flew at the breakfast table, dinner table and everywhere between. *Snap snap snap* with the silver tongs!

"Don't abuse those!" Becca complained, looking up from her laptop. She sat on a high stool at the cash desk of her store, Queensville Fine Antiques. "You're supposed to be arranging the display case, not getting fingerprints all over the goods."

Jaymie snapped them in Becca's face. "Stay silent so I can ask *cat got your tongs?*"

"You are nuts!" Becca said, bursting into laughter. She closed the laptop and slid it under the sales desk. "You've been spending too much time with Jocie."

"*Tongs of Innocence, Tongs of Experience* . . . whoops! My English major is leaking out." When was the last time she had thought of Blake's poetry? Probably her last university English Lit final. "Why is it tongs and not tong?" Jaymie wondered aloud, brandishing the silver implement like a sword. It flashed in a brilliant pin spotlight. "And what do you call two of these? I mean, two tongs?"

"Two *pair* of tongs," Georgina said, having overheard Jaymie as she trotted in the front door from a lunch date at the Queensville Inn. "Bloody awful out there," she complained.

"It's March, in Michigan," Jaymie replied. "We go from shorts and T-shirt weather to a blizzard in five seconds. Remember that warm spell in February? We're lucky we had it, or the river and lakes would be completely iced up."

Georgina stomped her booted feet and unbuttoned her coat. She paused and wavered slightly in place, then straightened her back, squared her shoulders and went on, her voice frosty: "About the tongs; it is like two *pair* of pants or two *pair* of scissors. If you were an English major, surely you'd know that."

"That's my cue to get out of here," Jaymie muttered to her sister. She used a cloth to wipe her fingerprints off, then set the silver tongs in the display case, locked it up, and headed for the coatrack. "Catch you later?" She was going over to the Queensville home she co-owned with Becca to sort through some of her kitchen collection seeking vintage tongs for her historic house display. In the boxes and boxes and *boxes* of vintage kitchen stuff she had stored in the Queensville house attic and basement and storage room there were bound to be several pair. Whether they would be suitable or interesting was another matter entirely.

They were in the middle of a cold snap, so she retrieved her coat, mittens, scarf and slipped on her boots, escaping as quickly as possible into the chill. If she lingered too long, Becca would surely gripe about those boxes of vintage kitchen stuff. It was taking over the Queensville house, her elder sister complained. There would be no room for humans soon if Jaymie kept up her collecting.

She strode down the walk toward the town center. From there she'd thread through the streets toward the house. Because she was trying to walk more, she had left her new-to-her SUV at the Queensville house; it replaced the last one that had been wrecked.

Her thoughts circled back to the problem of too much vintage kitchen stuff. The massive collection *was* getting out of hand. *It's all Jakob's fault*, Jaymie thought, grinning at the notion of blaming the ballooning collection on her hubby. There was some truth in it. It was at his store, The Junk Stops Here, that she found many of the irresistible vintage kitchen tools, bowls and etcetera that sang her the siren song that all collectors heed. She should not be her husband's best customer, though. That was on her.

She heaved a sigh and stuck her hands in her pockets as she slowed her stride to pick her way down the icy sidewalk. Valetta Nibley, her best friend and confidante, was in the same predicament. Her love of mid-century kitsch was getting out of hand. Becca had hinted more than once that Val would have to move out of her house soon if her collection increased at the current rate. The joy of collecting would soon be dimmed, Jaymie feared. They would both have to stop.

What to do with it all? It was mostly stored in boxes, and that wasn't ideal. She sighed again, and her breath came out in a crystalline puff. Her cell phone buzzed. It was Mrs. Stubbs, her old friend and frequent co-investigator. There wasn't anything in Queensville that the woman didn't know or remember or couldn't find out in her vast village acquaintance.

"Jaymie, are you there?" she shouted.

"I'm here!" Jaymie replied, holding the phone away from her ear an inch.

"I have a problem and need your help."

Her cousin, Miss Lois Perry, supported a feral and stray cat colony in the Winding Woods neighborhood of Queensville, Mrs. Stubbs explained. That was a tonier part of the town on a bluff overlooking the St. Clair River. The various felines had, Mrs. Stubbs said, mostly been neutered and given shots in a TNR (trap, neuter, return) program, which ensured the health of the cats and also that they would create no more unwanted litters of kittens.

But the overseers of the colony, George Hellman and Bonnie Smith, would be away for the rest of March and into April, Mrs. Stubbs said. Lois, who contributed money to the feeding and care of the cats, had promised to find someone reliable to feed the colony while they were gone.

Jaymie bit her lip; a request was on its way, she was sure of it.

The colony caretakers did the feeding twice a day. Food and water must be provided regularly, especially in such cold weather. Lois, in her nineties, couldn't do it, and Lois's niece, Morgan, was laid up with a sprained ankle. It would be unsafe for her to stroll along the bluff to the cat colony with bags of food. She couldn't even drive yet on her own and needed a lift everywhere.

Lois was at her wits' end, so Mrs. Stubbs had promised to help find someone. "Do you know anyone who could help? Maybe some enterprising young person?" She paused, waiting.

Jaymie sighed. Life was busy busy busy. But then she thought of those cats, in wet, blustery, icy March. The wind was cold coming off the river. A kind animal lover was looking out for them the rest of the year, they just needed a little help for the short term.

And Jocie would adore it.

"We'll be going away late in March for spring break, but until then I'd *love* to help," Jaymie said.

And that was her first mistake.

• • •

Jaymie checked the storage boxes at the Queensville house for tongs, sighed over the boxes and boxes of kitchen stuff she had no use for but could not bear to get rid of, and set aside a few interesting pairs. Who knew there were so many types? She had forgotten half of what she had, but there were tongs for salad, cake, sugar cubes and to use at a buffet. There was a pair shaped like chicken feet, and a long pair she thought might be meant to move coals in a fireplace. *Tongs for everything. Tongs a million.*

Stupid puns again! Argh!

Done for the moment, and with the boxes back on shelves in the basement, she sat down at the table in the kitchen and called Miss Perry. Mrs. Stubbs had already called her cousin to say that Jaymie was taking on the task.

"If you're free, come over now and you can meet George Hellman," Miss Perry said. "He'll be relieved we have someone to take care of it. He's here now, feeding and tidying. Come right away." She hung up.

Command performance. Okey dokey.

• • •

The new SUV purred and she enjoyed driving it through Queensville, past the Queensville Inn to River Road, which gently ascended from the village to a wooded prominence that overlooked the river. River Road moved away from the waterway briefly, circling around an enclave of historic, stately homes, most concealed from each other by bends, turns and trees. After curving around the Winding Woods neighborhood, River Road resumed its track along the St. Clair and descended to less lofty heights.

The best view of the river was commanded by Nutmeg Palace, Miss Perry's large, intricately painted Queen Anne, which was stately in its regal splendor and isolation. From the upstairs one could look out over the river and to Heartbreak Island. When the Queensville Heritage Society had first started searching for a house to buy and convert to a historic home attraction, they had considered one in Winding Woods, but the homes, most over a hundred and thirty years old, were out of the society's price range, every single one elegantly outfitted and perfectly preserved, like wealthy dowagers with precise surgical face-lifts every half century or so. Because of the heavy woods surrounding it, only the widow's walk and turret rooms were visible until one rounded the bend of Winding Woods Lane, the great loop off of River Road that was the highest and furthest point of Winding Woods, with Laurel and Linden Streets the only others in the enclave.

Miss Perry's neighbors were Haskell Lockland, president of the historic society, to her south and the Zanes to the north. Or . . . maybe not the Zanes. She recalled hearing that the couple had sold the house and retired to live full-time on Heartbreak Island. Jaymie rang the bell and Miss Perry tottered as she swung it open.

"Follow me!" she said, waving her cane. "Don't take off your boots. You'll need them." She stumped through the house with Jaymie who, after stamping the snow and grit off her feet, trailed her to the back door. Miss Perry wobbled out to the patio. "George! *George!*" she shouted, the bitter wind catching her voice and whipping it off toward the river.

Jaymie peered out and searched the distant bluffs over the river, noticing in the distance an older man stooped over a small wooden structure. "Is that Mr. Hellman?" She pointed.

"It is. Why can't he hear me?"

"The wind carries your voice away. I'll go out and meet him."

"You do that, dear, but don't call him Mr. Hellman. He'll laugh in your face. Call him George. Bring him back here for a cup of tea and you can get acquainted."

Jaymie strode out into the wind, along a snowy path cut between drifted snowbanks. She turned in a circle, examining the other houses, or what she could see of them, from the back. They fronted on Winding Woods Lane. There was Haskell Lockland's, or what little she could see of it, the second floor above the hedge that divided the properties. A path sloped from his land to the bluff. The most prominent feature of his house was the second-floor glassed office, with probably the best Queensville view of the river. A bright light glowed in the glass-enclosed room. Lockland was house-proud, especially of his gorgeous office, so the light was never turned off. He wanted others to admire his home, even from a distance. His property was fenced on the other side of the hedge to keep out the riffraff.

The former Zane property was to the north of Miss Perry's, but Jaymie couldn't see that at all from the back, as it was concealed by Miss Perry's home and the high hedge, and by the fact that Winding Woods Lane curved away past the elderly woman's home. Her property was the largest of the three, though her house wasn't. Once one got to the bluff overlooking the river, the former Zane property came into view.

She headed toward the bluff, part of which was public property, though other portions were owned by the homeowners. There had been quarrels over walkers using the paths to cross private land, but for the most part locals were okay with it. Jaymie examined the cat colony buildings, a collection of shelters with several cats huddled inside them, perched on top, and a few winding around the man's legs. He straightened and watched as she approached.

"Hi, my name is Jaymie Leighton Müller," she said, but didn't stick out her mittened hand. His work-gloved hands were full, with a stack of blankets under one arm and a big plastic tub of food in the other. "I'm a friend of Miss Perry. I understand you need a helper to look after the colony while you're away?"

He nodded and eyed her, his eyes the pale blue of the wintry sky, his hair tufts of white sticking out from under a gray knitted watch cap.

When he didn't respond, she said, "Would you introduce me to your friends?"

He nodded again, but she had the impression he didn't trust her, and she wondered why. It hadn't occurred to her that she'd be there on trial, but clearly, she was. Most of the cats watched them warily, but a couple still wound around his legs. She crouched and one that had been watching from a distance, a little calico with one ear notched, approached and sniffed her outstretched hand.

"Sadie likes you," he said, his voice creaky. "You don't even have a treat. Me, she won't come near, but she likes you."

"Maybe she smells my daughter's little female cat."

"You got a cat?"

She nodded, sitting down cross-legged in the snow and letting Sadie sniff her all over. "I have a three-legged Yorkie Poo named

Hoppy, and my daughter's cat Lilibet." Sadie climbed into her lap and Jaymie smiled, stroking her head with a light touch, happy when Sadie head-butted her hand. "Aw, you sweet thing!" she cooed, cradling her. She picked her up and unbuttoned the top button of her coat, tucking the little cat inside, where it squirmed, but then settled.

That was enough for Hellman, who nodded in approval. He grinned a gappy smile. "Mebbe she don't like men. S'pose that could be. Glad we got someone to fill in. Thought I was gonna have to cancel my trip."

Jaymie stood, but the movement scared Sadie. She squirmed and struggled until she was out of bondage and leaped away, joining her cat friends.

"Bonnie Smith and me, we take care of the colony."

"I know her." Bonnie had recently shuttered her knitting shop for good after a huge December and January sell-off of her goods. No one had wanted to buy the establishment, so it was up in the air what the Knit Knack Shack would become.

"Which is why we don't have anyone to look after the colony while I'm gone. Bonnie's already most of the time in Florida. That there is Purl," he said, pointing to an all-white cat and spelling her name out for Jaymie. "Can't spell it P-e-a-r-l, no, that won't do for Bonnie, it's gotta be P-u-r-l. That there is Aran," he said, spelling that out too as he pointed to a skinny plain gray unaltered male. "Gotta get him fixed if we can catch hold of him. And that fella is Clark Cable," he said, pointing to a handsome, aloof tabby.

"Gable?"

"Nope. Cable. Some kind of knitting joke."

"Oh! That's why *Aran* is spelled the way it is. That's a knitting stitch too."

"And then there's Fluffernutter," he said, pointing to a brown and white fluffy cat by two gingers. "Next to him is Jammy and Marmalade, the dark ginger and the lighter one." He squinted and pointed to a chocolate point Siamese who was next to a big, fat varicolored cat. "That's PB—Peanut Butter, ya know, the brown Siamese—and PoBoy, the tortie."

"I thought all torties were female?"

"He's a rare 'un . . . one in three thousand, so I've heard it said."

She eyed him. "And *you* named *these* ones, right?"

He chuckled. "You caught on, huh?"

"You must like sandwiches and sandwich spreads. I'll try to remember their names."

"Oh, you're not gonna. There are others that aren't around right now."

"I can solve the memory dilemma," Jaymie said, and used her cell phone to take pictures of the skittish cats, labeling each one with the names she remembered, asking George when she got confused. "And of course, my darling little Sadie," she said, taking a snap of the little female who again wound around her legs. "She must have been named before the themes?"

"Nope. She had a collar on her when we found her, with the name Sadie on it."

"Aw, doesn't she have a family, then?"

"No one has claimed her. We had her scanned but she's not chipped. We tried to find her family, but no luck. We'll keep trying."

Jaymie straightened and glanced around. "Last I remember, none of this was here," she said, taking in the feeding stations, shelters, and the latched storage box. "There was one stray, I seem to remember from when I helped Miss Perry out a couple of years ago, when she had some trouble."

"Ah, that was *you*! I remember hearing about that. One became a whole lot more. Me and Bonnie started this up two winters ago. Coupla cats hung around people's doors. Miss Perry worried about them." He glared darkly at the row of houses that followed Winding Woods Lane, some visible, some indicated only by hedges and shrubs. "Not all the folks hereabouts have taken to it. We've had some trouble."

"I'm sorry to hear about it."

"Let's get you trained up."

For the next cold half hour he showed her the locked storage box—a deck box from the marina, perhaps—where he kept the hard food. He inspected the containers to make sure mice had not nibbled through the plastic. They filled large bowls and set them around the colony, then he filled water bowls with a plastic pitcher of water he had brought from home.

There was also a stack of soft, dry blankets and towels. "You take these barbecue tongs, you see," he said, snapping a long metal pair of tongs that he had taken out of the deck box, "and you get right down and pull out the dirty blankets from the shelters." He demonstrated on a nearby shelter, pulling out a dirty, matted cloth that he then deposited in a shopping bag. "And put in fresh ones every coupla days." He grunted with difficulty as he took a clean square of blanket with the tongs and poked it into the shelter. He got back to his feet with a sigh. PB came over immediately and sniffed, then climbed into the shelter and happily kneaded the soft bedding. "Otherwise the blankets get damp and freeze in there." He thrust the shopping bag at her. "You might as well start with the laundry of this and the others."

She took over and did all of the shelters, ending up with a bag jammed full of dirty cloths.

Wet cat food he kept in his car, George said, as he opened some cans and scraped food into bowls. "It freezes up this time of year, if you leave it in the deck box."

This was more involved than she had expected, but it was important for the cats, who crowded around the bowls. Occasional growling and swatting broke the peace, but there was plenty of food for all. "I understand Miss Perry has a heated watering station so they have access to water?"

"Yup. She keeps an eye on things as best she can. She's got a pair o' binoculars that she used to use to watch the goings-on on Heartbreak Island," he said with a chuckle.

"Goings-on?"

"You know, hanky-panky on the beach. She's caught a few things she oughtn't," he said, giving a dark look across the river to Heartbreak Island.

"What do you mean?"

"Some folks don't like to check in at customs, you know? Bring stuff over the border they shouldn't."

"'Stuff'? Like what?"

He shrugged and evaded the question. "She uses the binoculars now to spot when one of the cat crew has a limp, or a sore spot. She can watch the ones we don't see, the shyer ones." He straightened from locking the deck box and took a spare key off his chain. "Now, don't you lose it. I got one master at home, and Bonnie's got one, but

I don't like them floating around, y'know? I worry someone's going to take one of the keys and steal the cat food."

She slipped it on her key chain with freezing fingers that had trouble with the ring.

"Or do something worse," he added grimly, squinting at the deck box.

Worse? Jaymie thought for a moment. "You don't mean someone would tamper with the food, do you?"

"I don't like to think it, but people aren't always what they seem. Some of the nicest hide some dark thoughts." He looked over her shoulder and his mouth twisted in a grimace. "Drat. Here comes trouble."

ఴ **Two** ఴ

JAYMIE TURNED AND SAW A GUY WEARING A RED PARKA, black jeans and an unhappy frown, striding across the hard-packed snow toward them.

"I thought you were going to wait for me!" he yelled. "I *told* you I'd take care of the cats."

George Hellman took a step back. Jaymie, though concerned, held her position.

"Parker, you aren't reliable. I found someone else," George said. "I told you I'd be here at noon and you didn't show up."

"I was busy on my boat!" he exclaimed.

"Yeah, well, Mrs. Müller here is going to help me out."

"I can do it." He turned to Jaymie and held out his hand. "Give me the key. I'll take care of it."

She examined him, from the black knit cap on his head, the red parka with the black patch on the left upper reinforced yoke—a red skull grinned out at her from the patch—to the black jeans and impractical black boots. "I'd *like* to help."

"I *told* him I'd help out while he's gone," he said, dropping his hand. "I was delayed a bit. No big, right?"

George Hellman said, "It's a big deal for the cats if they don't get their chow. 'Specially in this weather. If I miss because of a blizzard, at least I know I put down extra in the morning, or vice versa." He turned to Jaymie. "Keep an eye on the weather. If it looks like there's going to be a storm, leave out extra food, and a big bowl o' chow on Lois's back porch in case you can't get back."

Parker Hellman stared at Jaymie and held out his hand again, snapping his fingers. "I'll take the key. No need for you to worry about it."

She didn't like having fingers snapped at her as if she was a dog refusing to give up a toy. Jaymie glanced at George, who shook his head. She turned back to his nephew and said, "I'm looking forward to doing it, so . . . no."

"Can't count on you, Parker," George said, shaking his gloved finger at his nephew. "Look what happened at Christmas, when I counted on you for the cats."

"That was a mix-up. I told you—"

"Bullfeathers! You didn't feed 'em for days! Dr. Kasimo—that's the vet who takes care of the colony," he explained in an aside to Jaymie— "had to come out here and feed the poor critters 'cause you took off. Good thing Lois noticed and had his number or those poor cats woulda starved to death. He had to come here three days in a row. And what do you do when you finally decide to show up? Start a fight with him."

"I woulda done it!"

"But you *didn't*!"

Cats were slinking away, sensitive to the increasing tension in the dispute. Jaymie didn't like it either.

"It was a mix-up. How many times do I have to tell you that?" The fellow muttered an expletive and whirled, striding away, yelling over his shoulder, "You never did cut me slack. Jeez!" He stomped away like an ill-tempered teen even though he was in his thirties, at least, and a moment later the roar of a motor and squeal of tires on bare pavement echoed and dissipated, leaving an uneasy silence behind.

"A fight with the doctor?" Jaymie said as cats returned to their bowls.

"He started a fistfight with Dr. Kasimo. Lois called the police on Parker, but it ended up the doc is the one who got in trouble, until they sorted it all out."

"What happened?"

"Doc was defending himself, from what Lois says. Parker grabbed him by the coat collar, and when the doc tried to get loose he hit Parker on the chin. My nephew had a cut, so they took Doc into custody. I was so mad. Doc has been good to us and that's the thanks he gets. They sorted it out, but I didn't like it. I haven't talked to Parker much since." George leaned down and gave one last caress to PoBoy, who leaned into it. "We'd best meet up with Lois. She'll have been watching with the binoculars and want to know what gives."

They gathered up the bags of dirty bowls and blankets, Jaymie said goodbye to the cats, especially pretty Sadie, then, as they walked back to Miss Perry's house, she tried to lighten his glum mood. "Some of the cats are friendly."

"A few, but it depends on who's around. They'll scatter if they sense trouble." He glanced over at her. "You got a way with them. None of 'em will come to Parker."

"I notice almost all of them have a notched ear," she said. "Why is that?"

"Tells us at a glance which ones have been fixed. It's done while they're under anesthesia. It heals real quick."

"I see."

"I'll give you Dr. Kasimo's number. He's a good guy. He helps us out with the neutering. We pay as much as we can, but there's never enough money, what with food and shelters."

"He does it for free?"

"It amounts to that, a lot of the time. We're always behind on the vet bill, but it doesn't stop him from doing it. He knows we'll pay him. If there's any of 'em sick or injured, call him."

"How do you decide if you should fix a cat or not? Couldn't one of them belong to somebody?"

"When a new cat joins the colony, we watch him for a while to see if he's a stray or feral." George paused to catch his breath, setting down the bag of dirty bowls he carried. Jaymie picked it up and they walked on, as the older man continued to explain. "If he's unfixed, and he's going to stay with the colony, we trap him, check to see if he's chipped, then we get him shots, neutered, keep him a coupla days with a foster family, then let him back out with the colony, if that's what he wants. If not, if he adjusts to staying inside, we try to find a home for him."

As they reached Miss Perry's back door, Jaymie asked, "What's the difference between feral and str—"

"Come on, you two, get inside out of this cold." Miss Perry was at her back door and she beckoned with a vigorous wave, keeping a shawl wrapped tight around her thin frame. "C'mon in. I've got tea made. Coffee for you, George. And Tansy's tarts for everyone. Jaymie, you'll take one home for that adorable little girl of yours, and one for your hubby too. Let's go sit, and you tell me what that darned Parker wanted."

They deposited the bags of bowls and blankets near the door and shed their coats and boots. Then in Miss Perry's sitting room, a small, dim nook at the back of the house, with bookshelves lining one wall and a big modern TV facing her easy chair, George and Lois commiserated over the difficulties of having a nephew like Parker.

He had been in trouble in the past. "I keep hoping he's tryna go straight. I've bailed him out a couple of times. He owes me." He brooded a moment while he took a deep gulp of coffee. "He keeps saying he's gonna clean up his act, and sometimes I think he means it, then he screws up all over again. You're lucky you got a niece, Lois, and not a nephew."

"I don't know what I'd do without Morgan. She lived here a year or so, but she's moved in with a boyfriend right now."

"That's news to me," Jaymie said. "What's his name?"

"Ethan Zarcone."

"What's he like?"

"I don't know a lot about him," Lois said, exchanging a look with George, who shrugged.

Jaymie, not sure how to follow up on that, changed the subject. "Did I hear that Lan and Phillipa Zane sold their house and moved to their property on the island?"

"They sure did. Thought I'd be glad to see the last of them, but someone bought it to rent out and now instead I've got someone ten times worse over there," Miss Perry said, casting a dark look to the north wall, beyond which were the offending neighbors.

"Who is it and what's wrong with them?"

"Immigrants!" she bellowed, setting her teacup down with a clatter.

Uh-oh. "Uh, where are they from?"

"It's some darned weird Englishman and his bimbo American wife. Not our kind of people at all. Trashy. Fellow wears robes and scarves and long hair and has his nose and eyebrow and who knows what else pierced."

Jaymie snickered. She'd have to meet this guy for sure. "What are their names?"

"Hmmm . . . Bricker? Brewer? Last name is something like that, but all I've heard him called is Bog."

"Bog?" Her eyes widened and she laughed.

Miss Perry stared. "Why is that funny?"

"In British slang, *bog* is another word for the toilet. I can't imagine that's his name."

"That's what his wife calls him. He calls her Duckie."

"Bog and Duckie. I *have* to meet them," Jaymie muttered.

George was silent, having sunk into a blue funk about his nephew. Jaymie, to perk him up and include him in the conversation, reiterated the question she had started to ask earlier. "So, I was about to ask . . . what *is* the difference between a feral and a stray cat? Aren't they the same?"

"Not at all. A stray is a cat that has or had a home," Lois said. "I've always called the cats I fed around here strays, but I was straightened out by Bonnie and George."

"Go ahead, explain the rest, Lois," George said, taking a tart and biting, gooey filling running down his fingers.

Lois handed him a paper napkin. "Strays might be scared of people, but they want to be with them. They'll hang around trying to get into the house," she explained. "A feral cat is wild, probably born wild, or gone that way. Maybe George already told you, but when a stray joins the colony, Bonnie takes a picture and searches missing cat notices on the local internet thingie."

"The Queensville-Wolverhampton community page online," Jaymie said, and Miss Perry nodded.

"I've got several cases of cans of wet food in my car. I can put them in yours, if you like," George said. "And I keep a couple of cat carriers back there too, in case a cat is injured and needs to go to the vet."

Jaymie had taken her notebook from her purse and jotted down everything she'd need to remember. She also got the vet's phone number and home number. "When are you leaving?"

"Sunday afternoon. I'll be coming out here that morning for one last feed and to say goodbye to the kids. That's what I call them, my kids," George said.

Lois smiled. "Sentimental old fool."

Jaymie got ready to go. Once she had the cat carriers and cases of cat food in her SUV, she drove home carefully, eyeing the gloomy sky with trepidation. They had been in a prolonged cold spell that the weather service promised was about to break, but there were no signs of a shift in the temperature yet.

Once back home at their cabin in the country, it was time to organize and pack. Becca and Kevin were returning to her house in Canada for a week to visit with Grandma Leighton, so Jaymie, Jocie and Jakob were staying in the Queensville house for at least the weekend, and maybe the whole week, if Jaymie decided to get ambitious and go through her kitchen collection. There was something about staying in the mellow yellow room of her youth that gave her a lift nowhere else could. Jocie was over the moon, because it meant she was within walking distance of her friends Gemma, Peyton and Noor.

It required planning, because there were not just the humans to consider, but Hoppy and Lilibet too. Hoppy loved the house in town because it meant he could run around outside in the fenced backyard with no leash. Lilibet was not so sure about it, usually spending the first night huddled behind the sofa in the parlor, only tempted out by treats and entreaties.

She picked Jocie up from school, waited until she was buckled into her special seat for her small stature — Jocie was a little person — then pulled out of the parking lot. "Guess what?" she said, flicking a glance at her daughter in the rearview mirror as they drove. "I have a special task to do for a while that you may be able to help me with."

Jocie squinted, skeptical. The last time Jaymie had spoken of a special task she needed help with, it was cleaning out the freezer and washing it thoroughly. The time before that it was cleaning the basement of the Queensville house, a dusty, spooky place with cobwebs. The time before that it was cleaning the cottage on Heartbreak Island, Rosetree Cottage. So much cleaning! She would not be taken in by false brightness. "Is it cleaning a closet? Or the basement again?" she said with a dramatic shudder.

"No, this time you'll actually enjoy it. I'm going to be feeding cats."

"Feeding cats?" Jocie sat up straight with a quizzical expression, her mouth pursed in a pink bow of puzzlement.

Jaymie explained her new task, and by the time they pulled up to the cabin, Jocie was fully on board with helping when she could. More packing and arranging meant it was a frozen pizza kind of night. In the morning they would be moving into town for the weekend.

• • •

Saturday was "moving to Queensville" day. Why did she think this was such a good idea? Jaymie thought, blinking at the bright wintry light filtering in between the curtains. Her cabin bed was so warm and cozy. But Jakob was already up, Jocie was in the shower, and Jaymie needed the coffee she could smell. Badly.

She yawned, stretched and got up, after which it was coffee, feed the animals, walk Hoppy, breakfast, load the car, come back after driving out of the lane to retrieve the litter box, which they had forgotten in the rush, then come back again for Jocie's homework. And finally, in bright but frigid March sunshine, driving into Queensville. Jaymie had Jocie with her in the SUV, but Jakob drove his truck, as he'd need it for work if they stayed past the weekend. They pulled down the back lane that provided parking for all of the Queensville homes along their street and the one that ran parallel one street back, and parked side by side on the parking pad that barely fit the two vehicles.

Trip Findley, their across-the-lane neighbor, greeted them. Jakob waved as he hoisted his and Jaymie's suitcases, carrying Jocie's knapsack as well and shepherding his daughter through the unlatched gate and up the stone path. Jocie awkwardly toted Lilibet's carrier into the house.

Trip was putting down clay kitty litter in his little parking spot off the lane. "What are you folks up to?" he asked as Hoppy danced about at his feet begging for attention.

Jaymie paused from unpacking the back of the SUV and recited their most recent itinerary, then mentioned that to top it all off and add even more to her to-do list, she would be taking care of the cat population up on Winding Woods Lane.

"Hah, Lois roped you in, did she?" Trip said, tossing the plastic scoop into the pail and bending over to scratch Hoppy behind the ears. "I knew she'd trick someone into doing it. She already asked me when she found out George was going away. You *know* I'd do almost anything for Lois or Martha," he said, naming the cousins, "but I draw the line at feeding a bunch of mangy strays. No sir. Don't much like cats. You sure you want to do it?"

"Why?" she asked, watching his face. He knew something.

"Haskell Lockland don't like the cat colony. He's always going out to harass the folks doing the feeding."

"Haskell, harassing someone?"

"That's what I heard."

She wasn't completely unaware. She knew from past conversations that he didn't like stray cats, and probably even less now that there was a whole colony of them practically in his backyard, however . . . "I can't imagine him harassing anyone." Haskell was a gentleman.

Trip shrugged. "Mebbe. Mebbe not. But I heard those cats are kinda wild. Been chasing off the Queensville Walkers . . . you know, the folks that walk the river trail."

Jamey bit her lip, trying not to laugh at the absurd picture of cats chasing hikers across the icy, frozen expanse above the St. Clair. Her experience with the felines had been that they were content to watch from a distance, preferring to stay away from humans. Perhaps the humans who had been chased had been pelting the cats with stones, or something equally unfavorable. Whenever she heard a rumor attached to "someone," it was suspect.

"I met George Hellman. He seems friendly."

"Nice feller," agreed Trip.

"I wasn't fond of his nephew, Parker, though."

Trip darkly said, "That Parker Hellman is a menace."

"In what way?"

"He's had his share of trouble, let's say."

"I heard he got in a physical fight over the cat feeding at Christmas."

"Huh. I wouldn't have said he was the violent sort, more like messing up all the time," Trip said, hefting the container of cat litter. "He messes up then makes excuses."

"I'm only going out to feed the cats once or twice a day. That should be okay, right?"

"Oh, sure. Daylight hours, safe as houses."

"I'm kind of looking forward to it," she admitted.

"Hmph. Watch out for the smugglers!" Trip said, waving his scoop in the air as he let himself back through his wood gate.

"Smugglers? What does that mean, Trip?" Jamie called after him.

A laugh floated over the wood fence, drifting on the frosty air.

He was teasing, something he had delighted in doing to Jaymie when she was a little girl and gullible. He told her once that he used to take girlfriends to watch submarine races along the St. Clair River, something she proudly announced at school to laughter. She rolled her eyes and got a box of food out of the SUV.

Jakob returned and finished unloading the car while Jaymie helped Jocie arrange the pet bowls and set Lilibet's litter box up in the kitchen, while the pet beds were put in the parlor near the fireplace. Both animals would end up in Jocie's room upstairs, but at least they had a choice. Jocie got on the landline—a great novelty for her, to use the phone that had hung on the kitchen wall forever— and called Mia, her new friend, to tell her about the colony cats. Afterward, while Jaymie scanned the contents of the fridge to see what there was for lunch, Jocie plunked down at the kitchen table.

"Mama, who pays for the cat food? And the vet bills?"

"The volunteers that look after them, Miss Perry—you remember Miss Perry?—and George, and Bonnie Smith, though she's not in town much since she closed the store. I know that the vet does the medical stuff for a lower fee, and sometimes for free, Mr. Hellman said."

"But it must be expensive, right?"

"I suppose."

"Mia and I are going to raise some money. We're going to make more bath bombs and sell them to the teachers at school."

"What a good idea!" Jaymie said.

๛ **Three** ๛

JAYMIE LOCKED THE BACK DOOR OF THE QUEENSVILLE HOUSE and put her arm around Jocie's shoulders. There had been a little fresh snow overnight, but Jakob had already shoveled the path to the back parking lane and whisked the powder from her SUV. Sunday had dawned sunny but was again frigid. Her husband was already gone. He had a day and evening planned with one of his brothers and a buddy, a long-postponed birthday party for Helmut, who had been given tickets that included dinner in Detroit, then box seats for a Red Wings game. They might come home that night, or crash at a motel and be back the next day.

Jocie and Jaymie had the day to themselves. First, they were heading out to feed the cats, and then they would attend the heritage society meeting at the historic house. Jocie could have gone to a friend's, but she was too excited about visiting the colony after seeing Jaymie's photo gallery of cats.

They parked in Miss Perry's driveway, where another car sat, melting snow sliding off the roof. As they approached the door it opened and a young woman, slinging her purse over her shoulder, exited. Morgan was at the door. "Hey, Jaymie. This is my friend, Quin . . . Quinley Gustafson. She dropped me off here today. I've got another few days with this danged boot before the doctor says I can drive."

Jaymie greeted the other young woman, who was examining her with a bright smile. She was younger than Morgan or Jaymie, probably in her late twenties, slim, dressed in tight jeans and a blue puffer jacket. Her blonde hair was topped by a pink knit cap with a blue pom-pom. She looked down at Jocie and her eyes widened.

"Aren't you the cutest little munchkin!" she squealed.

Jocie examined her with distrust. "My name is Jocie."

"Aren't you precious!" she said, tweaking Jocie's pudgy cheek. Jocie reared back and glared. "Welp, I gotta scoot," Quin said. "Morgan, hon, I have to go to Wolverhampton to pick up my meds and some test strips. Time to calibrate my monitor. I'll come get you later, okay?" She waggled the cell phone in her hand. "Give me a holler if you need me." She bounced away and got in her car, squealing out and fishtailing on the icy street.

"She seems nice," Jaymie said.

Morgan, leaning on a cane, smiled. "She's been a godsend. So nice to see you, Jaymie! Aunt Lois was saying you might be here today feeding the kitties. Hey, Jocie! Remember me? We met a while back."

"Nice to see you, Miss Morgan," Jocie said politely.

"Is George here yet?" Jaymie asked. "He said he'd be feeding the cats before he left, and I thought I'd trail him one more time."

"He's out there now, if you want to go around the house. Aunt Lois wants you all to come back for tea after you're done."

Jaymie led Jocie around through the gate along the side of Miss Perry's house, kicking away the fluffy new snow as they walked. They cut across the lawn, through the arch, and then out to the open area by the trail that in summer was traipsed by dedicated river hikers. She could see George from a distance, and facing him, Haskell Lockland, clad in his elegant tan Burberry trench coat, which was lined, Jaymie knew — because Haskell made sure everyone saw it — in the iconic plaid sateen. It was too cold for a trench coat. Haskell was shivering, tying his Burberry plaid scarf around his neck more tightly.

"Jaymie, you're here. I hear you've volunteered in this mess," he said with a distinct lack of enthusiasm. "I thought you'd have better sense than to offer to feed these pests."

"They ain't pests!" George stoutly insisted.

"They can't help being homeless," Jocie said, fists on her hips, glaring up at Haskell. "Like people who don't have a home."

Startled, he warily glanced from child to man and back.

"My daughter's right, Haskell. These cats are here because humans failed them."

The man's expression was puzzled, his mouth a round O of confusion. He then said, "I don't think I follow you, Jaymie."

"Humans failed them," she repeated as Jocie took her hand. "Their owners dumped them, or lost track of them, and in some cases didn't neuter them, resulting in litters of feral kittens. They need to eat like my cat and dog at home." She took in a deep breath. "I'd better get a move on to help George. See you at the meeting later."

He nodded but would not be swayed. "I am not hard-hearted, I hope you know that. But these cats are a menace. Something needs to be done about them. They traverse my yard and torment Aloysius."

"What is an Aloysius?" Jocie asked.

He twisted his lips into a smile that didn't reach his eyes. He tried his best, bending over and saying, in a gentler tone, "Aloysius is my purebred Pomeranian. You would love him. He is adorable, and cuddly and friendly." He straightened. "Jaymie, he was badly scratched by one of these mangy beasts."

"Was your dog chasing the cats? They will defend themselves."

"They have no right to be in my backyard. Don't you think my neighbors would complain if Aloysius was wandering their property? And rightly so. It's not fair to my poor little doggie that I must keep him in when one of those cats is in my yard. My yard is fenced. I can't think how they are getting in."

Jaymie bit her lip. "Haskell, you do know that cats can easily climb fences, don't you?" Jocie giggled, but smothered it at a look from Jaymie.

"They can?"

"Of course. The cat probably chased something into your yard. A mouse. Or a rat."

"Or a bird," Haskell said. "You can't tell me that these strays don't kill birds."

Jaymie stayed silent, because he was right. She didn't know what could be done, though. Obvious solutions didn't bear considering.

"Haskell, your mutt would learn his lesson if you let him out and the cats faced him down," George said, tossing his keys in his hand. "Wouldn't kill Aloysius to learn some manners. Every one of these cats has had his shots, y'know." Cats were milling about while some perched on top of the shelters. Others sniffed empty bowls.

"Most of them would run away, Haskell. Cats don't want a fight, not with a dog," Jaymie said. "Sometimes Hoppy goes a little too far with roughhousing and Lilibet scratches him."

"I still say those cats should not be in my yard," Haskell said.

"Betcha your mutt has met a skunk or two," George said, pursuing his point. "I'm right, ain't I?"

Grudgingly, Haskell admitted that Aloysius had been skunked.

"You gonna try to get rid of every skunk, raccoon and possum in the whole state of Michigan?"

"Don't be ridiculous."

"Then why pick on the cats? These cats aren't pets at the moment, and a few were likely born wild like those skunks and possums."

This confrontation was going nowhere, and no one's mind had been changed. Jocie had wandered off and was befriending some of the cats. "Say, Haskell, I understand you've got some new neighbors here," Jaymie said to distract him, pointing toward the house that was to the north of Miss Perry's. Nothing he loved better than gossiping about neighbors.

"*Those* people!" he said, with another harrumph. "The Brewers, Rick and Patty. Rock and rollers. Apparently, he was the bass player of a British group, the Berk Scouse Brothers."

"Hey, I've heard of them," Jaymie said. "A punk group in the eighties. I was told their names were Bog and Duckie, though."

"Ridiculous nicknames. I refuse to call them that. He's as old as I am but dresses in leather pants, long scarves, and an open shirt to show his tattoos. *She* dresses in miniskirts. Too old for that."

"You're never too old to dress how you want," Jaymie replied.

"Hah! Wait'll you see 'em." Haskell whirled and tossed over his shoulder, "I'll see you at the meeting this afternoon, Jaymie. We've got some news you're probably not going to like."

"What does *that* mean?" she called after him, though it was pointless to ask. Haskell gloried in secrets and would not tell more until he had an audience.

George, who had already swept the soft snow away from the shelters and the open feeding area, said he'd show Jocie the ropes while Jaymie went back to her vehicle to get the canned food, which she had forgotten. Ten of the large cans, he told her, for the morning feed. He unlocked the big wooden bin by a bush near the property line and reached into it with the pair of long barbecue tongs, pulling out a bag of kitty treats that was buried in the depths. He gave Jocie a handful of the delicacies, and soon she was swarmed with cats, doling out treats to the friendliest and tossing some to those who wouldn't approach.

Together they fed the felines, and George named those that had been absent the day before as Jaymie took photos. "There's GC, for Grilled Cheese," he said with a chuckle, pointing at a one-eyed marmalade cat. "That's Hoagie," he said, of a matted old gray cat that hungrily wolfed down the soft food. "He's missing a bunch of teeth, so be sure he gets a whole can of food to himself, though he does okay even with the kibble. And that, there, is Reuben."

Reuben was a handsome tom, thick-necked and glowering, his eyes a piercing gold. He hunched at a distance, watching them as Jaymie lifted her phone, zeroed in on him, and snapped a photo, captioning it with his name, as she did with the others. "He won't eat 'til we go," George said. "He needs to be fixed. He's the cause of half the overpopulation, old Romeo that he is."

"Speaking of eating," Jaymie said, "Miss Perry would like us to come back to her place for tea and cookies. Morgan said so."

George picked up the empty cat food cans, tossing them into a bag. "Can't. I gotta get going. I got a long drive ahead and need to get started. I wanted to see the gang before I left." He hurried away, tossing a happy farewell over his shoulder.

Jaymie and Jocie finished up. There was no sign of Sadie, the sweet tortie, but maybe next time, she promised her daughter. As they walked across the snow, being careful not to slip, Jocie said, "Why was Mr. Haskell in such a bad mood? Why doesn't he like the cats?"

Jaymie took a moment to formulate her reply, trying to be fair to everyone. "If one of the cats had scratched Hoppy, I suppose I wouldn't be too happy."

"But you said yourself that Lilibet *has* scratched him before when he got too . . ." She searched for the word Jaymie had used once. "Boisterous. When Hoppy got too boisterous. They have a right to defend themselves, don't they?"

"Sure, honey, but it's complicated."

"That's what grown-ups always say when they don't know how to explain something."

"That doesn't mean it's not true. Life is complicated, Jocie. There is more than one side to a problem. *We* see animals that need to be fed and cared for. I believe that we owe them that. But feral colonies are controversial to some people who think they harbor fleas and mites and other infestations. And some people are upset that the cats kill birds and chipmunks."

"But they used to be kept to kill mice and rats, isn't that so? Luuk says that in medieval Europe, when they got some weird idea about cats being evil and killed a bunch, that's when the plague happened, *maybe* because the cats weren't there to kill the rats that carried the fleas."

"*Luuk* said that?" Luuk was the son of Bram and grandson of Arend and Lise Brouwer, who owned the land across from the Müllers. Bram Brouwer's quiet eleven-year-old son was one of those "still waters run deep" kind of boys, she supposed, but he and Jocie had become friends over the last year.

"He says it might not be true, that it's maybe a story that sounded good, so people spread it. He said people like their history to be neat and make sense, but making sense is what *we* need, not what truth in history needs."

Jaymie's eyes widened. That was a deep statement for an eleven-year-old. Agree with it or not, it was an interesting take on things.

"He likes history and reads a lot. We talk about where we've been. He's been to the Netherlands, and I've been to Poland. He taught me hello in Dutch, and I taught him hello in Polish."

"Maybe it's true, about the cat population decline being responsible for the plague. I do think I heard that once."

"Mom, cars kill birds all the time. So do windmills. Birds die when they fly into glass buildings in big cities. We don't get rid of *them*, do we? Maybe we should ask people to give up their cars or tall buildings. It's funny that they worry about the birds when it's convenient, but forget about them when it's inconvenient, like when it's about glass windows and cars."

Jaymie bit her lip, trying not to smile. "That is all true. If I get complaints about the feral or stray cats killing birds, I'll remember what you've said."

Inside they took off their boots and coats. Morgan was limping around the kitchen making tea and putting a tray together, wearing an inconvenient but protective walking boot, while Lois watched a game show. Jocie watched TV with Miss Perry while Jaymie helped Morgan in the kitchen.

After chatting about the cats while they waited for the kettle to boil, Jaymie said, "I hear you've moved and have a new boyfriend. How is that going?"

"All right, I guess." The young woman cast a sideways glance at Jaymie. "What has Aunt Lois told you?"

"I heard his name, but that's about it," Jaymie said, remembering the exchange of glances between Lois and George Hellman.

"His name is Ethan Zarcone. We have a little place in Wolverhampton right now. He wants to buy a house together."

Jaymie frowned. "What does he do?"

"He's into investments."

"What does that mean?"

"He invests, I guess. For people," she said with a shrug. "I don't keep tabs on him."

"Where are you working now?"

"I got a job at another car dealership." She had worked at her husband's dealership until he was arrested and they divorced. "That's how I met Quin; she works maintenance at the dealership. Isn't she nice?"

"She is," Jaymie said.

"She's been a doll, taking me all over the place, even out to school. I'm taking night classes some evenings, working toward becoming a radiology technician. I want to work at Wolverhampton General."

"That's exciting, Morgan!" Jaymie exclaimed.

"I need something to look forward to. People have been so nasty."

"Who? And why?"

"*People.* People still act like I was responsible for that trouble with Saunders." She shivered. "I have nightmares of being locked in that car trunk. I don't know how you do it."

"Do what?"

"Investigate." Morgan hesitated. "I'd have nightmares *all* the time."

"Oh, honey, I'm so sorry." She reached out and hugged Morgan, who awkwardly shifted on her booted foot. "I compartmentalize it. I've had a few bad dreams, but having someone to talk to has helped." Jakob was always there for her, even in the middle of the night to soothe nightmares. "I'm sure having a new beau helps?"

She didn't respond except to shake her head. "Anyway, *Ethan!*" she said, false brightness in her tone. "You'll like him." Morgan paused in rummaging for teabags and glanced over at Jaymie, her expression darkened. "Please, don't mention him to Auntie Lois. She doesn't like him."

"Why?"

"Because he's friends with Parker Hellman, George's nephew," she replied with an exasperated sigh.

"I met Parker. I wasn't a big fan. Is that all she doesn't like about Ethan?"

With a mulish expression on her pretty face, she slammed down the teabag container and glared at Jaymie. "Ethan's a . . . he's a good guy. He's . . . he's misunderstood."

Jaymie frowned. Why did she stammer?

"Why don't people believe I know what I'm doing with my life?"

"Morgan, I didn't say you didn't know what you were doing with your life," Jaymie replied gently. She let a moment pass and the young woman calmed. "Investing; it sounds so vague. Does Ethan actually work?" She took cookies out of a plastic tub and arranged them on a plate.

Morgan poured boiling water into the teapot and got down an acrylic cup from the cupboard. "He's between nine-to-five jobs right now."

"What kind of job would he apply for?"

"I don't know." She glanced at Jaymie and shrugged. "He's trying to get this investment business off the ground, I guess. I try not to tell him what to do. Guys don't like that."

She hadn't suggested Morgan tell him what to do, but it was an interesting shift.

"What does Jocie like to drink? Is milk okay?"

"Sure. Especially since there are cookies. Let me carry the tray and you go in and sit, put up your poor foot!" She realized Morgan hadn't yet told her how she was injured. Jaymie carried the tray into the sitting room. Jocie was sitting on the floor in front of the TV as it wailed and flashed in the background, game show chatter about *a new car* and *a home spa*! All shouted in very *excited tones*!

"How did you hurt your foot?" Jaymie asked as Morgan rested the boot on a footstool.

Miss Perry, alert and focused, said, her tone insinuating, "Yes,

Morgan, why don't you tell Jaymie how you hurt your foot?"

Slewing her gaze between the great-aunt and niece, Jaymie sensed discord. What was going on? As Morgan had complained, Miss Perry did *not* like Ethan, but she had a feeling it had little to do with Parker Hellman.

Morgan sighed. "It was an accident. I fell out of the car."

"You *fell* out of the car?" Jaymie, eyes wide, stared at her. "Whose car? Were you driving? How fast were you going? How did *that* happen?"

"It's my own fault," she said. "We were arguing—"

"Morgan and Ethan were arguing in a moving vehicle," Miss Perry said.

"I made a stupid threat, so he leaned over me and opened my door."

"While it was *moving*?" Jaymie said. Miss Perry's antipathy for Ethan was beginning to make sense. "Didn't you have your seat belt on?"

Morgan sighed and her eyes teared up. She looked away, biting her lip until it was red. Jaymie glanced at Jocie. Maybe this was too intense a conversation for her daughter.

"I shouldn't have threatened to leave," Morgan whispered.

"That's why he opened the car door?"

She nodded.

"But how did you fall out of the car?"

"I didn't fall, I *jumped*."

"You jumped?" Jaymie didn't believe her. It made no sense.

"It was my own fault, I told you." Her manner brooked no argument. "Moving on, what are you ladies doing with the rest of your day?" Her bright tone was forced, but relentless.

"We're going to the historic society meeting out at the heritage house this afternoon," Jaymie said, following the change of subject Morgan clearly wanted.

The young woman's story was odd, and Jaymie didn't believe it. But it was not her business, when it came right down to it. Besides, this was neither the time nor the place to dig deeper, not with Jocie there. Mrs. Stubbs often used an old expression: little pitchers have big ears. Jocie had a certain tilt to her head that led Jaymie to believe that was true in this instance.

"That's nice," Morgan said absently, stirring a packet of sweetener into her tea, clanking her spoon in the mug.

"We're looking forward to feeding the cats, Miss Perry," Jaymie said.

"I'm relieved someone reliable is doing it," she said, casting a glance at Morgan. "Parker swore up and down he'd take care of it for George, but I wouldn't trust that boy as far as I could throw him."

"I'm not a big fan of his either," Morgan said in a stilted tone. "He gets Ethan into all kinds of trouble."

Miss Perry rolled her eyes.

"George told me that Parker was supposed to do it once before when he was away, but he forgot, or misunderstood," Jaymie said. "I guess you had to call the vet, Miss Perry? George was not happy with his nephew." She didn't mention the physical altercation that had apparently resulted from it.

"Parker tries to say he only missed one day, but he hadn't been there for three days, and I was getting frantic. That was Christmas and you were away, Morgan." Miss Perry fussed with her cookie, which was crumbling in her lap.

"How do you know he wasn't there for three days?" Morgan asked.

"I watched for him. Those poor cats were coming right up to my door, the bold ones, anyway. I fed the ones I could and finally phoned the vet to help out." Miss Perry carefully wet her finger and picked up the crumbs bit by bit, licking the tidbits off her fingers. "There sure have been odd goings-on lately out on that river, I'll tell you that," she said, finally brushing her hands and folding her paper napkin. "I see lots out there at night."

Jocie swiveled and took another cookie. "What do you see, Miss Perry? Tell me!"

"Submarine races," Miss Perry said with a gusty chuckle. She dropped a wink at Jaymie, who grinned, remembering Trip and his tales.

"What are you doing looking out there at night?" Morgan said, her brow wrinkled. "Aunt Lois, maybe that's not a good idea."

"Why?"

"Someone may think you're snoopy."

"I *am* snoopy! At my age I'm *expected* to be snoopy," Lois snapped. "It's the code of old people. Young folks don't know it, but once you reach eighty they sit you down and make you sign a pledge to snoop into everyone else's business, and then they issue you your binoculars and a notebook to write it all down."

Jocie stared up at her wide-eyed, but Miss Perry winked at her. She smiled, but turned her attention back to the TV.

"Remember what happened last time." Morgan referred back to a couple of years before when Miss Perry had almost died at the hands of a killer, who happened to be Morgan's ex-husband.

"Pshaw!" the woman said with a wave of one arthritic hand. "That had nothing to do with my nosiness."

"So, you were telling me the other day about your new neighbors," Jaymie said with a smile. "Bog, the Englishman, of the infamous group Berk Scouse Brothers, and his wife Duckie Brewer?"

"What a pair of whackadoodles!" Miss Perry exclaimed. "He's a lunatic. All alone outside at midnight, braying and laughing like a loonie bird!"

Jaymie cast a glance at Jocie. "It's possible that he was on a cell phone call, Miss Perry."

"Don't spoil my fun!" she retorted. "What have I got if I can't complain about the younger generation?"

Younger generation? From Haskell's observation Bog Brewer must be over sixty.

"No one should keep you from being your own miserable self," Morgan sniped. She bit her lip and her eyes watered. "Sorry, Aunt Lois. My foot is hurting today, but that's no excuse for being snippy." She limped over and placed a gentle kiss on the woman's forehead, one hand on her shoulder. Miss Perry put her hand over her niece's. Something passed between them as Jaymie watched, exchanged worried glances. An undercurrent of some worrisome sort was there.

Jaymie stood and gathered up the cups and plates. "C'mon, kiddo," she said to Jocie. "We have to get going because I have a historic society meeting, and you have to come with me, so let's get a move on!"

⌗ Four ⌗

THE QUEENSVILLE HISTORIC HOUSE WAS IN THE MIDST OF SPRING cleaning, so rugs had been rolled up and a chandelier had been removed for maintenance. Jaymie had, the last couple of times she had come, found it oddly bleak after the glamour of the holiday season. But today it was filled with warmth and people and life, as the largest historic society meeting of the year got underway.

A long table with coffee urns and laden with containers of cookies and squares lined the back wall. Jaymie set her tub of treats on the table. She was experimenting with a vintage recipe she'd found for a no-bake bar made with crushed graham crackers, sweetened condensed milk, and a mixture of maraschino cherries, raisins and other goodies. They were kept chilled. She hoped they didn't warm up too much in the heat of the full house or they would get awfully sticky.

Her friends were there and fawned over Jocie. But the girl sat with her favorite person, Mrs. Stubbs, while Jaymie mingled, trying to get a sense of what Haskell had been hinting at.

She sidled up to Val, who was perusing the treat table. Val was dressed in an A-line jean skirt, sensible shoes, and her favorite sweater, the one Jaymie had given her a couple of Christmases before. She glanced over at Jaymie and pointed at the tub of treats. "Experimenting?"

"I found this recipe in a vintage cookbook and it sounds intriguing. It's going to be my next 'Vintage Eats' column if everyone likes it. Val, I've got a question."

"I knew there was something going on in your brain. What's up?"

Jaymie took her aside from the rapidly filling room to the cool of the kitchen. Mabel Bloomsbury was there filling a tray with cream pitchers and sugar bowls, but she gave Jaymie a sickly smile then hurried out, carrying the tray. "Is Mabel okay?"

Val watched after her. "I don't know. That was weird, right?"

"It *was* weird. She didn't even say hello." Jaymie told Val what Haskell had said about hearing news she wasn't going to like. "Do you know what that's about?"

36

Val shook her head, pushing her glasses up on her nose. "What can he mean?"

"I don't know. It worries me."

The sound of the gavel opening the meeting echoed from the other room, startling her. The conversation would have to wait. They scurried through and took their seats. Petty Welch, who dated Haskell Lockland on and off and had become involved with the historic society because of that, was the recording secretary. She stood at the lectern and read the minutes of the previous monthly meeting of the whole membership, then discussion was opened on the floor. It was mostly about the successes of the holiday fundraiser, Dickens Days. Questions were raised and answered, suggestions were offered and recorded to be discussed. Jaymie was mostly occupied with keeping Jocie from fidgeting in her seat and urging her to stay still. The treasury secretary, Imogene Frump, relayed what profit had been reaped from the December festival, now that accounts had been tallied.

It had been a huge success, as always.

Haskell Lockland took the lectern, cleared his throat, and looked at his fellow board members, who were seated at a table in the front of the room. Jaymie got a bad feeling when Mabel Bloomsbury, red-cheeked, would not meet her gaze. She had been so odd earlier in the kitchen, avoiding her. It occurred to her that the treasury subcommittee had met a week ago. Subcommittee meeting minutes were not read out to the entire membership, though they were printed and available on request. It had to be something to do with the treasury subcommittee, but what?

Haskell again cleared his throat and talked for a while about the important work planned for the Queensville Historic Manor that spring and summer. They were doing a study on Victorian gardening, and the gardening committee had made a proposal to feature Victory Gardens, those staples of the world wars when citizens were encouraged to plant gardens to supplement rations and boost morale. It was a way for folks to get together to trade seeds and share information. He read from notes prepared for him that the committee felt it was a great way to engage the public, with food prices so high and the value of quality vegetables and fruits in the news every day, and they were even considering, on the back acres, having garden plots for Queensville residents to use.

There was general agreement, and volunteers were encouraged to sign up to help with the work.

"Now, on to some difficult decisions those of us who you have voted in have had to make. We are in a state of donor and volunteer fatigue. As much as we'd like to do it all, regarding Queensville history and heritage, we can't. And so the treasury subcommittee has come to the difficult and even, some may say" — he said, casting a glance at a teary-eyed Mrs. Bellwood — "heartbreaking decision that we can only fund one large event per year, and Dickens Days is it. That means that last year's Tea with the Queen event was our last."

"You can't do that!" Jaymie shouted, jumping to her feet. Tea with the Queen was an annual tea party carried out on the lawn of Stowe House, a historic home in downtown Queensville. It coincided with the Victoria Day holiday weekend celebrated in Ontario and beyond. Locals and tourists alike came, took tea on the lawn, then strolled the town, visiting the shops. "Haskell, people come by the busload from seniors' facilities, nearby historic societies, small towns from Ohio, and over the border. You'll be disappointing so many people. You *can't* cancel the Tea with the Queen event." There were a few scattered *"you go, girl"* and *"yes!"* comments, and even a smattering of applause. "It's a great moneymaker. And it draws a tourist crowd, even more so than the Dickens Days. It signals the launch of the summer tourist season."

Finally Haskell hammered with his gavel. "Jaymie, you can't speak until you are recognized by the chair!"

The meeting devolved, for a few minutes, into chatty factions shouting at each other, with the pro-tea forces arguing vociferously with the anti-tea group.

Hammering again, Haskell told everyone to come to order. "Jaymie, you're simply not right. Dickens Days *far* outearns the Tea with the Queen event."

"Because it's a full month, Haskell. You know that! *And* it's more expensive to run. Tea with the Queen is one long weekend, but on the basis of per-day earnings, I challenge the notion that any single day in the Dickens Days month outearns a day during the tea. Dickens Days as an event is far more costly and comes at a busy time of year for everybody. You all know that," she said, glancing around the room. "It's hard to get enough volunteers every single December."

"Too late, Jaymie," Haskell said, speaking loudly over her final words. "It's been voted on and is settled."

"Actually, Haskell, that's not true according to the society bylaws," Petty said, standing. Jaymie watched her, noting the twinkle in her eye and the quirk of her smile. She caught Jaymie's eye and winked, clearly enjoying contradicting her occasional beau. All eyes were on the petite gray-haired dynamo. She met Jaymie's gaze. "This was a treasury subcommittee vote, but society members are allowed to challenge as long as they have a second."

"I challenge it!" Jaymie said.

Val jumped to her feet and held up her hand. "I second!"

"No point in wasting time, then. We can do a show of hands to take a full membership vote right here and now," Petty calmly said as Haskell shot visual daggers at her. "All in favor of Jaymie's proposal to continue the Tea with the Queen event, show hands."

Many shot up, but was it enough? Jaymie scanned the meeting, then saw Mrs. Bellwood stand.

"Far be it from me to put *my* voice in," she said, in her plummiest Queen Victoria tone, with a malicious glance at Haskell. "But I think the treasury subcommittee ought to be ashamed of itself, voting the event out of existence without even consulting the membership. Shoddily done, sir," she said, pointing at Haskell. "Shoddily done! You bullied people into agreeing, *and* you waited until I was visiting family in Arizona before you did it. *Shame* on you!"

More hands shot up, and there was clapping. Jaymie's eyes watered as the show of hands became a forest of limbs. Jocie was crowing and clapping, as were others.

When it settled down, Mrs. Stubbs said, her clear dry voice cutting, "Haskell, I'd say if you want another term as president, you ought to go along with the masses. You're on shaky ground."

With bad grace Haskell said to Jaymie, "All right, young lady, if you think we ought to continue, I nominate *you* for subcommittee chair to head up the whole event. *Then* we'll see who's right."

"But . . . but that's only two and a half months away!" Jaymie protested.

"*And* we don't even know if Stowe House will be available to use this year," Haskell said with a chilly smile. "So that's yet another problem, but far be it from me to interfere. You go ahead. But you'll have to figure that out first, or an alternative site." His smile died. "And the event had better make *more* money than last year, that's all I can say."

• • •

"What have I gotten myself into?" Jaymie muttered to Val as they perused the treats. Date squares, hmmm. No, she'd already done those in the column. Raisin Squares, Dream Bars, Nut Bread, Mallow Squares . . . nope, nope, nope and nope. She had done them all so far in her column. She wandered past her no-bake fruitcake squares and happily noted the tub was almost empty. That was good.

She turned to her friend, who hadn't answered. Val was staring, perplexed, at Petty, who was smiling up at a younger man, who bent over her talking earnestly. "Who is that guy?" Jaymie asked.

"You don't know him," she said absently.

"Clearly, since I asked who he was. Who is he, and why are you so perturbed by Petty talking to him?" She watched the pair. "*Flirting* with him," she amended, as Haskell eyed the two with distaste.

"His name is Ethan Zarcone."

"Oh! I know the name. You don't look like you approve. What's up?"

Sourly, Val said, "He's a small-time hood, always out for a shortcut or a quick buck. He's been no end of trouble to his family. I ran into his sister Olivia a few days ago. She said her mom is worried that Ethan is spiraling again."

"Spiraling? What did she mean?"

"Olivia said Ethan swears he's gone straight, but that is exactly what he always says when he's heading for the worst trouble."

That was not good, given that Morgan was now dating him. Perhaps she was mistaken. It didn't happen often with Val, but it was possible. "How do you know the family?"

"I babysat the four of them when they were kids and still see

Olivia every once in a while. Ethan always did have a nasty streak a mile wide." She frowned and relented. "I shouldn't say that. When he was little he was not actually nasty, more pushing limits, seeing what he could get away with. And he got away with a *lot*. His mom felt she had to go easy on him because of some health problems. Gabriella worked her butt off her whole life, and still does, according to Olivia."

"He was always trying to get away with stuff, you say," Jaymie mused.

"That's him in a nutshell. I don't imagine he's changed. His type never do."

Jaymie watched Val for a moment, surprised by her remarks, then turned to examine the pair, Petty regarding him with charmed attraction. "I don't know him, but I know *of* him," she said, then filled Val in on her conversation with Morgan and Miss Perry earlier in the day.

"What is he doing here?" Val fretted. "I wouldn't have thought a heritage meeting would be his scene."

"Come with me," she said, threading her arm through Val's. "I want to talk to Petty, thank her for her support. Maybe we can find out what's up."

"You know, if we don't watch it *we're* going to start being called the Snoop Sisters instead of Miss Frump and Mrs. Bellwood."

"Do you care?"

"Nope."

"Neither do I," Jaymie said. She glanced over. Jocie was with Mrs. Stubbs, having an intense conversation, so she led Val as they drifted closer to Petty and Ethan. "Petty!" Jaymie said as they approached. "Sorry to interrupt," she said, glancing at the handsome man with her, then turning back to her friend. "I wanted to thank you for your support. I would be devastated if the Tea with the Queen event was canceled forever."

"I hope it didn't land you in hot water, Jaymie. I know how busy you always are, and now you're saddled with the whole event on such a short timeline. Are you going to be able to do it?"

"She'll have help," Val said. "We're in it together." She turned. "Hey, Ethan, remember me? I babysat you and your siblings when you were a kid."

"Auntie Val," he said with an ingratiating smile. "How could I forget? You were the coolest."

"Was I? I doubt it. That was the summer I was home from pharm school and needed a job. Your brothers and sister were good kids, but what I recall most from that summer was me telling your parents your long list of daily infractions."

He still smiled, but his expression had gone cold. "I'm sorry for what I put you through. I was a bit of a hellion," he admitted with a rueful chuckle.

Petty stroked his arm. "Little boys are scamps."

He smiled down at her. "Shall we go speak with Mr. Lockland? I'm anxious to talk to him about . . . about that project I told you about."

"But he's still talking with that other gentleman."

"I'm sure he won't mind," Ethan said, cupping her elbow and turning her in Haskell's direction. "In fact, I . . . I think I know that fellow and I'm sure he won't mind."

"What project is that?" Val said, brightly, riveting Ethan with her steady gaze. "I'm fascinated. It's to do with Queensville's history, I'm assuming, since you're at a heritage meeting?"

"I'm not quite sure what it is," Petty said, pausing and looking up at Ethan. "What did you say it was? A scheme involving vacant historic homes in Queensville? You were asking if I knew who owned what, and I told you Haskell would be the one who could give you more info on that."

"Let's not bore these ladies with the details," he said.

"I'd love to hear about it," Val claimed. "Do tell, Ethan! Haskell is still busy but he never leaves until the last person is gone. You've got plenty of time. Let us in on the secret!"

Jaymie examined him. He was handsome, with beautiful full lips, a sweep of curly dark hair that drifted over his forehead and long-lashed dark brown eyes topped by thick dark brows, drawn down over his piercing gaze. He could have posed for the statue of David, that cold marble perfection in male form. And yet he was vitally human, not statue-like. There was an endearing sprinkle of light brown freckles over his aquiline nose. She could see the attraction for Morgan because he was exactly the kind of guy *she'd* have fallen for before her marriage to Jakob.

Petty gazed up at him with an infatuated smile, waiting for him to answer Val. For a woman her age and with her levelheadedness to be smitten said something about the guy's charm, but he left Jaymie unimpressed.

He had answered Val, evading specificity, and there was a pause in the conversation. Jaymie said, "Ethan, I'm acquainted with Morgan Perry. I saw her today and she told me that you two are dating."

"We . . . date on occasion," he said easily.

"It sounded more serious than occasional from her. She said you two live together and are going to buy a house together."

His gaze fastened on her and dawning recognition lit his eyes. "Wait, I know who *you* are. You're that chick who solves crimes. Cool." His tone was contemptuous and dismissive. "My buddy Parker said you were taking care of the stray cats up Winding Woods."

"Why would he tell you about that?"

He smiled, a wintry expression. "I've heard you like to stick your nose into other people's business."

Petty pulled away from him and eyed him with dawning wariness. Val smiled, an even colder one than Ethan's, and gave Jaymie an approving look, nodding. Exposing frauds was like catnip to her.

"I'm not nosy, if that's what you're saying. Or maybe I am." Jaymie cocked her head to one side and eyed him. "I don't like people I care about being taken advantage of or hurt." She paused, then said, "That's quite the injury Morgan has. A sprained foot is no joke. Poor girl, limping around with a boot and a cane."

"Oops, my phone's on vibrate and I'm getting a call," he said, feeling his pocket. "I gotta take it. Excuse me, ladies. Petty, I'll catch up with you later." He hastily "answered" his phone and headed toward the door, brushing past Haskell and the gentleman to whom he spoke so keenly.

Petty watched him go, then turned to Val, crossing her arms over her chest. "Okay, Val, what was that all about?"

"He was a little jerk when I knew him as a kid. I'm recalling it all more clearly now. Maybe time softens those memories, but specific instances are coming back. He was not just disrespectful—I could deal with that—but mean, pinching his sister then blaming his younger brother for it, and generally making my day miserable. But when I told his mom about his behavior, she shrugged it off."

"He was so charming," Petty said.

"How did you meet him? And what was he doing *here*?" Val asked her.

"I met him at a local business luncheon I attended for Cynthia and Jewel," she said, referring to the two vintage store owners she worked for. "We talked, and he took me out for coffee. He was charming. He and a partner have a business proposal for the village, something hush-hush about the historic homes that are empty and for sale. You know, Stowe House, and the old Glidden place, and that big house on River Road. I said Haskell Lockland would be the one to talk to, and that the best place to catch up with Haskell was here."

Jaymie eyed her with curiosity. "I don't mean to snoop, Petty, but wouldn't it have been easier to set up a meeting between them?" Petty didn't answer. "Would that have been too awkward? Are you and Haskell not dating?"

"I thought here would be easier. I could introduce them, rather than call Haskell up and ask a favor." She shrugged and met Jaymie's curious gaze. "And no, we're not dating. Haskell's set in his ways. I like life a little more fun, more spontaneous."

Val grinned. "Haskell could never be called spontaneous."

"So Ethan didn't meet Haskell yet tonight," Jaymie said, clarifying.

"No, I was waiting. Haskell's been talking to that fellow for a half an hour." And indeed Haskell still stood talking earnestly to a gentleman in an immaculate navy-blue three-piece suit and red patterned tie with a gold bar clip. The fellow was tall and reed thin, his sparse graying hair swept to one side. As neat as he appeared, his face was haggard, though, lined with a lifetime of hard living, a scar trailing down his cheek. She squinted. It almost looked like he had a tattoo beside one eye, a dagger, perhaps.

"But now Ethan has left," Val pointed out. "So he couldn't have wanted to talk to Haskell *that* badly."

"It's odd." Petty eyed Jaymie. "Tell me about Ethan's relationship with Morgan."

She relayed the little she did know. "Her new friend, Quinley Gustafson, might know more. They seem pretty close. I wonder who that guy is?" Jaymie asked, watching the two men.

"I'll find out." Petty strolled over and joined Haskell. As she did the tall fellow broke away, with a handshake and a nod for Petty. He exited the historic house.

"I'm about done in," Jaymie said. "I think I'll retrieve Jocie and we'll toddle off now."

"I'm sticking around for a few," Val said. "I'll talk to Haskell about the next general election for the leadership of the heritage society."

Jaymie grinned at her friend. "You're not going to threaten him, are you?"

"Not at all. I'm shocked you would say that," she exclaimed, one hand on her sweatered chest. "I am going to remind him, though, of how Mayor Fletcher has always used the Tea with the Queen event in his brochures for Queensville summer tourism. And how many businesses in our town rely on the summer tourist trade. And how many Canadians come over that weekend and stay at the Queensville Inn."

"Go get 'em, tiger!" Jaymie said. "And while you're at it, find out who that was. I'm curious now. A stranger at a heritage meeting? It's odd."

"Will do."

She rounded up Jocie and they descended the steps, following the flagstone walk out to the parking area. She heard loud voices and turned. Ethan was standing by a sedan in conversation with the tall fellow who had been speaking with Haskell. They were not arguing, but there was some disagreement or tension between them. She could tell by the men's stances and expressions. A few words floated on the cold breeze . . . Jaymie cocked her ear, but all she could hear was *"introduced me"* and *"leaving me out in the cold"* from Ethan, whose voice was louder.

Huh. Interesting. They clearly knew each other. So why didn't Ethan go over and join the conversation?

✐ Five ✐

JAKOB HAD COME HOME LATE AND EXHAUSTED, mumbling about leaving the other two guys in Detroit because he didn't want to stay away overnight. He tumbled into bed after a kiss good night. The next morning he arose groggy, but ready to face the busy week ahead. They had decided to stay at the Queensville house for the week, since Jocie was having so much fun being close to her town friends and had a project that she could more easily work on with them from the yellow brick Queen Anne.

Jocie was in school now, ferried there by Peyton's mom, who would then pick up both girls later as they were working on that project together. Jakob was at work, and Jaymie was going to feed the cats. Miss Perry was not home, as Morgan and Quin had taken her to an appointment in Wolverhampton. Jaymie parked in the drive, opened the back and filled a bag with clean bowls, cans of cat food and a few old blankets she was going to put in the shelters. Music blasted but she could hear voices over the racket. It was an unlikely scenario for a frigid weekday in Winding Woods.

As she filled the bag the front door of the former Zane home flung open, and a familiar figure—Ethan Zarcone—raced out, pulling on a dark blue parka as a voice followed him, spewing an almost incomprehensible diatribe laced with obscenities.

"*. . . gormless bloody wanker (incomprehensible) get outta my house before I get the rozzers on yer knicky trail and (expletive) up yer bum, ya (expletive and then incomprehensible.) . . .*"

Zarcone spotted her, but ducked down, pulled his hood over his head, and speed-walked to a shiny black sedan. He got in, slammed the door, then screeched down the road as a potbellied gray-haired man in socks, a T-shirt and unbelted robe flew out the door with a pot of boiling water that he threw into the air. It was so cold the water crystalized into a frosty cloud and disappeared. Panting, the man saw her and gave an exaggerated bow, flung the pot into the bushes, then reentered the house, slamming the door behind him.

That was quite the introduction to who she figured must be Bog Brewer. Why was Ethan Zarcone in his house and why was Bog yelling at him? Questions to which she would likely never have answers.

An icy blast of arctic air almost pushed her off her feet, but she recovered and followed the walk around to the back of Miss Perry's house. Cats were pacing and watched her expectantly. Some were crouched in the shelters that local handyman Bill Waterman had built, according to George Hellman, from scrap lumber and pallet wood. They were in a variety of styles, but all were sanded and painted. She could see glimpses of painted flowers and bright splashes of color, but most had been swaddled in tarps bungied to the shelters. She counted ten or so cats. Sadie was there, but unlike before she kept her distance, hunching warily in the door of one of the shelters. Maybe she had only been so friendly because George was there.

All of the cats looked uneasy. The music was getting louder: a thudding beat, a wailing guitar, a screeching singer, a cacophony of pseudo song. Words were shouted in a raucous accent, expletives howling on the arctic wind that swept up from the river. Jaymie hustled around the open area, her hands freezing as she pulled the tabs on the cans of wet food. Once she had the canned food spilled out into bowls, which were swiftly circled by the cats, more arriving at the sound of cans opening, she took the larger bowls to the locked bin and filled them generously with hard food, putting some out in the open, but trudging back through the snow to place a couple in the sheltered area by Miss Perry's back door.

She then gathered the dirty bowls, loaded them in a bag, and set the bag down on the path away from the bluff. With the barbecue tongs George kept in the locked bin, she reached into the cat shelters and retrieved the dirtiest of the blankets and pushed fresh fluffy ones in as snow crystals started to blow horizontally along the drifted snow.

Great, a March storm was blowing in. Time to hurry along.

At the far edge of the cliff overlooking the St. Clair River she glanced down at the icy floes that were beginning to cluster and did a double take. There, on the flats, a man walked, scanning the water's edge. He turned, and even from a distance she could tell that it was Parker Hellman in his bright red parka. What was he doing down there? He saw her and waved casually, then turned away and started ascending the path. She thought he was going to come talk to her and hoped he wouldn't be nasty or try to convince her to leave, but he veered away and avoided her completely by cutting through Haskell's property.

Odd. Haskell wasn't home, fortunately, because he was picky about his property.

She mulled over why Parker would avoid her but couldn't think of a reason. Neither could she imagine why he was down by the river. She was packing up to go when the music abruptly ceased. From over the hedge she heard Bog Brewer's voice again raised in anger.

"You trollop, shaggin' that smarmy effin' Yankee trolldoll."

"Boggie baby, you gotta believe me." It was a woman's voice, a high-pitched wheedle. "I never did a single thing with him. Honest! Honey, please . . . you *can't* believe it!"

Silence. Jaymie shrugged and started to pack up when the Brit stomped out to the cat colony. "Hey? Can you hold on a moment?" Jaymie yelled, holding out one hand. The rocker stopped dead in his tracks. "Mr. Brewer, can you please not stomp around the cat colony? The cats are having their breakfast. In this cold they need the calories in the wet food before it freezes. And especially this old guy, Hoagie, I want him to be able to eat it all, since the poor darling is toothless." Jaymie tried a disarming smile. "I'm Jaymie Müller. And you're Bog Brewer. Did I get that right?"

The man smiled, his yellow gappy teeth making for a lopsided grin that was friendly enough. "Poor old moggy," he said, watching Hoagie. "I can relate. Teeth hurt all the time. Makes me cross."

"Are you okay, Mr. Brewer?"

He shrugged. "Arf n' arf." He kept his distance as he lit a cigarette, the smoke drifting on the wind. He introduced himself properly as Rick Brewer, *"but call me Bog; everyone does."* He and Duckie were renting the house until they found one to buy.

"What kind of house?"

"Somethin' big. Maybe outta town. Gonna renovate and put in a studio, y'see. Gonna start recording 'ere, in the U.S."

"Wow, that's interesting. Why?"

He looked off into the distance. "Got my reasons."

"Did you record in England before?"

"Yep."

He had returned to surly silence, so she let silence fall as she watched the cats finish their meals. Then she cast him a side glance and said, "I saw Ethan Zarcone leaving your house. Do you know him well?" She didn't let on that she had overheard the part about Duckie cheating with Ethan.

Bog's face darkened. "What a berk 'e is. Bloody plonker. Came moochin' round talkin' up soom investment or other. Arsked me a bunch o' questions about the 'ouse we rent, was we gonna buy it, 'oo was the owner. Thinks coz I'm a rocker I don't 'ave a bleedin' brain in me 'ead. I know better than to put my money in the likes of 'im."

Investment . . . like he had been going to talk to Haskell about. "What kind of investment, exactly?"

"Soom business about property. Carn't say I let 'im get far," he said with a grimace. "Saw 'im fer the wanker 'e is right off. M'lady's not so swift an' thought 'e was the cat's meow, so ta speak."

She smiled.

"I know you 'eard it all," he said, flicking ashes to the wind. "I'm not a violent sort, y'know, an' I know that my Duckie ain't shaggin' 'im. But good-lookin' smooth-talkin' guys like that take advantage of wimmin 'oo got no common sense. I lost it. If I'da 'ad a shotgun, he woulda had a hole the size of Big Ben in 'im. She was gonna give 'im 'er own money to invest. That arse ain't a man, 'es a transaction. Money in, money out."

Interesting. He did seem to have that effect on some women, as shown by Petty's infatuation. If Bog Brewer was right about Ethan, what did he want from Morgan? Jaymie wondered.

And who was the guy he was arguing with in the parking lot? That did not have the look of a tiff between strangers.

A buxom blonde trotted out clad only in a fluffy fur coat that she held closed with one bejeweled hand, and wellies on her feet. Her bare legs were reddening, and the wind tousled her cotton candy hair, pink highlights dancing about on the breeze. "Boggie, baby, come in from the cold," she coaxed. "You hafta know, I didn't sleep with Ethan. He's not my type."

She tucked herself under the old rocker's arm, and he got a foolish expression on his weathered face. He pulled her close to him.

"I know, Duckie, I know. Jealous old fool that I am. You know 'ow I get when I'm listenin' to the stuff from the old days. Get all raged up inside, me blood hot."

"Come inside, Boggie. You'll catch your death. Hey, I got a strange call from Alf."

"Duckie, why didn't yer say? I need to talk to 'im now. Is 'e on the line?"

"No, he had to hang up, he said —"

"Nup! Hush, Duckie." He cast a wary glance at Jaymie, and said, "C'mon. We gotta go inside in case Alf calls back."

She gave Jaymie a little wave and guided the old rocker toward their back door.

"Ta for now, Jaymie!" Bog shouted, with a forced tone of cheeriness, his voice floating back to her.

Jaymie stood still, frowning, watching the two pick their way across the snow. What was up with them? Who was Alf, and why was a call from him so important? Not that it mattered. It didn't affect her one little bit.

She turned back to observe the cats. Sadie had barely moved from her spot and wasn't eating. Jaymie approached, and the small cat gave a pitiable mew, moving with discomfort. Time to call the vet. In a stroke of good luck, Dr. Kasimo was finishing up caring for a horse. He'd come right away. Jaymie stowed the bags of bowls and blankets in the back of her SUV and waited for him. She was shivering from the cold by the time he pulled up in a gray SUV with his name on the side and introduced himself.

He was a tall, slim, good-looking Black man, wearing a black wool cap pulled down over his ears, and a black peacoat, with a red scarf and gloves. They shook hands and he said, "Let's go to little Miss Sadie," he said. "I've examined her before. She arrived at the colony already spayed so she was someone's cat at one point. George and Bonnie tried to find an owner, but no such luck."

Jaymie loped after him as he marched along the path to the cat colony. His strides were long, his medical bag swinging at his side. "I'm glad you were able to fit us in," she said.

"Me too. She's such a little thing. If she's not eating, there's something wrong." He went directly to the shelter she was huddled in and sat cross-legged on the ground. He stripped his gloves off, then took her into his large hands and cradled her, checking her butt, then feeling her legs and hind end. She squawked and wriggled, then bit him, fastening her little pin-sharp teeth on his finger. He frowned.

"What is it?" Jaymie said.

"She's tender in her hind quarter, but I'm not sure if it's a bruise—the cats do tussle, and she may have gotten in a fight or fallen off the top of a shelter—or it could be constipation. That can cause tenderness in the hind end and may explain her failure to eat. Either way, I don't know if we should be worried. It could be nothing, but she's already so tiny, I hate to think of her out here not eating." Cradling Sadie, he said, "What I'd like is for her to be under observation for a while. Can you take her home with you? Do you have pets?"

"I do, I have a dog and a cat who may—" Her phone rang and she apologized, then answered. It was Heidi wanting to meet her for lunch. Jaymie explained what was going on, and what she was trying to figure out. "I'll have to take her home, but I'm not sure how I'm going to handle it, with Hoppy and Lilibet."

"Oh, Jaymsie, don't even worry about it," Heidi said, using her pet name for Jaymie. "Why don't I take her? I've got this big house to myself."

"*Would* you? Oh, Heidi, you're such a doll." She gave a thumbs-up to the doctor. "Can you come now?"

"I'll be there in two minutes."

She hung up. Jaymie explained to Dr. Kasimo that her petless friend would come and get Sadie. While they waited, the doctor made a call to the stable. He ordered a couple of bales of straw delivered for the shelters. When he hung up he said, "Straw is much better bedding for the cats. Blankets get damp and compact, making inadequate insulation for the cats sheltering in the huts. Bonnie used to order the straw, but George doesn't always do things quite the way I'd like. He's got the best of intentions," the vet hastily added. "He doesn't pay attention the way Bonnie did. They'll deliver two bales later today."

"Who will pay for it?"

"I'll take it off my bill. They're my best customers, so—"

"Wait, that wouldn't be Dani Brougham and Emma Spangler's

stable, would it?"

"It is. Do you know them?"

"Yes! We're good friends. My daughter and I went to their wedding." She eyed him. "But that is definitely further away than you implied when I called."

He shrugged and stood, still cradling the little cat.

She smiled at him. It was a further example of his kindness and care for the cats. "I'll be coming back this evening to do the second feeding, so I can distribute the straw into the shelters then."

The vet had frozen in place as he stared over Jaymie's shoulder. Jaymie turned. Her beautiful friend Heidi was trotting toward them, long blonde hair lifting on the breeze, snow spangling her turquoise wooly hat and coat, concern on her pretty face. She abruptly stopped when she got there and stared up at the doctor, who smiled down at her.

Jaymie watched as his brown eyes warmed, from concern over Sadie to appreciation for the sweet young woman in front of him. Heidi's blue eyes widened and she took a step back, breathing out a gust of frosty steam, a slow smile lifting the corners of her mouth. "Hi," she said softly, putting out one gloved hand. "I'm Heidi Lockland."

"Dakarai Kasimo," he said, shifting Sadie and sticking out his free hand. "Pleased to meet you." Their gazes lingered, their hands clasped.

Jaymie cleared her throat. The two jumped away from each other, Heidi's cheeks pinkening, from embarrassment or the cold wind was not clear. They explained to her what was needed, that Sadie would require careful observation.

"I've got nothing planned for the next few days," Heidi said brightly. She looked at Sadie and her smile softened. "Aw, what a sweetie," she cooed. "I've never taken care of a cat in my own home before." She looked up at the vet. "I could use some pointers."

"You've cat-sat at Val's before," Jaymie said with a frown. "This is basically —"

"You don't have a carrier," the doctor said. "And you can't take her in the car without one. I don't have to get back to the clinic right away. Why don't I bring her to you and help you get her comfortable? I can explain what you need to watch for."

"I'd love that," Heidi said, not taking her eyes off his face. "You could follow me back to my house."

Jaymie bit her lip, trying to keep from grinning. She had cat carriers in her SUV, but she was not going to get in the way of this budding friendship by offering one. "I'll leave you two to it, then," she said, and headed around Miss Perry's house to her SUV as a pale gray BMW four-door glided past and stopped in front of Bog and Duckie's house. Out of it emerged the mysterious gentleman from the historic meeting, the fellow who had monopolized Haskell's time. He carefully picked his way up the walk to the Brewer home, knocked on the door and entered.

Huh. Interesting. He had not appeared to be the kind of fellow an aging rocker would associate with, but maybe he was a lawyer or an accountant. She had to hurry, as she was meeting Val for lunch at the Emporium

• • •

"You could feel the electricity between them, Val!" Jaymie said, smiling at the memory of the veterinarian and Heidi's instant connection. "You know how sparks fly when you drag your feet across a rug? There were practically sparks on that cold, windswept plateau. And it wasn't because of how beautiful Heidi is, though there is that, of course. I think what impressed the doctor was how immediately she volunteered her help with Sadie. You know Heidi; she's the soul of kindness. And of course, the doctor is handsome, but he's also got this aura of competence. He's got the most elegant hands." Val chuckled at that description. "Don't laugh! He does. And he's kind, you can see it in his eyes and in the way he handled little Sadie. That's what Heidi was responding to, I think, that genuine gentle kindness."

Val was locking up her pharmacy section at the back of the Queensville Emporium before they went for lunch. She carried a tote bag with sandwiches and a thermos of tea. "Come on, let's go before that phone rings again," she said. Mondays were busy at the pharmacy, but Val always took her lunch hour.

"Where are we going?"

"Never mind, follow me."

Jaymie tagged along like she did her whole life when Val led the way, walking into the stiff breeze, snow crystals blowing into their faces. Down the main street, past Becca's store, past some others, and to the Knit Knack Shack. Eyeing it in puzzlement, Jaymie was surprised when Val took out a key and led the way to the front door, unlocking it and heading inside. She turned on lights as they proceeded. The place was still set up as a yarn store with a twirling rack of a few unsold pattern books, and some leftover yarn in labeled bins and discarded on the floor. This was stock left over from the final sale, balls of weird-colored yarn—fuchsia and puce and khaki—tossed about like a giant cat had been playing.

"Let's have our lunch back here," Val said, proceeding to the cash desk Bonnie had used. Val perched on the stool behind it, while Jaymie pulled over a stool from the wall and sat opposite her friend. Bonnie had loved a good chin wag, as she called gossip, so she always kept a few stools for friendly visits. Val laid out their sandwiches and poured tea. Mystified but famished, Jaymie wolfed down her tuna sandwich and drank tea. Val would talk when she was ready.

"How are plans for the Müller holiday store coming?" Val finally asked of the Christmas store Jaymie and Jakob had been working toward in the last year on a plot of land they had bought adjacent to the Christmas tree farm property. "You haven't talked about it for a while."

"It was hung up in red tape, at first—zoning and all that—and now we're a little worried about the timing, with the economy the way it is. Though Jakob says, when is the economy ever perfect? We're delaying work on it for at least a year. Jakob and his brothers will farm the land instead, for now. We *are* going to have a pumpkin field in the front acre, which I'm looking forward to, and so is Jocie. They've started the pumpkin seedlings in the Müllers' greenhouse, with all the cousins working on it."

"That's a great idea. But just an acre?"

Jaymie laughed. "That's what I said, until Jakob pointed out that you can grow up to three thousand pumpkins on an acre."

"Wow! Who knew?"

"I didn't. Jocie's thrilled; for an FFA project she's going to grow her own pumpkins in a little patch near the road. She swears she'll grow the biggest pumpkin of all of us. The cousins are going to compete. This fall we'll have a pumpkin patch party, to gauge interest going forward." She eyed Val curiously, sensing something behind her questions. "You know, you could come right out and tell me why you brought me here."

Val fidgeted, red-cheeked. "Okay, but you have to promise me you won't say yes if you don't have time. You're so busy all the time, and this spring you'll have the Alicia forest trail project to work on. And now Haskell has dropped the whole Tea with the Queen event into your lap."

"I promise not to overcommit myself no matter what you ask." She had the fingers on one hand crossed, but didn't say that. She was often overbooked but thrived on the variety. "Now speak! I'm dying of curiosity."

"I was thinking we could be partners in a new venture. We could open up a vintage shop and tea room right here, in this storefront."

⌖ Six ⌖

JAYMIE STARED AT VAL. "A *WHAT?*"

"A tea shop. Lunch and afternoon tea, open at eleven, closed by five. But selling vintage stuff, too, all the vintage clutter in both of our homes. And the stuff we both long to buy at auctions and yard sales. And the stuff that comes into The Junk Stops Here every day that you lament you and Jakob have to sell dirt cheap because you don't have the right customers for it." As she spoke, her eyes glowing behind her glasses, she spoke more quickly, warming to the topic. "Think about it, Jaymie! Teacups and tea sets and all the pretty stuff we have no room for in our daily lives." She clasped her hands to her bosom. "Old embroidered tablecloths and aprons and linens I keep buying at estate sales. And cookbooks, even." Softly, she added, "And vintage china cat figurines."

"Oh," Jaymie said softly, letting out her breath, taking in the idea. A tea shop. A *vintage* tea shop. "*Oh!*"

Val sat on the edge of her stool and leaned across the counter. "Jaymie, we could serve tea and treats and decorate with pretty vintage stuff in the main room, and then in the other rooms we could sell my kitschy stuff, and your kitchen stuff." She stopped and stared, openmouthed, into the distance. "I have a *great* idea! We'll call it the Kitschy Kitchen."

The hair on the back of Jaymie's neck stood up and she got goose bumps that were not solely because of how cold the yarn store was. "The Kitschy Kitchen! Val, that is *brilliant*! But it would be expensive, wouldn't it? And who would work here every day? I mean, *you* can't, *I* can't, who —"

"Violet can," Val quickly said, naming her sister-in-law, the widow of her late older brother. "And you can take a day now and then, and so can I. Vi wants to move here from Canada to be closer to Brock and me and the kids. We're all the family she has. She's retired and bored. I've already asked her, and not only does she want to do it, but she also wants to invest."

"You've already thought this out and made plans," Jaymie said, a little hurt.

Val reached over and put her boney hand on Jaymie's. "I wanted to be sure it was viable. I've already talked to Helen, too," she said of her pharmacist colleague who had been filling in at the Queensville pharmacy. "She's up for more hours, so I can take time off. Bonnie's going to be back next week. If we decide to go ahead with it, I'll put in a formal offer. Why don't you talk it over with Jakob tonight? We'll get together tomorrow and make plans."

"You've given me a lot to think about."

"I know, but I don't want to pressure you. There is no obligation, one way or the other."

"But the idea makes me happy. I would be excited."

Val smiled and swiped at tears under her glasses. "I thought you'd say it was the stupidest thing you'd ever heard, like Brock did."

"Tcha, Brock! What does *he* know about tea and kitsch?"

"Not a thing. Now, let's walk around the place and I'll tell you my thoughts."

• • •

". . . and I'd have a place to get rid of all of that stuff that's accumulating at the cabin and in this attic and basement." Jaymie lay on her side in Jakob's arms, watching his eyes as he thought about the store she and Val proposed opening together. She didn't need her husband's permission, but not only did she value his opinion, they were a family. Every decision made by one of them had implications for them all. She had thought of nothing else, even as she fed the cats their evening ration and distributed the straw that had, as Dr. Kasimo promised, been delivered.

He considered it for a few minutes. "I'm a little worried about how this works with your other commitments, especially since Haskell has saddled you with the whole Tea with the Queen event. I know how important that is to you." He searched her eyes. "You already do so much."

"I won't say I'm not concerned, but that *is* a short-term commitment. I have no intention of taking it on every year alone. I need to prove to Haskell that we can make it even more successful than it already is. He's blind to it because it isn't his favorite." She burned even thinking about his dismissiveness, and how he had influenced the whole treasury subcommittee to vote against going on with it because he didn't see its value. "The two can work together. Every year we have an overflow of guests from the tea event, people who didn't prebook and are left out. If we have the Kitschy Kitchen up and going—"

Her cell phone rang. She reached behind her and picked it up, frowning at the name that popped up. "Miss Perry? Is everything okay?"

"I don't know, Jaymie," the woman said, her voice quavering. "I saw lights a while ago down on the river flats."

"Lights? What do you mean?"

"I was upstairs sorting through boxes in one of my rooms. It takes me a while to get up there, but what else do I have to do? Anyway, I was sitting by the window taking a break and looking down to the river—"

"With your binoculars?" she said, smiling at Jakob.

"Of course. I saw a light bouncing around, and heard the faint sound of a boat motor. Who the heck would have a boat out there at this time of night and in this weather?"

"Call the police!"

"I suppose I should. Thought I'd get your opinion before I did it."

"Do it! Call the police and tell them exactly what you told me!" She paused, then said, "Miss Perry, are you okay? Do you need me to come out there?"

"Oh, gosh no, honey. Thank you, but I'm fine. Doors locked up tight, security lights on. I'm even using that alarm system I had installed two years ago."

"Call me if you need me." They hung up. Jaymie brought Jakob up to speed, then went back to what she had been talking about, the Kitschy Kitchen. "It could work with the Tea with the Queen event, which is always sold out. We turn people away, usually, but this way we could point them to the Kitschy Kitchen for their tea fix!" With a sigh of happiness, she lay down by his side again.

"In fact . . ." Her brain spun with ideas popping. She sat upright again, her heart pounding. "Oh, Jakob! I could have the little trailer brought over," she said of the trailer she had renovated into mid-century kitschiness, ". . . and park it behind, to serve a patio crowd tea in summer!" She clasped her hands together. "And you know how the vintage and antique stores we already have are beginning to get a real reputation around Michigan and Ohio and even into Ontario. We'd be a part of that!" When she again gazed at him, he was smiling. "What?" she said.

He pulled her down to him. "Whatever gives you this much joy, I'm all for it." He touched her face, then leaned over her and kissed her deeply. She melted into his arms.

Later, as she was falling asleep, she was jolted awake by a thought. Miss Perry hadn't called back. She stared into the dark, recalling Parker in his red coat walking along the flats by the river, looking out over the water. What was he looking for? And did it have anything to do with Miss Perry's lights?

• • •

It was frigid on the St. Clair River near midnight. Here it was March, and he was *still* doing what he swore to stop doing! Was he some kind of idiot? Or did he cave when people told him what to do?

Nah, neither. It was the easy money that kept him coming back. The trolling motor sputtered and coughed like an asthmatic pug. This one last drop-off, Parker Hellman thought, and he'd have enough money that he could cool it for a while, maybe fall off the edge of the earth, hunker down and hide out. He kept thinking it, but now was the time to do it. His partner was overpromising help to dangerous people and getting in deep. Parker didn't like it at all, but when had his buddy ever listened to him? He was one of those guys who claimed to think big. *If you want to make it big,* he said, *you have to be willing to get dirty.* But he expected everyone *else* to get dirty while he stayed clean, manicured nails, trendy clothes and all. He had it all under control, to hear him tell it. Parker had told him this was it, the end. He'd do anything for his pal, but he'd put his foot down this time.

"Hey, when're we gonna get there?" his passenger asked, restlessly moving about in the little boat, tipping it dangerously with his fidgeting.

"Stay still, will you?" Parker hissed. "Or we'll end up in the river."

"I'm bloody freezin' 'ere!"

"It's March in Michigan. You're coming from Canada. Did you not think it was going to be cold?"

"Get stuffed, y'wanker. I know 'ow cold it gets. But I only ever go from the 'ouse to th'car an' back. Trade wiv me, willya?"

"Oh, for . . ." Parker cut the motor for a moment, struggled out of his coat, and handed it to his passenger. "You'll pay me more for this," he muttered, shivering as his passenger groped in the dark and put a wad of bills in his pilot's hand. "Be careful of the jacket, though," he added, thinking of the impact the red parka with the skull crest would have if the guy wore it in the wrong company. "Shed it the moment you can. It could get you in trouble with the wrong people."

"Whatdya mean?"

"Never mind."

"You didn't tell anyone I was coomin' over 'ere, didya?"

Parker paused, then grunted a hasty lie. "'Course not."

"Better not 'ave."

"I'm just saying, get another parka and ditch this one. Bring it back here and leave it where I tell you." He started the trolling motor again and turned the bow, heading upstream toward shore.

"I thought we was goin' ta Queensville?"

"We are. But I'm *not* dropping you off at the freakin' marina," he muttered, hyper aware of how quiet it was, and how sounds carried on a calm cold night. "It's too dangerous." He went through the usual explanation, with the warning about the cats and the key and the wooden box, the bag of all the guy would need, and how to get to his destination. "Be careful with the flashlight. Old bat up in one of the houses is snoopy as hell." He ran them aground, and his passenger clambered out. "Push me off, will you?"

His passenger complied, then straightened, watching the little boat chug out on the river. He turned, and using the little flashlight he had been given to find the way, he started along the gritty river shore toward the hill path.

Out of the frigid shadows an assailant darted and clubbed him on the back of the head with a heavy stone. He cried out once, fell to the river beach and lay still. The assailant checked for a pulse. Fading, fading, and . . . none. He straightened and regarded the coat, thinking of taking it, but couldn't risk the time and trouble it would take. Blood on it now. He turned and strode a ways away, then heaved the rock into the river.

Parker heard the outcry and splash, but didn't think much of it. Not then, anyway. That would come on the morrow, when he learned about the body, confronted his partner, and set in motion a series of events that would take one more life.

৶ Seven ৶

BECAUSE SHE WAS WORKING AT BECCA'S ANTIQUE STORE that morning to give Georgina a break while Becca and Kevin were in Canada for the week, Jaymie left the house early, letting Jakob get his and Jocie's breakfast. He would then take her and a couple of her friends to school. It was six thirty and dark as she drove to Winding Woods Lane, a frigid still morning. She went around a black car at the curb and parked in front of Miss Perry's house.

Bundled warmly in a parka, scarf, gloves and warm boots, she got out the cat necessities and slung the tote bags over her arm. She carried a flashlight because away from the road, along the river, it would be pitch dark. *Dark* came in gradients, town dark not being nearly as absolute as the pitch dark where there were no streetlights.

Plunking down the canvas totes of food on the snow-packed cliff, by the light of the flashlight beam she set out clean dishes and filled them with food, then filled the water dishes. She crossed to the big wooden locked container and frowned, puzzled. The barbecue tongs that were usually inside were sitting on the ground. She shrugged, unlocked the box and put the tongs inside, then fished around for the one large bowl to use in addition to the other water bowls.

She felt something inside and gasped, then shone her flashlight inside. Well *that* was weird; a fabric shopping bag. She pulled it out and opened it, shining the flashlight inside. There were heavy gloves, a wallet stuffed with American money, granola bars and some other stuff. What the heck? That hadn't been there the day before. What was going on? She left the bag in the box. She'd call George later to see if he knew what that was all about.

She could hear the river sounds, an occasional splash, and a car revving and roaring down the street beyond the row of houses. "Slow *down*," she muttered. Who would drive so fast around here?

Drowsy cats were cocooned in the shelters, the fresh straw giving them a warm insulating layer against the cold. The doctor was right; straw was better than blankets. She tucked the wet food close to the shelters, hoping it didn't freeze. Maybe she'd close up shop and take a break halfway through the morning to check on the bowls. The cold snap was supposed to break soon. She hoped so.

As she was gathering the dirty bowls and tossing them in the empty bags, she heard an odd sound, like a guitar riff, drifting on the wind, dissipating, then chiming again. It stopped. Then she heard it again with a vocal accompaniment of the repeated phrase *that's right* and then *that's neat* over and over. Where the heck was *that* coming from?

She gripped her flashlight and followed the sound to the edge of the sloping cliffside, hearing it louder and repeatedly. Then there was the sound of a voice, someone talking, then silence again. And then a minute or so later the repeated musical phrase. This was weird.

She played her flashlight beam down on the flats below as the musical chime stopped, then started again. Words floated to her on the breeze from the river as she examined the shore, the dark water rushing by, ice glinting in her beam. She spotted a figure huddled there, dressed in a red parka. Someone was in trouble.

She dropped the bag of bowls with a clank and hustled to the sloping path that led down to the water's edge, stumbling and sliding on ice, tripping on gravel and branches that caught her coat and snapped. She hoped she wasn't too late. Red parka? Oh no! Was it Parker Hellman down there? A hum of fear coursed through her. She made it to level ground, then stumbled and slipped along the path toward the water, focusing her light on the figure.

When she got there she saw that it was not Parker Hellman. The fellow was still, his head bashed in and bloody, his phone ringing with those weird musical phrases repeated. This time a woman's English-accented voice left a voicemail. *Tolly, answer me, ya git! It's not like you to not answer. Didya make it to the States? Shoulda bin there hours ago. Did ya find 'im? What did 'e say? Tolly, don't do this to me. Call me, ya bleedin' berk!*

Jaymie grabbed the guy's shoulder, rolled him over and shone the light on him, the beam hitting a balding pate fringed in long gray hair and covered in snow crystals above a pale saggy face marred by acne scars and threaded with broken capillaries. His nose had been broken in his past, and his lips were curled back in a frozen grimace, revealing yellowed long teeth.

This was a stranger, an older man, but he was wearing Parker's coat, or one that looked exactly like it, right down to the black crest with the red grinning skull. He was dead, stiffening in the frigid March morning.

• • •

The sun was rising. Jaymie observed it from the back of a police cruiser that was surrounded by emergency vehicles with lights flashing: cop cars, a fire rescue vehicle, an ambulance. It had been a little over an hour since she found the body. She stared out the car window toward the east as the sun topped the trees that lined the cliff, at the bottom of which she knew was the red-coated body of a stranger, an older man with no ID on him, nothing but the burner flip phone. It had rung again but died in mid-ring, as if the charge had gone from it, or the cold had finally put it out of commission. That happened often in Michigan, cell phones not appreciating the frigidity of outdoor winter temperatures. If you were smart, you kept them in pockets close to body warmth.

She recalled the ring tone and hummed it in her head, and the two competing phrases: *that's right* repeated again and again and *that's neat*, ditto, set to crashing music. Odd.

Bernie, her police friend, was not present at the scene, nor was Detective Vestry, the two sources of info she could usually count on. She was to stay put and someone would come to get her statement. Uniformed officers passed by, too busy to answer her shouted queries. Her phone had been taken, but a young officer came to the car and handed it back to her through the window. She called Georgina to tell her why she would not be opening the antique store. Georgina, groggy, said she'd put a sign in the window, and for Jaymie to come in when she could.

Jaymie then called Jakob, who was mostly concerned for *her*. Once he knew she was okay, he asked that she keep him up to date. Anxious and unnerved, she called Val, who expressed appropriate concern and also asked to be kept updated. Jaymie then called Heidi. After explaining briefly but in no detail what happened, they moved on to talking about Sadie. "How is she?"

"She's still limping, but oh, what a cuddle bunny! She slept with me last night. I had to help her up to the bed, and then I worried she'd fall off, so I put blankets on the floor all the way around the bed, but she was fine. She managed to jump down, and Jaymie, she knew exactly what to do in the litter box! I can't believe that sweet little girl was out there in that cold lonely place."

"Did Dr. Kasimo stay and tell you all about how to care for cats? All the stuff you know because you cat-sat for Val before?"

"I know, I *know*!" she said with a tinkling laugh. "But never in my own home. I did say that. He was so sweet. He stayed for a cup of coffee and we talked. And *talked*! I have never talked so much with a man. Then it was getting late so I made dinner."

"You *cooked*?" Heidi normally brought store-bought desserts or snacks to potluck dinners they attended.

She giggled. "I *can* cook! I usually choose not to, but I make a mean vegan omelet and salad." She sobered. "He's vegan too. I was so surprised. I've never met a guy who was."

Jaymie was speechless at Heidi's rapidly shifting moods, happy, sunny, thoughtful. And a little fearful? This was a Heidi who had gone through a profound connection. Jaymie's heart beat a little faster. That was so exactly what happened when she met Jakob. She hoped it went as well for these two.

An officer approached the car. "I have to go. I'll talk to you later, sweetie," Jaymie said, her eyes welling, her voice clogged. Finding a body was never easy and invariably left her sad and teary.

The officer opened the door. "You can go on home now, ma'am," she said.

Jaymie climbed out of the car into the frigid air. Tears froze on her cheeks and she sniffed. "So who is it? Who is the body?"

"I'm not at liberty to say, ma'am. Where will you be?"

"I suppose I'll go to work. I'm at Queensville Fine Antiques today."

"Detective Rodriguez would like to speak with you. He'll be in touch."

Jaymie stood staring at Miss Perry's house. Quin pulled up and Morgan got out of the car, limping over to Jaymie. Quin followed, eyeing the police cars and hubbub with interest.

"What's going on? Is Aunt Lois okay?"

"She's fine. I saw her at her window and she waved to me."

"So what's up?"

Jaymie jammed her hands deep in her pockets. "I found a body down on the flats when I came to feed the cats this morning."

"You found a *body*?" Quin exclaimed. "Who was it? How did it happen? Did he drown?"

"How did you know it's a he?"

Quin stared. "I guess I assumed. You mean it's a woman?"

"No, it's a man." Jaymie relayed briefly what happened, keeping it simple. She had found the body and called the police.

"I'm going to make Aunt Lois breakfast, and then Quin will take me to work. Come in and at least have coffee, or tea."

"I'm supposed to be opening the antique store, but it can wait a bit." Bog Brewer came out onto his porch and picked up his newspaper, then stared at the police cars. Jaymie waved to him, and he beckoned. She turned back to Morgan. "You go on in. I'll join you in a minute."

She trotted over to the neighboring house. Bog, bleary-eyed, stared in dismay at the conglomeration of cops. When she reached him, he said, "What the bloody 'ell is goin' on? That Perry woman's okay, ain't she?"

"Yes, she's fine."

"Then whot's up?"

"There was an incident down on the flats by the river. I found a body." She watched as a local TV station truck arrived. It would be all over the news soon.

"Bloody 'ell!" he exclaimed. "'Oo was it?"

"I don't know. A stranger to me. I'd better go. You're going to freeze out here in just your robe."

"Yeh. Awright . . . go on now. Get warm."

She started to walk away, humming and then breaking into the refrain she had heard on the ring tone, as it was obsessively threading through her brain. *That's right, that's right, that's right, that's right, that's neat, that's neat, that's neat . . .*

"Whot's that you're singin'?" he called after her.

She turned back to him. "A phone ring tone I heard."

"Where?"

"On the flats, I—" She stopped. Too much information. She stared at him. His eyes had gotten big and he dropped the newspaper at his feet. As she stared, he bent over, grabbed the newspaper, and scuttled back into his house, slamming the door shut behind him. What was that all about?

☙ Eight ☙

JAYMIE ENTERED THE PERRY HOME AND TOOK OFF HER BOOTS. In stocking feet she padded down the hall to the back kitchen and sitting room area. Morgan paced in the hall, red-faced, phone in hand. She glared at her aunt, who sat in a dining chair by the back door watching the police gathered beyond her property on the bluff. Quin perched on a stool by the kitchen door.

"Parker, if you get this message, *call me!*" Morgan yelled into the phone.

"What's going on?" Jaymie asked. Morgan was fine moments ago.

"Morgan has switched on witch mode," Quin said, crossing her arms over her narrow chest.

Morgan eyed her friend, but then muttered into her phone, "Ethan isn't answering his phone and I need to talk to him. He never came home last night, and if I find out he was with you, Parker, I'll . . ." She saw Jaymie watching her and turned away.

Jaymie could only hear *boat* and *body*, but that was enough to concern her deeply. Why did Morgan feel compelled to tell Parker about the body on the flats? And what was she saying to him about a boat?

Call me! Morgan hissed, and then hit the off button on the phone, which she slipped into her sweater pocket as she limped into the kitchen to make tea and her aunt's breakfast. Quin slipped off her stool and followed her friend.

"Miss Perry?" Jaymie said.

The woman turned, her mouth clamped in an angry frown. "Jaymie. Are you okay? All they'd say was that you found a body on the flats."

Once more she explained as simply as possible without going into detail. "Did you tell them about seeing lights down there last night? Did you end up calling the police?"

"I did. I've been thinking about it a lot, and I have a theory." She got up and tottered toward her little cocoon, the sitting room. "Come sit with me, and I'll tell you what I think."

Jaymie was about to follow but she saw Morgan, in the kitchen, with Quin talking to her. "I'll be with you in a sec, Miss Perry."

Morgan clanked dishes around in the fridge, and stared into it, blankly. "You appear to have a lot going on," Jaymie said, entering the kitchen and eyeing the two friends. "Tell you what, I'm in no hurry to leave. Why don't I make Miss Perry her breakfast?"

"That's nice of you, Jaymie," Morgan said. "I hate to dump this on you but I *am* worried about Ethan. He never came home last night and he isn't answering his phone. I have to go to work."

"Morgan, settle *down*," Quin said irritably. Her mood appeared to have shifted. "You've been a wreck all morning. Calm down."

"Calm down? *You're* the one who said it was odd that he never came home," she snapped. "I told you he was probably with Parker, but now you've got me worried."

Quin, huffy, turned away. "Okay, all right, I thought . . . but never mind. I was *trying* to comfort you, but I can see I'm in the way."

Jaymie eyed her, frowning. With a few short statements she had turned the argument around to being about her.

"Maybe I'll go," Quin said. "I'm sure with Jaymie here you can find your own way. She can take you wherever you want to go. I'm in the way." Her tone had flashed from irritable to angry.

"You're not in the way," Morgan relented. She took her friend aside and murmured to her. Quin nodded, shouldered her purse and headed to the hallway half bath.

"What's going on?" Jaymie asked.

"I'm sorry I'm so worked up. This is all . . . I need to . . ." She trailed off, staring ahead, tears in her eyes.

"Morgan, what is going *on*?"

"I'm worried. I don't know what to do about—"

Quin came out of the half bath stuffing a small zippered pouch into her purse. "Let's get out of here," she said to Morgan. "Jaymie offered to stay, so we can go now."

"You're right," Morgan said. "I have to find Ethan."

"Why?" Jaymie asked, puzzled by the urgency. "I know you said it's because he didn't come home, but what does that—"

"I need to know what's going on with him. Aunt Lois likes a poached egg on whole wheat toast. Can you do that?"

"Of course I can do that," Jaymie said, cross at Morgan's evasions. "Probably better than you." She took a deep breath. "I'm sorry, it's been an upsetting morning," she said when she saw the hurt on Morgan's face.

She drew her away from Quin. "I couldn't help overhearing some of what you said on the phone," she murmured, shooting glances at the slender woman, who was not watching them and yet was hyperaware, Jaymie could tell from the set of her narrow shoulders and the angle of her head. She was fussing around in her purse. "In your message to Parker you talked about a body and a boat," Jaymie murmured. "Is there something you should be telling the police?"

"Of course not," Morgan said. "You misheard."

"Morgan, please, are you worried that Ethan is involved?"

"Of course not!"

But she looked away. Jaymie knew from experience that the other woman would only talk when she was ready. "You do what you need to do, but I'm here if you ever need to talk."

Morgan said goodbye to her aunt and departed with Quin. Jaymie made her friend breakfast. With the tray set between them, breakfast for Miss Perry and tea and a cheese tea biscuit in front of Jaymie, the older lady explained what she witnessed the night before.

"I saw those lights, and I told you I thought I heard a boat motor."

"But the police didn't investigate."

"They did *not*," she said tartly. "Probably thought I was a fool old woman who was seeing things. I told you I see lots going on down there. Especially late at night in the summer and fall. But that stops over the winter. It's so darned cold." She shivered and pulled her ratty cardigan closer around her shoulders.

Remembering what Trip Findley said, Jaymie suggested, "What about smuggling?"

"Smuggling, but of the human kind. People have been coming over the border with Canada for years, people who can't come in legally."

Jaymie frowned. "What are you saying?"

"I wonder if the lights I saw and the motor I heard was either a boat leaving this side of the river, going across, picking someone up and bringing them back here, or vice versa."

"But how did this guy end up dead? There was no boat on the

shore, so was someone waiting for him? To kill him?"

"Maybe," Miss Perry said, then took a bite of poached egg. "Mmm, this is so good. Morgan never gets the yolk right, runny but with no sloppy egg white. She either overcooks it or it's like eating slime."

"I'm glad you like it. My Grandma Leighton taught me how to cook eggs perfectly." Jaymie broke off a piece of tea biscuit and ate it, then drank some tea. "I have to admit, I'm puzzled. What kind of place is the riverside to commit murder? Why *there*? If you hadn't heard a boat, I would have thought the guy was down there walking and fell." And if she hadn't noticed that his head was bashed in, she didn't say. "Or that his body had been deposited in the river and washed ashore."

Miss Perry eyed her. "I know you're holding back, Jaymie, but I won't ask you what it is. I overheard one of the officers talk to another. They think my hearing's not good, but I had my hearing aids in. He said it looked like the poor fellow had died where he fell."

"I wonder if Haskell would have heard or seen anything?" Jaymie mused.

"He didn't come home until late, after I heard the boat."

"Miss Perry, when I was feeding the cats earlier yesterday, I saw Parker Hellman down on the flats, walking. Why would he be down there?"

"I don't know."

"It made me wonder why he was so upset when George denied him cat feeding duty. He doesn't seem like an animal lover to me."

"You think it might be tied into this death?"

"I don't know," Jaymie admitted. "But I'll mention it to the police." It troubled her that he wasn't answering his phone, according to Morgan's frantic words. Was he the killer?

Miss Perry met Jaymie's gaze. "I'm worried about Morgan," she admitted.

"Me too. Were you two arguing?"

Miss Perry flapped on hand. "Not so's you'd notice. We bicker all the time, you know that. I think she's flaky and she thinks I'm an interfering old biddy." She paused, shaking her head. "But I do worry. That girl has the worst taste in men."

What she had overheard from Morgan's message to Parker concerned Jaymie, but she was not about to divulge that until she had thought about it. "Do you think Ethan Zarcone is dangerous for her? There is something going on there, but I can't figure it out. Does she love him? Is she afraid of him? What gives?"

Miss Perry sighed and mopped up the last of her egg yolk. "She was always contrary as all get-out. I told her once when she was twelve to be careful on the bluff, and what does she do but jump off it and break her arm."

Jaymie rose and collected the plates and cup. "I'd better get going. I'm supposed to be opening the antique store."

As she went to her SUV, it occurred to her that when she had arrived that morning she had to drive around a dark-colored car parked on the road. Where was that car, and when had it departed?

℘ **Nine** ℘

JAYMIE DUSTED THE ANTIQUE SHOP AND THEN SETTLED DOWN with a fresh binder to begin planning for the Tea with the Queen event. First she had to find out whether Stowe House, their traditional venue, would be available to them, because if it wasn't, it changed everything. It was complicated. At one time, she had known, and even dated, Daniel Collins, the owner of the historic home, who had given them permission to use the house lawn every spring for the tea. He had been trying to sell the house for years, and indeed it was rumored to have been sold at one point. That sale fell through, but recent rumors indicated it was again close to being sold. Maybe Brock Nibley, Val's brother and the busiest local realtor, would be able to help.

Val called and Jaymie filled her in on what had happened since they last spoke. She also asked if Brock could help her out with the Stowe House matter.

"I'll call him and ask. If you've got a minute I'll come over so we can talk," Val said. "I'll take my break now instead of later. Put on the kettle for tea."

Five minutes later they sat at the dining table in the front window of Queensville Fine Antiques sipping tea from a couple of pretty and inexpensive transferware teacups depicting English castles. Jaymie explained her discovery of the body in more depth, then went over what Miss Perry had talked about, the human smuggling aspect.

"There *have* been a few arrests made of people who came over illegally that way."

"It's a problem on Heartbreak Island," Jaymie said. "It happens every summer, in both directions. But this time of year?"

"I know," Val said, frowning down into her cup. "Someone who needed desperately to come over to the U.S., I suppose?"

"And then got randomly murdered?" Jaymie bit her tongue; the police hadn't exposed it as a murder yet, so she shouldn't be throwing the word around. "We don't know that's what happened. It could be something entirely different."

"Like what? A dead body shows up on the flats in the middle of winter. How many possibilities *are* there?"

"I can think of a few," Jaymie said.

"I'm sure you could." Val took a sip of her tea. "How *did* he die, do you think? Was he drowned?"

"Not drowned," Jaymie said. "His head was bashed in, it looked like to me. Someone out there is missing him terribly. I heard a woman leaving a message for him — *if* the phone is his — and she was worried. She called him 'Tolly.' What kind of name is that?"

Val frowned. "I've heard that name used before but I can't think where."

"I suppose the phone could have belonged to his killer. In that case Tolly could be the murderer's name."

"Good point. That sure would make it easier to solve the crime."

"It's never that easy, though, is it?" Jaymie sighed and sipped her tea. "Logically, the phone is likely the victim's. I'm worried, Val." She explained what she overheard of Morgan's message to Parker, and how Ethan had not come home. "I heard her say *boat* and *body*. What is up with her?"

"She was probably telling Parker what was going on, about the body, and that Miss Perry had heard a boat motor."

"Why would she do that?"

Val pondered that. "I don't know why that would be important to tell him unless — " She broke off and glanced at Jaymie.

"You can say it, Val. Unless he was involved," Jaymie said. "He or Ethan." She pushed her concerns away and sat up straighter, smiling at her friend. "On a happier note, I talked to Jakob last night about the tea and vintage shop and he told me to follow my heart."

Val watched her expectantly.

"Val, of course my heart says *yes please!* I'm in!"

"Yay!" They laughed and hugged and congratulated each other, and then made some quick plans for the Kitschy Kitchen.

"Let me get Violet on video." Val called her sister-in-law on video chat.

Violet Nibley was a British-born woman in her sixties. She had been a widow for years, as Val and Brock's older brother had tragically died far too young. She had never remarried and had no children but kept herself busy with work and hobbies. A seamstress in her youth, then a baker for a pastry shop, she had worked at a restaurant managing the dining room for the last few years of her work life. Her résumé was perfectly suited to running the Kitschy Kitchen.

Now retired, she had recently decided she was not ready to stop working. Her notion to move to Queensville from Canada was mostly because Val, Brock, and Brock's two kids, Will and Eva, were her closest family. They had maintained a close bond for all these years. Their new joint venture would give her a purpose, she had told Val.

On the video Jaymie saw the slim Englishwoman, her clipped accent from the north of England a reminder of her youth that she had never lost. Her gray hair was a cap of tight curls, she wore a lot of lilac and floral prints, and was always fidgeting, never still. Even on video chat she embroidered while she spoke.

Together they celebrated their new venture and tossed around plans. Until the deal with Bonnie was final, though, it was up in the air. Jaymie, her stomach full of butterflies, had a mind that was wildly spinning. Or maybe it was the start of her day, so shocking, that had her reeling.

Val was filling Vi in on what had gone on and mentioned the name Jaymie had overheard.

"Tolly? Now *that* is a true English nickname," Vi chirped. "Short for Bartholomew, you know. Or sometimes Oliver. Or even Tolliver."

"Really? I'll tell the police that," Jaymie said. "They still don't know who the guy is, as far as I know. The message I overheard that was left for 'Tolly' might mean the guy is Tolly, or it is Tolly's phone and that guy is the killer or . . . who knows. It had such a weird ring tone!"

"You didn't tell me that," Val said. "What did it sound like?"

"Uh . . . listen to this." Jaymie sang a few bars.

Violet, on the other end of the phone, hopped up and down in her chair. "Oh! I know what that is."

"What is it?" Jaymie and Val said together.

"It's an English pop song from the seventies, 'Tiger Feet' by the band Mud. Our Billy — me older brother, you know; poor lad died in the nineties — looved it. I was a wee bairn but we danced about the lounge to it." She sang the song with a warble, and when she got to the chorus, it was a repetition, mostly, of the two phrases *that's right* and *that's neat.*

"That's it!" Jaymie cried. "But who would have that as their ring tone?"

"Someone who loved English pop songs of the seventies, I guess," Val said.

"Any Englishman over sixty-five," Violet said with a laugh. "I doubt it even charted in the U.S. I must leave you two as I have so much planning to do! My house closing is Friday, and I've only started packing. Let's talk more tomorrow about the tea shop. I have *oodles* of ideas. Ta for now."

An Englishman over sixty-five, like Bog Brewer. Jaymie pulled her laptop toward her and input a brief search of Bog's band, Berk Scouse Brothers, and there it was: Berk Scouse Brothers was made up of Bog Brewer, a couple of other guys, and . . . the drummer, Tolly Jones. Jaymie gasped and pointed it out to Val. "And there's a photo. It's an old one, though."

"Could he be the body you found?"

She squinted and stared. "I suppose. Val, I was singing that 'Tiger Feet' phrase when Bog asked me where I'd heard it. You should have seen the look on his face when I told him. Then he bolted back into his house." Did he know that his old bandmate, Tolly Jones, was dead? Why wouldn't he have asked her for information if he was concerned? Why didn't he ask her about the tune?

She read up on Bog Brewer, his past marriages—three, all divorces until the most recent one, four years ago, to Duckie, aka Patty—and his two kids, one girl, Lily, and one boy, Fred—and his legal troubles, including being sued for the rights to song lyrics by a former unnamed bandmate. Interesting, but largely irrelevant.

Val returned to the pharmacy and Jaymie went back to working on a plan for the tea event, while thoughts of the Kitschy Kitchen whirled through her mind and mingled with her thoughts about the name she had heard. The moment she could, she'd pass it along to the police.

That opportunity came midafternoon. Detective Rodriguez entered the antique store, stamping his shoes on the mat and glancing around. He was a man in his late forties, stocky, black hair slicked back from an olive-complected round face. He reintroduced himself to Jaymie, shaking her hand across the cash desk.

"Why don't we sit down at the dining table in the front room," she suggested, circling the desk and leading the way. "Can I get you tea or coffee?" she said over her shoulder.

"No, I'm good, thanks." He pulled off his winter parka and hung it on the coat tree by the front door. He was dressed in a faintly rumpled dark gray suit over a magenta dress shirt. Knotted at the throat was a gray and magenta paisley tie. Very Columbo-ish in his rumpled air, Jaymie thought. They sat. He pulled a small notebook out of his pocket and consulted it, then he asked her about her past incidences of finding bodies and her involvement in investigations. As she explained he made notes with a stubby pencil.

"Going down to the river in the dark was a risk. What led you to take that chance?"

"I guess I didn't think of risk, I just reacted to a situation." She heard a defensiveness creep into her tone. Jaymie was beginning to get a worried sensation in her stomach. What was this all about? "You can ask Detective Vestry about me," she finally said, by way of saying someone would vouch for her character.

"What I'm asking is," he said, meeting her gaze with a neutral expression, "did you have reason to believe there was a body on the river flat before going down there?"

Shocked, she reared back, her mind spinning. "Of *course* not! As I told the officer I first spoke to, I heard a phone ringing, or a ring tone, or whatever—"

"So you decided to scale down there in the dark and investigate? That does not sound like the reaction of a reasonable person, to me."

"Maybe I'm not reasonable, then," she snapped, then took a deep breath. Folding her hands on the table in front of her, she said, "You're wrong. Anyone, worried that someone was in trouble, would have done exactly what I did."

"Not true in my experience."

"I wouldn't have had to be the one to find him if the police had investigated Miss Perry's call about lights on the river."

He eyed her with a furrowed brow. "Can you explain?"

She told him about Miss Perry's late-night call about lights and a boat down on the river flats. "She called the police, but no one showed up to investigate."

He jotted a note. "Interesting. There wouldn't have been many officers available, unfortunately. There was trouble at Shooters last night, a huge brawl, so it was all hands on deck for that."

"Trouble at Shooters?" That was a bar on the highway frequented by her friend Clutch Roth and his biker pals.

"I can't imagine it's your kind of place."

"I don't hang out there, but I know people who do. Was anyone hurt?"

"Not to my knowledge. Just a conflict among bikers. There are some new guys in town. I've got a couple of officers trying to track down their elusive leader, Raider Dobbs. I hear his name, and sources say he's running the show, but he's never around. Can we please continue, Ms. Müller?"

"Call me Jaymie, please."

"Let's get back to what happened. Even if officers had responded to Miss Perry's call, why do you think the body would have been there then? How do you know that?"

"I *don't* know that," she said, sighing in exasperation. "Detective, may I tell you in my own words what happened, and why I did what I did? And other information that has since come to light?"

"Be my guest," he said, a smile tugging the corner of his mouth.

She explained from the beginning, then moved on to why she was there so early to feed the cats, because she was scheduled to open the antique store. "I had finished putting out the food and was picking up the dirty dishes to take them away when I heard this odd sound." She paused and glanced out the front window to the street. "It was so quiet out there. The wind was coming up from the river, as it does, and it carried the sound of that strange ring tone."

"You knew it was a ring tone?"

"What else could it be? It repeated again and again, just that one musical phrase and lyrics, then it stopped, then started again. I took my flashlight and scanned the riverbank and saw a red coat. I was worried. The day before I saw someone walking down there wearing an identical coat and —"

"Whoa, wait, you saw someone with the same coat? Did you recognize them?"

She hesitated, but there was no point in denying it. If it got him in some kind of trouble, so be it. "It was Parker Hellman, an acquaintance, the nephew of George Hellman, for whom I'm feeding the cats."

"Did he see you?"

"Sure. He waved to me." She explained how and why they had met, and Parker's anger at the duty of feeding the cats being given to her.

"Did you ask him why he was down there walking around? Don't you find that odd on a freezing March day?"

"It *is* odd. He was staring across the river. People do walk along there sometimes, though. People fish off the riverbank, and hike."

"In March?"

"Not many this time of year," she admitted. He was silent, watching her. "But no, I didn't have a chance to ask him about it. He came up the path, but he veered off, went a different way and disappeared."

"Do you think he was avoiding you?"

"Why would he?"

He didn't answer her question.

"It did look like he was avoiding me," she said. "He cut through Haskell Lockland's property, and no one does that."

"So when you saw the red coat on the body, did you think it was him?"

"It did occur to me, but as soon as I saw the body I knew it wasn't Parker."

"Did you touch the victim?"

"I turned him over to see if he was alive." Tears blurred her vision, and she swiped them away. "I suppose I knew he was dead even before I turned him over, but I didn't want to assume." It was beginning to sink in, that a life had ended in a terrible way. She retrieved a tissue from a box on the cash desk and sat back down, dried her eyes, blew her nose, and said, "Do you know who he is yet?"

"I have no comment on that."

"I think I can help." She explained about hearing the message on the cell phone, the video call with Violet, how her finding the body came up in conversation, and how she mentioned the name Tolly. Violet had offered that it was short for Bartholomew or Oliver or Tolliver, but it was Jaymie humming the ring tone that had helped with identification. She explained their circuitous route to deciding that the body might be that of Tolly Jones, drummer for the Berk Scouse Brothers.

"I don't think I follow. Why would you think that?"

She had learned the hard way that holding back didn't help, so she explained Bog Brewer's odd reaction when she hummed that tune. "And that led me to look up his band online. I found out his drummer's name was Tolly Jones."

He nodded as he wrote notes. Tapping his pencil on the table, he eyed her. "What's your take on this, Ms. Müller?"

She wasn't prepared for the question. "What do you mean?"

"Your impression of what happened. How the body got there. Why this Tolly Jones, if it's him, is on that riverbank."

She repeated how Miss Perry had seen lights and heard a boat motor down there the night before and how it wasn't the first time. She thought Rodriguez ought to talk to her because she was a sharp cookie. She relayed her conversations and how they had speculated on human smuggling. She wondered aloud if maybe Tolly Jones wasn't allowed in the U.S. for some reason. Who locally could have helped him? Parker Hellman, maybe? And if so, how did he end up dead? Surely the intent of human smuggling was to deliver the person alive. "I might have it completely wrong. It's possible that the guy is someone else, and that Tolly Jones is his killer and dropped his phone there by accident." She shook her head. "But I don't think so. I think that poor man *is* Tolly Jones. And if it is, the connection with Bog Brewer *has* to mean something." She fell silent and eyed him.

"Is that it?"

She nodded. "That's all I can think of. For now."

"Chief Ledbetter was right about you," he said, slapping his notebook shut, stuffing it in his jacket pocket and standing.

"Wait, what? You know the chief?"

"Sure. We met at a retiree's dinner. I like to talk to all the guys who grew up and policed around here. I wasn't raised in the area, so it's helpful."

"And Chief Ledbetter mentioned *me*."

"He sure did."

"What do you mean he was right about me? What did he say?"

"Enough." Rodriguez smiled. "He said enough. Thank you for your cooperation, Ms. Müller. Jaymie. If you think of anything else — and I'm sure you will — please call me." He left his card on the table, shrugged on his coat, and departed.

⌘ Ten ⌘

GIVEN THE EVENTS OF THE MORNING, JAYMIE DIDN'T PARTICULARLY want to take care of the cat colony alone. Jakob was home but watching Jocie, who had Peyton over. Heidi called. When she heard of Jaymie's predicament, she volunteered to meet her at Miss Perry's. After dinner Jaymie set out in the dark, driving up to Winding Woods. Feeding the cats was turning into more of a chore than she had expected, but she didn't regret it. The cats needed care.

No one could have anticipated murder.

Heidi was already parked at the curb when Jaymie arrived. The two hugged and Jaymie held her friend at arm's length, examining her face in the pale glow of moonlight. "You look happy," she said.

"Aren't I always?"

"Happier than usual."

Heidi laughed. "Let's get these kitties fed!"

The evening, thank goodness, was clear and calm, though very cold. Their flashlight beams bobbing, they circled the house to the back and heard a *halloo!* It was Miss Perry at her back door. She had the door open, with a blanket around her shoulders. She was already wearing a long nightie, flannel pants and slippers.

"You girls be brisk about it," the woman said. "It's a bitter night out there. I worry about the cats on nights like these."

"Miss Perry, please, get back in the house and get warm!" Jaymie admonished.

"I will, I will. Just so you know, I saw lights again. Those police have all gone, but I saw lights out there."

"It could still be police keeping an eye out," Jaymie said, casting a glance in that direction.

"Maybe. Maybe not. You girls be careful." She headed back in and closed the door but sat in her chair watching out.

The two women lugged the bags with the clean bowls, canned cat food, and the jug of fresh water. Heidi updated Jaymie on Sadie's progress as they went. The little cat was still limping, but she had made herself at home, taking over the window seat, chattering at the birds that came to Heidi's feeders.

They headed through Miss Perry's backyard to the cat colony, picking their way carefully across the icy flats to the shelters, which were barely visible in the flashlight beams. It was slow going, with such burdens, so Jaymie quizzed her friend on her growing friendship with the veterinarian. Heidi was uncharacteristically coy. The conversation ended as they reached the colony, after which the only talk was directions from Jaymie.

The cats were mostly huddled in their shelters, pairs of glowing eyes visible as the animals watched them. A few ventured out to get the soft food, including old Hoagie. Jaymie crouched nearby to make sure he had a good fill, because the food would otherwise freeze solid in no time. She even refilled his bowl and watched, in satisfaction, as he wolfed it down. Her calm presence seemed good for him. Afterward he walked close to her, brushing by her legs in a "body kiss" before heading to one of the shelters and burrowing into the straw inside. She wondered, was it possible to find a home for the old boy? A place to live out his golden years in comfort? She'd ask the doctor next time she saw him for his opinion. Or maybe she'd ask Heidi to pass on the message, she thought with a smile.

"We can pack it in now," Jaymie said. A wind whipped up from the river, over the frozen bluff and across the flat frozen expanse. Something snapped and flapped nearby in the gusts, like a flag in a stiff breeze. "What *is* that noise?" she asked.

"I don't know." Heidi played the flashlight beam along the edge of the bluff toward the path downward. "What's that?"

"What?"

"That piece of cloth," she said, pointing at a patch of blue in the beam. "I think it's one of those tarps they use to cover boats in the marina."

"Do you think so? Maybe it blew up here and got caught on a bush," Jaymie suggested. But the marina was quite a ways away. "Or it could be from one of these shelters." She swept the beam of her flashlight across the colony, but no shelter was exposed. "Maybe it's from one of the houses nearby." People covered their outdoor furniture with tarps sometimes to protect them from the winter weather. "Maybe we can weight it down or haul it away. I don't like the idea of a tarp blowing around and scaring the cats, or covering one of the cat shelters."

They set down their bags and trudged across the open snow, both with flashlights pointed at the flapping material. It *was* blue, but it wasn't big enough to be a tarp. It was . . . Jaymie gasped aloud and then moaned *oh no*. It was a person!

Jaymie raced to help but again, for the second time in twelve hours, it was too late. Shivering and weeping, Heidi had to be sharply told to give Jaymie her flashlight and to get her cell phone out and call the police, while she turned the fellow over to see if he was indeed beyond help. He was long-limbed, wearing jeans and a blue parka, hood up over his dark hair. She trained the flashlight beam on his face.

His skin was frosted, his lips blue, his eyes closed, long ice-rimmed eyelashes fanned over his cheeks. Tears rose in her eyes, blurring her vision as she sat back on her haunches, listening as Heidi babbled on the phone. She knew who this was. The dark hair, the thick dark brows, the features, like the carved marble of a David statue.

"Jaymie, help me," Heidi wailed. "I don't know how to describe where we are! I mean, I know how to find it while driving, but I don't know what to call it!"

She rose and snatched the phone from Heidi. Jaymie told the 911 operator their exact location, and that the police and EMTs had been there that very morning for a similar report.

That's when the shots started. A boom-boom-boom fired, echoing across the river and back. Heidi screamed. Jaymie did too, and heard the 911 operator yelling into the receiver *"What's happening?"* Immediately after, she heard the operator shouting into her dispatch radio *"Shots fired."*

But as the booms continued, colorful starbursts lit up the sky over the river. Fireworks! Jaymie shouted into the phone to the 911 operator that it was not gunshots, but it was too late. Chaotic moments passed in confusion as Jaymie tried to make herself understood, to no avail, given the loud explosions. Sirens blared and officers shouted commands, swarming the open area as Jaymie and Heidi huddled by the body.

Hands up, Jaymie yelled at the officers with guns drawn. They shouted at her to not move and keep her hands up, all while starbursts of fireworks broke overhead. Heidi wailed and Jaymie couldn't comfort her. Miss Perry must have had her door open, because even above the din Jaymie could hear her in the doorway shrieking from a distance, and a dog barked and howled as other people shouted from the direction of the other houses and the street.

Bernie was the senior responding officer and took command of the situation. Given that the ongoing explosions were clearly fireworks, and after establishing with Jaymie that no shots had actually been fired, she swiftly ordered the others to stand down. Jaymie babbled an explanation as their efficient friend called off the SWAT team–like response. She ordered officers to secure a perimeter around the body.

She allowed Jaymie to comfort Heidi for the moment. Jaymie trembled as she held her weeping friend to her chest, letting her sob out her fear.

"Heidi, it's going to be okay," Bernie said in a calm, authoritative tone that stopped their friend from shuddering. She eyed the body from their current distance. "You've checked and he is beyond being revived?"

Jaymie nodded. "Oh, he's d-dead, Bernie. Stone-cold dead. *Frozen* dead!"

"We'll check ourselves, of course," Bernie said, and strode off with another officer. She returned. "You're right, he's long gone." She then spoke into her two-way radio, a string of numbers alternating with names and words. She refocused her attention. "Tell me *slowly* what's going on!"

One final loud *kapow* thundered like a cannon, echoing back to them from across the river. Far above them a glittering starburst in a waterfall effect exploded against the black night sky. Jaymie winced, holding Heidi, who was again shivering and sobbing, to her tightly. Finally, as Heidi took in deep gulping breaths, her shuddering waning, Jaymie related how they came to find the body.

"So we called 911, and that's when all of this started." She waved one hand, indicating the now-finished fireworks display. She patted a calmer Heidi's back as she watched officers heading in the direction of where the fireworks had been set off. "Hey. *Hey!*" she yelled. "Don't scare the cats— oh, shoot. It's too late for that, isn't it?" she muttered. They had probably rocketed off in all directions at the sound of explosives. Who the devil set them off? All that and a dead man, too.

"One more thing," she said, eyeing her police officer friend. "I know who the dead guy is. Was."

Bernie eyed her in surprise. "Yes?"

"His name is Ethan Zarcone."

It was going to be a long night.

• • •

Minutes later, sitting yet again in a cruiser parked at the curb, a bookend to her lengthy and horrifying day, Jaymie saw police officers enter Bog Brewer's place. Heidi was in another car, of course, so they wouldn't be able to "arrange" their stories. Ridiculous, given they had been together at the cat colony, so if there was a story to be checked, they could have done it then, but she understood the need to keep them apart so their testimonies would be untainted should it come to that. This wasn't her first rodeo, as the saying went.

She twiddled her thumbs as she waited. How long would this take? It had been, what . . . a half hour, at least? In front of the nose of the cruiser in which she sat, Morgan's car screeched to a halt at the curb. The young woman leaped out, yelped in pain, then shouldered her bag. She spotted Jaymie in the police car and mouthed *what's going on?*, but Jaymie couldn't answer, of course. She shrugged.

Poor Morgan; she'd soon discover that Ethan was dead. Jaymie sighed, leaned her head against the headrest and closed her eyes, wishing it were morning and she was home. She spent a moment praying the cats were all safe.

Detective Rodriguez opened the car door, bending over to peer in at her. "Ms. Müller, what a surprise to see you again, so soon."

"You can still call me Jaymie." She sighed and sat up straight. "No offense, but I could have done without this meeting, especially in the wake of the fireworks. Was it Bog Brewer's doing?"

The man looked over his shoulder at the Brewer house. "Apparently, he had leftover fireworks from Chinese New Year and chose tonight to set them off for his own entertainment. I pity dispatch right now, because I'm sure they're fielding dozens of angry calls."

"He couldn't have warned people?" Jaymie said in disgust. "What is *wrong* with him? There are a dozen cats who are probably scattered because of his behavior." Jaymie stared at the house and wondered, did Brewer set them off as some kind of message to someone? It was a thought she'd have to come back to. She scrubbed her gritty eyes. "Is Heidi okay? Poor kid. She's never found a body."

Leaning into the car, he watched her eyes and said, "Unlike your, what, a dozen or more now?"

"If you put it that way it sounds weird. I swear I don't know how I do it." She met his gaze. "How did Ethan die, Detective? And the other guy, Tolly Jones . . . are the deaths connected?"

"I have no further comment. Be happy I satisfied your curiosity about the fireworks. Officer Jenkins gave me your preliminary statement, but I'd like you to come see me at the station tomorrow to give a full account."

"Of course. But I'm not going home until I see for myself that those cats are okay." She folded her arms over her chest. "I mean it. I made a promise. They are my responsibility, and I'm worried about them. I won't get a wink of sleep unless I know."

"I'll have Jenkins escort you."

Jaymie shifted to climb out of the car, then straightened. "How is Morgan taking the news?"

"Morgan?"

"Morgan Perry. Miss Lois Perry's niece. Ethan Zarcone was her boyfriend."

"Her *boyfriend*?" The detective watched her.

Uh-oh. "They're, uh, living together."

"Maybe that's why she fainted when she saw the body."

"She what?"

He sighed. "Not the officers' fault. We're waiting for the medical examiner to arrive, so the body hasn't been bagged yet. She stormed out of her aunt's house—limped out; something's wrong with her foot—and to the scene, started yelling at the officers, asking what was going on. I guess a friend called her to tell her about the fireworks and the police swarming her aunt's home, which is why she drove up here in such a hurry. When she saw the body she crumpled into a ball right there. She recovered moments later, but didn't say he was her boyfriend."

"She was probably scared." Jaymie frowned and thought. It was odd that Morgan wouldn't admit knowing Ethan. Why?

"I'll get Officer Jenkins to escort you to the cat colony, but keep to your task and then go."

"Okay, all right." He didn't need to be surly about it, she thought. "Detective, I can't help but wonder, why did the killer leave his body there, at the top of the bluff? It doesn't make sense."

He paused, staring into the distance. "Good point. I don't know why." He stood still for a long moment, frowning, then said, "I'll see you tomorrow." He strode away, spoke to Bernie briefly, then continued around the house.

Jaymie stretched out her tired back. She had texted Jakob with an explanation. She would be home as soon as she could be and was grateful to be going to the Queensville home rather than the longer drive out to the cabin in the country. Bernie had been chatting to Heidi, her best friend, leaning into the cruiser window, but now straightened and approached Jaymie. "You better now?" she asked.

"I am. Thanks to you. I don't know how to express my appreciation for how you handled things, Bernie."

"My job," she said briskly. "Come on. We can go find out how the cats are faring."

"On my way back, can I stop and talk to Miss Perry?"

Bernie eyed her with a squinted gaze. "I suppose, but keep it brief."

They circled the house in the dark. Bernie guided Jaymie past the scene, now lit with powerful white lights on telescoping stands attached to battery packs. A photographer took pictures, as the medical examiner waited on the sidelines speaking with the detective.

She avoided the body. Instead, she turned her attention to the cats, prowling among the shelters in the bitter cold, relieved to see that Hoagie, at least, was still ensconced in his shelter with one of his feline friends. It would break her heart if this horrible night resulted in cats dying from exposure. She checked her phone photos and did as accurate a head count as she could. There were a few missing, but she wasn't sure what could be done about it.

She explained to Bernie, who thought for a moment. "We'll be knocking on doors this evening in the neighborhood. If it's not against procedure, I'll have the officers mention the feral cats and how there may be some frightened and trying to take shelter."

"I'm not sure what the neighbors will think. Some of them don't like the cat colony."

"It's all I can offer, Jaymie."

"I know. Thank you."

Bernie left her at Miss Perry's back door and retreated to the crime scene, where the medical examiner was now at work.

Miss Perry and her niece, head bowed and sobbing, sat together in her sitting room. Jaymie silently made tea, then came and sat down by Morgan, flicking a glance toward Miss Perry, who took the hint and said, "I'm going to look out the back door again. I want to know what's going on. Probably can't see a damn thing, but you never know."

Once she was gone, Jaymie softly said, "I'm so sorry, Morgan." Jaymie handed her a tissue.

She blotted her eyes and blew her nose. "Do you know what happened? How he . . . how he died?"

"He was already dead when I found him, that's all I know." She let Morgan take a deep breath and regain her composure, then said, "Why didn't you tell the police that Ethan was your live-in boyfriend?"

"I suppose *you* told them?"

"It never occurred to me that you wouldn't have, so it came out, yes."

"After this," she said, pointing at her foot, "I was afraid . . ." She looked away.

"Morgan, did Ethan cause your foot injury?"

Her eyes welled and she nodded, whispering, "I haven't been completely honest. Oh, Jaymie, I don't know what I'm going to do. Ethan wasn't always a good guy. He was involved in something illegal, and I knew it. He said I needed to keep my mouth shut, or . . ."

"Or what? Tell me!"

She stared sullenly away. Jaymie watched her, wondering what was going on in her mind.

"He said he was involved with some people who were used to getting their own way."

"Okay. So?"

"Ethan said if I opened my big fat mouth too much I'd get him killed."

❦ Eleven ❦

"WHAT WAS HE INVOLVED WITH?"

"No, it's . . . I can't—"

"You have to tell the police whatever you know, Morgan. You *have* to!"

She shook her head violently. "I don't *know* anything."

"Why would he make that threat, then?"

She was silent.

"You're fibbing, Morgan," Miss Perry said from the doorway. "I can always tell. You've got the same shifty look you had when you told your mom you were staying with me when you went on spring break with your friends. I wouldn't cover up for you then, and I can't now. This is *murder*."

Morgan stood and her gaze slewed from one to the other of the women. "You don't understand, neither of you."

Jaymie said, "If Ethan was involved in something that got him killed, you could be next."

"She's right," Miss Perry said, toddling into the room and sinking down into her easy chair with a groan. "You have got to think about yourself."

"Your best bet is to tell the police what you know."

Clutching her hands together, Morgan looked like she was about to flee. "He made me promise," she sobbed.

"He's dead, Morgan. You have to protect yourself."

"I'll think about it."

"You've got to do more than think about it. You're going to have to tell the police at some point. The longer you hold out, the worse it will seem."

"Is that a threat?" Morgan shot back.

"Of course not, but listen to me; don't hold back."

Miss Perry said, clasping her hands together, "*Please*, listen to her!"

Time to try a different tactic to loosen her lips. "Was Parker Hellman involved in whatever it was?" Jaymie asked. "Do you know *how* Parker was involved? Is that why you were trying to call him this morning?"

91

"I can't say."

"Did you see Ethan at all today?"

"I did."

"Where?" Jaymie asked. "And when?"

"In Wolverhampton. He came to see me at the car dealership, but I couldn't talk long. I was in the middle of a meeting when he pulled me out to tell me he had nothing to do with the dead guy by the river. And that's when he asked me, if the police came to talk to me, for me not to say anything. He kept looking over his shoulder, like he was afraid of being seen."

"Why would he say that, about not having anything to do with the dead body?"

"When I heard about it, I texted him to ask. I was scared."

"So you *were* worried about that."

"Him and Parker have this business, this . . ." She stopped, sealed her lips and shook her head.

"I've already figured out that at least a part of their business was smuggling people over the border. That's right, isn't it?"

She plopped down in the nearest chair and buried her face in her hands. "Let me *think*! Can't you let me think so I can decide what I should do?"

No denial; that was as good as an admission. Jaymie waited a moment, then asked, "Was Ethan alone when you saw him?"

"I think someone was in the car," Morgan said with a puzzled frown. "Quin was there. She might know."

"Quin? Oh, right, she works at the car dealership as a custodian. I thought she works nights?"

"She hangs around after her shift. We have coffee together most mornings."

"Was it a man or woman in the car?"

"I don't know. Quin spoke to whoever it was, though. She was at the car and handed over a package. I was afraid . . ." She lowered her voice. "I've been afraid that Quin is involved in something illegal, like . . . drugs."

Drugs! That would explain a lot, and might even be the business they were involved in. "Morgan, think. Could Parker have been in the car with Ethan?"

She chewed on her fingernail as she considered. "That would

make sense."

"But you don't know for sure." Morgan shook her head. Jaymie considered it. If Parker and Ethan had killed Tolly Jones together, perhaps Parker later killed Ethan to silence him. "Did you ask Ethan where he had been all night?"

"I did. He said he'd had business to attend to."

"Business in the middle of the night? Morgan, you must wonder—"

"No! I *don't* wonder," Morgan said stubbornly. "Ethan had nothing to do with the murder, I'm sure of it."

Miss Perry, silent this whole time, sighed and said, "Your ability to pick highly flawed men is a kind of genius. What did I hear someone say once? Your picker is broken."

Jaymie flicked a glance at the older woman, wishing she had withheld her critique. Morgan had stiffened at her aunt's disapproval but hadn't replied.

"So Ethan and Parker were in the business of smuggling people over the border," Jaymie said to her.

"I didn't say that."

"But it's true," Jaymie asserted. Morgan reluctantly nodded. "So, given what happened to Ethan, aren't you at all concerned about Parker's well-being?" *If* Parker wasn't Ethan's killer, Jaymie thought.

"I don't know where Parker is, and I don't care. I don't know *what* to think right now!" She jumped up and limped out of the room, weeping loudly. A moment later the front door slammed shut. She was gone.

"What is she keeping secret?" Jaymie said aloud. "And how does it involve Parker Hellman?"

"I don't know. That girl was always a fool for the wrong kind of man. Why does she keep picking these losers?"

"Ethan was handsome," Jaymie said sadly. "He would have been my type, once upon a time."

"I wish she'd find someone like your Jakob."

"I dated my share of frogs before I found my prince," Jaymie said. "Don't give up on her. Even if she never finds the right guy, she'll be okay on her own. Look at Valetta!" Val had been single for a long time, and though she was currently seeing an old friend, she insisted it was still just friends, for the time being.

Miss Perry snorted. "Morgan is no self-sufficient Valetta," she said with asperity. "I'm tired. I'm going to bed. What is going on with the kitties? Are they all okay?"

Jaymie told her what she knew, then rose to leave. "Will you be all right on your own?"

The woman nodded. "With this lot of police officers on my doorstep? Of course. You go along to your hubby and get some sleep."

"I'll be back in the morning to feed the cats and make sure they're all accounted for."

"Don't go finding any more dead bodies," Miss Perry cracked grimly.

Jaymie exited and went over to talk to Heidi, who, now out of the cruiser, was talking to Bernie by her car. Heidi whirled when she saw her friend and hurled herself into Jaymie's arms. "Jaymsie, are you okay?"

Hugging and releasing her, Jaymie searched her friend's face in the glow of the security light on the house. "I'm fine. But how are *you*?"

She smiled tremulously and nodded. "Better. Bernie helped," she said. "I'm cold and tired. I need home and my new kitty to snuggle."

"I have to get back to work," Bernie said. "Take care of each other and I'll call you tomorrow, Heidi. I've got a day off; maybe we can get together."

"You bet," Heidi said. "Come over for dinner. I want you to meet Sadie!" Bernie returned around the house toward the crime scene and Heidi opened her car door, slinging her purse inside. "Are the cats okay?" she asked Jaymie.

"As much as I can tell. I hope so. I'll come out early tomorrow and check again."

They hugged each other, got into their respective cars, and Jaymie followed Heidi to the turnoff, where they went their separate ways. When Jaymie got home Jakob didn't say a word. He took her in his arms and rocked her against his chest, murmuring comforting nothings.

Finally he said, "Are you okay?"

"I will be," Jaymie said, shivering. The cold had seeped into her soul, but Jakob was giving her some of his warmth, sharing his essence, and she could feel it like a balm, comforting her deeply.

• • •

The next morning Jaymie kissed a sleepy Jocie goodbye, shared a longer kiss with Jakob, who was making oatmeal for their daughter, and headed out. After the horrible day she'd had, and feeling so terrible for the two dead men and their families, she hadn't slept well. The desperate phone message for Tolly rang in her ears all night, and Ethan Zarcone's frosted face haunted her sleep when she did manage to get some.

The connection between Ethan and Parker, and Parker being missing, troubled her. Disappearing like that inevitably made him appear guilty. It wouldn't be the first time that partners in an illegal business had a falling-out, with murder as a result.

But *was* Parker missing, or was he dead too?

It could not be a coincidence, Tolly and Ethan being found in virtually the same place a little more than twelve hours apart. But if she was going to posit that they were connected, then she had to examine the point of connection, Bog Brewer. He lived near the bluff. He was a former bandmate of Tolly's. Ethan Zarcone had been thrown out of Brewer's home the day before. Too many connections to discount.

What *was* Bog Brewer's connection?

Two deaths. Two *murders*, in one day!

She was pulling up in front of Miss Perry's home when her phone chimed. It was Val, and she exclaimed over Jaymie's experience the night before. "I'm so sorry, kiddo! Are you okay? Is Heidi? It must have been hard for her, she's so sensitive. What's going on down there?"

"Good question. You heard who it was that I found?" Knowing Val's connection to the family, she worried.

"I do. It's terrible. I feel for his parents, who are nice people."

"Where do they live?"

"I know they split up, but I'm not sure where either of them lives now. I can find out, if you like?"

Jaymie hesitated. "I can't think why I'd need to know, but if you happen to find out . . . no, never mind. This is out of my hands, none of my business. I have to go and look for cats, make sure they're all okay. All that police commotion and before that the fireworks —"

"Fireworks?" Val shrieked. "What the heck — ?"

Jaymie held the phone away from her ear and grimaced, then brought it back to her face, saying, "Didn't you hear about that part? I thought all of Queensville would have seen them. Oh, I've got stories! I'll drop in at the store and we can chat before I go give my statement to the police. I'll tell you all about it, but right now, I gotta go."

There was still a police presence, but it was muted, a couple of patrol officers. The weather had turned from bitterly frigid to damply cold, so maybe the snap was ending. She had the back of her SUV open and was loading fabric bags with bowls and food when she saw Haskell banging on Bog Brewer's door. Someone opened it and he went in.

She could guess Haskell was going to complain to Bog about the fireworks.

Behind the houses she noted that the police still had part of the bluff cordoned off. Jaymie assumed they had a uniformed crew down on the flats conducting a formal search. She scanned the cat colony area. It appeared that the cats were enjoying the weather, which was not as cold as it had been for the last week. Some were eyeing her hopefully from the tops of shelters. She now recognized most of the cats and mentally checked them off the list in her mind, thankful to see that a few who were missing the night before were now present. A couple more and she'd know they were all okay.

She removed the dirty bowls and put clean ones about, filling them with hard food as cats emerged from shelters and hopped down from the elevated shelves, descending on the food with focused gazes. A few spats erupted, but mostly they settled down in peace. She started opening cans and dishing the wet food into bowls, which brought *all* the cats running as they abandoned the dry food for the more luscious wet. *There* were the couple of cats she hadn't seen the night before! Now she knew they were all accounted for.

Except . . . she looked around for Hoagie and frowned when she didn't see him. Where was the old boy? She had brought him some special food from Lilibet's stash, as well as a bunch of treats to dole out. She ducked and investigated the accommodations, finally finding Hoagie, who was huddled staring straight ahead in the last shelter. She scraped the special food into a saucer and placed it before him, but he didn't move. Her stomach sank. She had seen that fixed sad gaze before on Denver when he wasn't well.

She sat down cross-legged on the wet ground in front of the shelter. "Come on, Hoagie, eat! You have to eat." She pushed it toward him, but he turned away his face with a low growl in the back of his throat.

"You're back."

She looked up as a shadow fell over her. It was Haskell. She clambered to her feet, still worriedly focused on Hoagie. "Of course I'm back. You don't just feed cats once and that's it."

"I wish you wouldn't feed these pests," he groused. "You know, feral cats are responsible for killing songbirds, threatening extinction for some."

She wanted to bite his head off, but feeding feral cat colonies was controversial for that very reason. "What is your alternative?" she asked, instead of being combative.

"What?"

"What's your alternative? To feeding them, I mean."

"Just don't."

"So let them die? Haskell, I understand what you're getting at, but these cats are homeless through no fault of their own. You *must* know that. I already told you so the other day. They are not a malevolent force to be exterminated."

He blinked in the face of her calm insistence. "I didn't say they were. But how do they end up out here?"

"People don't get their pets neutered and then abandon them. Those cats breed, and the kittens are feral. They try to find places where they'll be let alone. Feeding them is probably saving some of those birds you're so worried about. And neutering them is saving future generations of feral cats from being born. If you want to help, contribute to the neutering program. When we know where they are, we can keep them neutered and disease-free."

"But—"

"I'm serious, Haskell," she said. "Everyone is doing the best they can." A few years ago she would never have stood up for what she believed in. Having a daughter had shown her how important it was to model that behavior. "I'll ask again, what is your alternative? Do you want to let this old guy die?" Tears clogged her voice as she pointed down into the shelter at Hoagie, who still had not eaten. "He's toothless and older. He's not eating today and I'm worried. Is your solution to leave him to die, alone and cold?"

She knew that her statement was about more than the cat, though it was all true. She was also thinking about Tolly and Ethan, dying alone in the freezing cold. Yesterday's trauma would not dissipate quickly. She cleared her throat and swiped at her eyes.

Haskell hunkered down and stared at Hoagie. "What's wrong with him?"

"I don't know. Last night's commotion may have disoriented him, or . . . I don't know. I'm going to call the vet, Dr. Kasimo."

"I know him. He's good with Aloysius." He paused, then said, "So you'll leave him here and have the vet come to see him?"

"What alternative is there?" she said, trying to clear her throat.

"I could take him to Dr. Kasimo myself."

She stared at him in surprise. What was going on? Maybe he was feeling guilty about shutting down her Tea with the Queen event behind her back and was trying to make it up to her.

Or . . .

Or maybe he was truly concerned about Hoagie. She wouldn't let herself get cynical. She had been called naïve by people who preferred to assume the worst about people, but she'd rather keep on thinking the best until proven wrong. She would resist cynicism.

"Haskell, that would be nice if you'd take Hoagie to the doctor," she said, trying not to cry. She took in a deep shuddering breath, the emotional overload of the day before crashing down on her. "I'd appreciate it so much," she said, her voice thick with unshed tears. "I would do it myself, but I have to go to the police today to give my statement about last night, and your help will make that easier. George did give me a couple of cat carriers for that possibility."

"Then it's settled," he said, watching her and smiling. "I'd like to help."

He was a stick in the mud, as Petty said, but there was an unexpected kindness in him that touched her. They walked together back to her car, Haskell carrying the tote bag full of dirty dishes. "I understand from Petty that you two aren't together?"

He grimaced, carefully navigating a wet slippery patch across the flats, past a police officer who nodded to them. "She's made it pretty clear that I'm an old fuddy-duddy."

"I'm sorry."

He was silent.

"I appreciate what you're going to do for Hoagie," she said. "I really do, Haskell."

"I won't let it be said that I'm heartless. Because I'm not. I still feel, though, that we need to have a conversation about this cat colony. It's not my place to have the conversation, I suppose, but I know the mayor feels the same way."

It was her turn for silence.

He glanced at her. "Jaymie, I'm sorry about the tea event. I know people don't think I'm capable of saying it, but I *am* sorry. I miscalculated the impact of doing away with the tea. I still think it will have challenges. How can you manage? Stowe House is under contract now, I've heard. Someone bought it, I don't know who, so it seems pointless to continue the Tea with the Queen event if we can't hold it there. I'm not sure what you'll do if it's not available to use."

"Where did you hear that Stowe House was sold?"

"A broker friend of mine heard it from someone else."

"So you don't know who bought it?"

"No, sorry."

"I've got feelers out to answer that question. It's possible that the new owners will let us use it, at least this year." She put the bag of dirty bowls and the big container of hard food into the back of her SUV and grabbed one of the cat carriers. They returned to the cat colony, where Jaymie was happy to see that all of the cats had eaten and were now having their ritual post-meal bath. She turned to the man beside her. "Haskell, why did you go to see Bog Brewer this morning?"

"To tell him off about those awful fireworks last night! It scared poor Aloysius to death. Poor baby hasn't gone out except to tinkle this morning and then retreated back under the bed."

"What did Bog say?"

"He wasn't up, and that awful wife of his was no use."

Or was Bog not up to seeing people because of the death of Tolly, and the police questioning?

"Fortunately his friend was there, and he was very reasonable.

Said he didn't understand why Mr. Brewer behaved so."

"His friend?"

"Yes, nice fellow. Fitzroy, uh . . . what was his last name? I know he said it when we were introduced at the heritage society meeting."

"Oh, the nicely dressed fellow you were speaking to."

"Yes. Interesting fellow. Considering relocating to Queensville. So complimentary of our town. Charming, in that genteel English manner."

"So his name is Fitzroy . . . ?"

"Fitzroy, yes . . . what *is* his last name? Uh, wait, I have it!" He snapped his fingers. "Of course. Such a simple surname, too. Fitzroy Jones."

"Jones!" Jaymie stopped stock-still. "You're sure his last name is Jones?"

He nodded.

Jones was a common name; she mustn't let her imagination run away with itself. "Where is he from?"

"As I said, he's English. That's all I know."

English. And there at the Brewers' early in the morning? She tried to calculate the odds of two Englishmen with the last name Jones being in Queensville. "I have to go, so we'd better get a move on." She opened the door on the cat carrier. "I don't know if he'll go in to the carrier on his own, or how he'll react once he's in there."

"I'll tell you what I do with Aloysius. Or better yet, I'll show you." He took off his coat and approached the shelter. "Don't give them time to think about it." He reached in with his long arms, bundled his coat around Hoagie, then pushed the cat into the carrier, pulling his coat out and leaving the cat inside.

Once in, Hoagie moaned, a long growly sound, but he huddled in the corner and didn't fight the inevitable. That was worrisome, Jaymie thought. She closed the door and latched it as Haskell put his coat back on. "That was fast and efficient," Jaymie said. He was better at that than she would have thought possible. "I hope he's going to be okay. I don't like how he's not fighting the carrier at all." She crouched down and eyed him. "It'll be okay, Hoagie baby." She put her fingers in the door grid, but could not reach him to pet him. "Poor boy."

As Jaymie stood, Haskell picked up the carrier and said, "I'll take him now and see what the doctor says. I'll call you later."

✄ **Twelve** ✄

"JONES. FITZROY *JONES*. WHAT ARE THE CHANCES, VAL?" Jaymie said as she drove into town. She had her phone on the holder on the dash. "He has to be related to Tolly, don't you think?"

"It's a common surname, but he is about the right age and has the same last name. I can't imagine that he's *not* related to Tolly Jones."

"I know," Jaymie said grimly. "It's too weird to be a coincidence. I'm here; see you in a sec." She parked in front of the Queensville Emporium and entered as she hung up her phone.

Val had called in her colleague to substitute for her. Helen Pham was there and working on a prescription as Jaymie approached the pharmacy counter at the back.

"I'm going with you to the PD, kiddo," Val said as she shrugged into her coat. "And then I'm taking you to lunch at Wellington's Retreat."

"I won't fight you on it."

"I wanted to bend your ear more about the Kitschy Kitchen and help you figure out your Tea with the Queen event."

"Actually, I have some information and some questions you may be able to help with. We'll take my SUV then?"

They drove to the police department first, for Jaymie to give her statement on both bodies she found the day before. The interview was being videotaped, she was told, for future retrieval, and a second detective—a new woman on the force—sat in, taking notes. It was straightforward, but a different experience being interviewed by Rodriguez. Jaymie realized how personality variations played a part in police investigations. Vestry was closemouthed and secretive, not giving up much in an interview, but she and Jaymie had come to a détente through working together on the hiking trail in the woods opposite the cabin.

Jaymie had no such rapport with Rodriguez, but she told herself to relax and go with the flow, as much as that is possible in a murder investigation.

He had her relate her memory of the events in as straightforward a manner as she could recall, but then he went back to points he had made notes on. With his prodding and digging she recalled details she may have lost otherwise, or not thought to mention. She related finding both bodies, and all the extraneous details that felt, to her, like they were associated. She told him about seeing Parker Hellman on the river flats, how she knew that Morgan had been trying to call him to find out where Ethan was, but that he didn't seem to be answering his phone.

She had since learned that Morgan did see Ethan that day, before he died, she told him, watching his expression, which remained neutral. She told him that the coat that Tolly Jones was wearing was exactly like the one she had seen on Parker Hellman when she first met him. Zarcone had been trying to get a business proposal going in Queensville and had sought a way to influence those with impact in the town, people like Haskell Lockland. "I'm giving you everything I know."

"Good. Excellent. I wonder, would you do me a favor?"

"I'd have to know what it is before agreeing, Detective."

A rare smile creased his face. "I like that. Okay, here it is, and it's pretty simple. Chief Ledbetter says you're trustworthy. Will you keep your eyes and ears open? Tell me what you hear or see or suspect. You have a unique access to these people; your friendship with Miss Perry, Morgan Perry, her friend Quinley Gustafson, feeding the cats near Bog Brewer's property, having met Parker Hellman—"

"Do you know where Parker is yet?"

"I'd like you, as I said, to keep your eyes and ears open but do nothing," he said, not answering her question. "And I mean that, young lady. Do *nothing*! Report to me."

She nodded. "You didn't even have to ask. I would do that anyway."

He watched her for a moment, a worried expression in his eyes. "You have a habit of getting yourself in trouble by confronting perps."

"Not on purpose. Or at least . . . not without help," she said. "*Never* without help, unless I didn't know what I was getting into. I've learned the hard way that *you don't know what you don't know*. I'm bound to make mistakes." She smiled. "The police do too, sometimes." He almost smiled back; she saw him force himself not to. "I'd like to tell you, or ask you, one more thing, Detective." She relayed what she had learned about Fitzroy Jones, and his arrival at the Brewer house. "We both know that the first body is that of Tolly Jones. What are the chances that Fitzroy Jones isn't related to Tolly?"

"Duly noted, Ms. Müller." Rodriguez thanked her for her cooperation, and said she could call him any time.

As she stood, she asked, "Detective, I will ask once more: have you spoken with Parker Hellman yet?"

He was standing by the interview room door ushering her out and smiled. "Now, Ms. Müller, you know I can't answer questions like that."

"Okay. All right. I'm wondering where Parker is, that's all. I wonder if he's the killer. Or is he a victim?"

"Victim?"

"If we don't know where he is, he could be dead."

"You are surprisingly frank, Ms. Müller."

"I've learned to be. I can't help but wonder why he was down by the river on a frigid day examining the far bank."

He didn't respond.

"I will be keeping my eyes open concerning the whereabouts of Parker Hellman," she said, watching for a reaction. "And whether he was out in his boat the night Tolly Jones died."

His eyebrows lifted but he didn't reply.

"And I can't help but wonder, too, Detective, if Bog Brewer's fireworks display was a message, or a signal."

Again, he regarded her stolidly. She shrugged and said she'd call him if she learned anything more.

She joined Val in the parking lot, climbing into the SUV. They talked about the day before and she went over what she had told Rodriguez and what she had recalled. "When I found Tolly Jones, at first I thought he was Parker because of the coat color, but there was more to it. That coat . . . it had some kind of patch on the pocket. It read 'Crimson Skeleton Riders' and had a red skull on a black background. What does that even mean?"

"Sounds like a bike gang to me."

"Interesting idea. I'll call Clutch Roth," she said of her biker friend. "Maybe he'll know what it is. Anyway, the coat was Parker's or one exactly like it, based on that patch."

"Why would he have given the victim his coat?"

"I don't know. Detective Rodriquez is not saying if he knows where Parker is, but I suspect he doesn't." She then told Val, as they drove into Wolverhampton, about how Haskell had come to Hoagie's rescue that morning, taking the ailing cat to the vet.

"I'm amazed! Especially as he's one of the leading critics of the ferals."

"As much as I hate to say it, he does have a point, Val. It isn't a great place for the cat colony. For so many reasons! Jocie did an essay for her science class last year on endangered species of the St. Clair River–Lake St. Clair area. Haskell pointed out that feral and stray cat populations do real damage to birds nesting and raising young."

"Ideally they would be relocated, maybe?"

"I'd love to think we can find homes for all the cats, but I don't know if that's realistic. They're only there because that's where they are being fed, I suppose. I'll think on it. I'm pretty sure Heidi is adopting Sadie, which is nice. She's such a small cat, too easily bullied by the bigger ones."

Val glanced at her. "Miss Perry would miss the cats."

"Maybe she should adopt a couple."

They found a parking spot on the main street in Wolverhampton and walked down to Wellington's Retreat, a breakfast and lunch nook. It was warm and humid, with the delicious smell of baking biscuits and good coffee filling the air. They took a window seat — the place would fill up closer to the noon hour, but it was only eleven — and ordered tea, to start.

"This is a business meeting," Val said. "I have registered the business online with the state, so I'm starting the bookkeeping for the Kitschy Kitchen with this lunch. Therefore, I will pay and keep the bill for taxes!"

Jaymie smiled. She couldn't quite believe they were about to undertake such a vast task and commitment. Was she ready for this? She had been working in the vintage shops in Queensville for years and had seen what worked and what didn't. She had a deep interest in kitchen collectibles, and how much they were worth. So maybe she did have the requisite background. One summer she had worked as a server at the Queensville Inn, so she even had a little serving experience.

Val insisted that they forgo the fun stuff—planning the renovations and paint colors and kitschy details—for the mundane. The day they examined the former knitting shop Val had given Jaymie a tour. It was much bigger than it appeared from the outside and had a tiny one-bedroom apartment upstairs that had been unused since a tenant moved out a year ago. The apartment would be ideal for Violet. "It will be a part of her investment package, I was thinking. We can sort out numbers before she moves in."

Besides the main room that Bonnie used for her yarn store, there was a kitchenette and two bathrooms. Beyond that there were three large rooms that had been used as storage and an office for Bonnie.

"I thought one room could be devoted to kitchen collectibles. With a name like the Kitschy Kitchen, that should be our main draw. It sets us apart from Cynthia and Jewel's shops. And we could use the other two rooms for the rest of the stuff. Maybe even a vintage book nook! There's a big hall closet that could be renovated to hold shelves."

"That would be wonderful. How about a Kitschy Kids nook of kids' books and vintage toys?"

Val's eyes widened. "Great thought!" she said, scribbling the idea. "Get Jocie and her friends involved."

"What is our timeline for this?"

"I know it will be tight, and there's a lot on both of our plates, but I hope we can have it ready for a grand opening on the Victoria Day weekend, to coincide with the Tea with the Queen event. We'd have a ready-made crowd, all the tourists who come for the tea and then walk through the village to the vintage and antique stores."

That was a lot. Jaymie counted the time left before then. "That only gives us two months, and we don't know what kind of repairs are going to be needed. I don't think it's possible."

"Okay, we'll figure it out. Let's have a meeting at the store and see if we think it's doable, and if not, can we do *something* the Tea with the Queen weekend, so we don't miss all those tourists that come to Queensville that weekend?"

"I had another thought," Jaymie said, eyeing Val. "The space out back . . . what would you think of a patio, and my vintage trailer out there, with a Kitschy Garden area? Vintage garden stuff for sale and a tea terrace in summer!"

"That is a great idea!" Tears welled in her friend's eyes. She pushed her glasses up on her forehead, blotted the tears with a paper napkin, and sniffed as her glasses fell back down on the bridge of her nose. "I'm going to love this, every step of the way. I like being a pharmacist, don't get me wrong, but this is exactly what I've needed in my life."

"It won't be easy, though. Promise me that if you're frustrated or need input, or need me to butt out—or *in*—that you'll tell me. Complete communication, all the way."

Val reached across the table and took Jaymie's hand. "I will do that, my friend. And the same for you. We'll have this discussion with Violet too, I promise."

"Maybe what would work is to have an outdoor tea party that weekend, to complement the Tea with the Queen event, so attendees learn about the Kitschy Kitchen and when we'll be opening for real."

"As a matter of fact, why not make the Kitschy Kitchen one of the corporate sponsors of the event so it will be featured in the advertising copy?"

"Awesome!" Jaymie said, wriggling in her seat. "I'm so excited."

They spent lunch planning on paper how to apportion the work. Val, too excited to wait, had called Bonnie and made an offer on the building. She and her sister-in-law, Violet, were purchasing the shop/house from Bonnie at a negotiated price. When Bonnie came back up to Queensville, they could finalize the paperwork.

By the time Val paid the bill and they walked out into the cold March air, they had solid foundations laid and plans for a meeting with Violet when she came over from Canada next. Valetta was going to begin interviewing contractors for the work to be done on the kitchen. They agreed that the tea trailer would have to wait until after the official opening, but they could tidy the patio area so, weather and licensing permitting, they could hold a tea reception the weekend of the Tea with the Queen event. Jaymie was going to speak to the owners of Tansy's Tarts, the bakery on Heartbreak Island, to see if they'd supply their delectable treats to be served at the Kitschy Kitchen.

On the drive back to Queensville, Jaymie glanced over at her friend and said, "Did you get a chance to ask Brock about Stowe House?"

"I did. He says he understands that the house is under contract, but it hasn't closed yet, so details about the sale and the new owner are not publicly available."

"What about Greg?" Jaymie asked. Greg Vasiliev, a realtor in Wolverhampton, had been going out with Val for a few months.

"Not much of his business is in Queensville. I can ask them what other local realtors it may have gone through. Then I'll see if we can get a message to the new owners, if we find out who it is."

Jaymie dropped Val off at her house, then returned to the yellow-brick Queen Anne family home she co-owned with Becca. It was Wednesday. They were staying at the house until Sunday, when Becca and Kevin would return from Canada. She sat down at the table in the old kitchen and looked around, at the clutter atop the cupboards — mostly hers — and the clutter atop the Hoosier she had bought a few years ago at auction, also hers.

It was time to let go of a lot of this stuff. Becca would be so excited! There was a decluttering coming for this old house.

But right now it was time to work on her "Vintage Eats" column, her blog, and dinner! What to make, what to make?

And then an idea came to her: old-fashioned rice pudding! She remembered her Grandma Leighton's, which was a baked treat with a custardy foundation and raisins. You baked it, and then it was scooped from the Dutch oven into a bowl and doused with cream. Delicious!

She dug out the recipe from her grandmother's handwritten cookbook and set it up on the counter, propping it on a bookstand. She made notes and tried to decipher Grandma Leighton's looped handwriting. She squinted, figured it out, and wrote it out for herself.

So . . . rice, eggs, whole milk, and spices. She had everything she needed, except for the raisins the recipe called for. She thought for a moment. *Aha!* She had an idea. Now came the fun part, the cooking!

• • •

After dinner, Jaymie and Jakob stood at the sink doing the dishes. The kitchen was bathed in the warm glow of the single pendant light over the sink. Jocie was down at Peyton's working on a dance routine for their dance class. They kept an eye on the time. It was a school night and Jocie had to be home by eight, and in bed by eight thirty.

Jakob leaned over and kissed her cheek. She smiled up at him. "What was that for?"

"For how good the house smelled when we came home this afternoon," he said softly, watching her. "Sugar and spice and everything nice. That's you."

"I'll remember to dab nutmeg and cinnamon behind my ears next time we're going out."

"Every man in miles will be following you around."

Jaymie relayed her meeting with the detective and, hands in warm soapy water, she scrubbed the rice pudding baking dish, an old Dutch oven casserole dish in the Cornflower Blue pattern that her grandmother had bought new in the sixties. "It's different talking to Detective Rodriguez than it is working with Detective Vestry," she mused. "It got me to thinking that despite them all having similar training, detectives must bring a lot of their own personality to their work, you know?"

Leaning his hip against the counter, waiting with a tea towel in his hands, Jakob said, "I never thought about it, but that's likely true. You have a preference between them now?"

She considered it. "I don't think so. Different doesn't always mean better or worse, I guess. He had a way of taking me back. I'd remember a little more each time. It was effective. But Detective Vestry knows me now, and knows when there is more I haven't figured out yet." She handed him the casserole dish and plucked the glass casserole lid from the sink to scrub. "There's one thing still bugging me. Why did whoever killed him leave Ethan's body at the top of the bluffs? It doesn't make sense. They could have dumped him in the river."

"Unless the placement was meant as a message."

Jaymie paused, dish dripping. "A message. Huh. A message to whom, though?"

"Whoever did it may have known Morgan was at Miss Perry's often. And he was her boyfriend, so . . . Morgan?"

"Maybe. I'll have to think about that. I can't stop thinking about Parker Hellman, wondering 'victim or villain,' you know?"

"I hope not a victim."

"Me too." No more dead bodies, please, she thought.

Jakob then talked about his day, a trip to a house clear-out he and his employees were undertaking while his business partner, Gus, watched the store. Increasingly he was being called in to help clear out the estates of people who had moved into an apartment or retirement home, or who had passed. "It makes me wonder, how do their homes get that way? How do they end up so deep in trash and treasures?"

"Friends of mine, their mother was in kind of that situation. They cleared it out, but she ended up right back in the same trouble again. It didn't stop until the woman moved in with her daughter, who was able to make sure it didn't happen again." She glanced at him. "I'm aware that I've been gathering far too much stuff in boxes, both at home and here. You've been sweet, and haven't said a word, but it has to stop. It's overrunning the space in both houses."

. "I wasn't bringing hoarding up to point a finger, *liebling*. I promise you that. When we have worries we face them head-on, we don't hint around the edges."

She scruffed his beard with her soapy hand, leaving bubbles behind. "After a lifetime of my parents, you don't know how much I appreciate that. I think you are a big part of my new ability to face things head-on. I used to tiptoe around stuff, but now . . . *now* I can be brave." She kissed him on the lips then tossed some soapy water at him.

From there, as he dried the matching lid from the Dutch oven, the conversation naturally moved on to discussing the Kitschy Kitchen plans, a good part of her planned reformation from hoarding kitchen stuff.

"Tell you what," he said, returning from putting the Dutch oven away and accepting a dripping mixing bowl. "There are tons of boxes at The Junk Stops Here that haven't been gone through yet. I never have time. If you go through them and sort them for me, you can take whatever you want for your store. And you know that storeroom space that we don't use? You can store it all in there until you have the Kitschy Kitchen ready to open. It has a locking door. You'll have the only key."

"Oh, Jakob, I knew I married the right man for me!" she said, hugging him, soapy hands locked around his neck. "Who else would understand exactly what I need?"

They finished up, and she got ready to head over and feed the cats. Jakob watched her shrug into her coat and helped her put it on.

"*Liebling,* are you sure . . ." He stopped and watched her, uncertainly.

"Sure about what?"

"About going out there in the dark. I don't mean you're not capable and safe, but . . ." He shrugged, worry in his brown eyes.

She smiled. "I understand. If I feel unsafe, I promise I won't do it, or I'll drag someone along with me. Haskell, maybe. You have to stay here and go get Jocie." He nodded, but still looked uneasy. She had been in trouble before, and she understood his concern. "I won't take any chances," she said softly. "I promise I will ask for help if I get nervous."

She was in her SUV but hadn't pulled out yet when her phone rang. It was Heidi. "Hey, Kitten," she said, with a new joking pet name, "How's your new cat?" She set the phone in its holder on the dash and pulled out, driving through the quiet streets of Queensville.

"Sadie is so sweet! I love her so much. She won't be going back to the cat colony."

"Aw, you're going to adopt her!" Jaymie had suspected as much. "That's wonderful!"

"I am. Her leg is getting better. The doctor thinks it may have been bruised in a fall from one of the shelters or aggression from one of the other cats. She's so much smaller than the others. Bernie was here for dinner. She just left. Dak—Dr. Kasimo, you know—was here too. They got along great."

Heidi wanted to run her new love interest past her best friend. That was sweet.

"Dak said my cousin brought one of the colony cats in to the vet clinic. What is up with that?"

Jaymie turned onto the road that followed the river up to Winding Woods. "I know, right? You could have knocked me over with a feather when Haskell volunteered to help." Heidi and Haskell were second or third cousins. The Lockland family had a long history in Queensville, though Heidi's branch of it had moved to New York almost a century ago and made a fortune in real estate.

"I was surprised too, but he seemed genuinely concerned. How is Hoagie doing?" Jaymie asked. "Did the doctor say?"

"Dak was worried at first. Hoagie wasn't drinking fluids and that's a problem. So he gave him subcutaneous fluids at the clinic."

"Look at you with the veterinary medical speak!"

Heidi chuckled. "Haskell took him home late this afternoon to see how he does overnight. Dak told him about a prescription food that's irresistible. Hoagie ate some tonight, apparently. I went out today and found some licky treats for Sadie, so I stopped in and gave one to Hoagie. I got him to eat the whole thing!"

Jaymie smiled. Heidi was enjoying looking after the cats. "As far as anyone knows Hoagie is feral, but he doesn't seem wild to me, not like some of the cats that disappear as soon as humans show up. How has he been behaving?" she asked, as she parked on the road, glancing up at Haskell's house.

"He's in a spare bedroom. He's not dashing for the door, at least. I think he's going to recover."

"How is Aloysius taking the new housemate?"

"It's so cute, Jaymsie!" she cried, her girlish voice lifting in a laugh. Jaymie was happy to hear it, for she had feared how her friend would take what had happened the night before. "That little pupper lies by the door and whines. He wants to meet Hoagie so bad, but Dak told Haskell not to introduce them yet, to give it a while, especially while poor Hoagie is feeling so awful."

Give it a while? Jaymie was silent for a long moment then finally asked, incredulous, "Does that mean Haskell is going to keep him?"

"I don't know. Until he recovers, for sure." Heidi reassured Jaymie that she was feeling better after talking to Bernie. "But you're not going out there alone to feed the cats, are you? After two murders?"

"I'll be okay. I promised Jakob that if I ever started feeling uneasy, I'd get someone to go with me, and I will, I promise you, too." They said goodbye. Jaymie clambered out and started getting the food and dishes together, still eyeing Haskell's house and wondering if she should stop in and see Hoagie. She decided to leave it until after she had fed the cats.

She heard yelling and looked up, toward the Brewers' house. Bog, in boxers and boots, was sliding on some ice and landed on his butt as Ducky, wailing incoherently, trotted after him, throwing vinyl records like Frisbees. A gust of wind caught one and it flew up, then dipped, then landed on its edge and rolled down the sloping street, stopping at Jaymie's feet. What on earth . . . ?"

∅ **Thirteen** ∅

SHE SET THE BAGS OF FOOD AND DISHES DOWN ON THE ICY ROAD and picked up the record, reading the label in the illumination of a streetlight as Duckie sobbed and swore, shrieking a stream of blue invective. *Killing the Muse*, by the Berk Scouse Brothers. Huh. She moved toward the arguing pair, Bog awkwardly clambering to his feet. "Hey, folks, everything okay?"

Duckie stopped and blinked. Bog flicked ice from his knees and straightened. "Yeah, everything's jammy," he said, glancing back at his wife.

Her bottom lip quivered. "Boggie, baby, I'm sorry."

"S'alright, Duckie, struth. C'mere." She wobbled over to him and he took her in his arms. Over her head he said, "We're 'avin' a bit of a barney."

A barney? Must be a fight. "I'm sorry about your old friend, Tolly Jones," she said, watching his face. "I imagine the police have interviewed you about him?"

"Yah, th'rozzers were 'ere. Couldn't believe it were 'im, but they said as 'ow it were."

"Was he on his way to see you?"

"Nah, couldna bin. 'E weren't let in the U.S. 'E bodged things royal back in th'day. Rozzers nicked 'im on a charge of smugglin' horse, but 'e scarpered afore 'e went to the slammer."

"Horse?"

"Heroin, darlin'. I 'eard he served time, though, finally, in the U.S., an' that's why he weren't allowed back in. M'lady's freezin' her Bristols off. We're goin' back in."

"Bog, what about the guy who was at your house, Fitzroy Jones? Is he Tolly's brother?"

"Gotta go, luv!" he sang.

He was in an awful hurry. "Tolly and you go way back," she called out as he retreated. Suspicion sang through her bones. "You must be reeling from his death, and in such an odd place. Was he trying to get to you?"

No answer, but Bog had stopped in his tracks, Duckie still hanging off him. He glanced back at Jaymie, fear on his lined face. Had he killed his friend? Why *was* Tolly coming to Queensville?

"Bog, why did you let off the fireworks the other night?" *Was it some kind of message, like the deed had been done and Ethan was dead?*

"Just a lark," he grunted. "Needed a bit of a break, y'know?"

It didn't make sense as a message, she acknowledged, watching Bog's face, his uncertainty, the fearful expression. And he was erratic enough to do it as an anxiety release. *Someone* had snuck Tolly across the river, over the border, most likely Parker Hellman, she mused. That could be why he was staring across the river; he was wondering if he could get Tolly across in such nasty cold weather. The river hadn't frozen up yet, though, so he risked it? But why, and what happened that Tolly ended up dead?

"We gotta go in, freezin' me arse off." Bog tried to pull Duckie away, but she resisted, speaking to him with her expressive, tear-filled eyes.

Or . . . was it *Ethan* who had ferried the Englishman? Jaymie couldn't imagine it. "Bog, none of this makes sense," she said, staring at the pair. "Why was Tolly coming to see you? And why is his brother here, and why did he come visit *you*? There has got to be some connection with you, and you should be telling the police, if you haven't already."

"*Tell* her, sweetie pumpkin. You've got to talk to someone," Duckie urged.

"Shut it, luv," he said, squeezing her until she squeaked. "You're not 'elpin' Alf wiv that chatter so *shut it*." He turned her around and tugged her away, back to his house.

"Bog, who is Alf?" Jaymie followed, record in hand. "Bog! What about your record?" she called after him, holding it up and waving it about.

"Keep it, luv," he shouted over his shoulder. "I've got a dozen just like it."

She watched them enter the big house and shut the door. Maybe Violet would like the record, thrown at Bog himself by his wife.

Tending to the cats was a pleasure. They were all there, the shy ones elusive but present, the friendlier ones rubbing against her legs and purring. The flat expanse of snow was starting to thaw in the milder temperatures that had arrived during the day. A few tufts of brown grass poked through. It occurred to her that she wasn't concerned at all, this moment, because the cats would not be so relaxed if a stranger lurked nearby or trouble was brewing. She finished up then approached the back door of Miss Perry's house.

She rapped, and was surprised when Morgan answered and ushered her in. Her friend's niece must have arrived while Jaymie was taking care of the cats. She took her boots off at the back door, then toted the bag of dirty bowls and boots to the front door, setting them down for when she left. Miss Perry shouted at her to come have a cup of tea, because they had something to discuss.

When she entered Miss Perry's lair, the two women were sitting together, the elder holding the younger's hand. Morgan's eyes were swimming with tears, though they weren't spilling over. Yet.

"What's going on?" Jaymie asked, glancing from one to the other. "What have you heard?" She thought immediately of Parker, because she had a bad feeling about his disappearance.

"We haven't heard a thing. Sit." Miss Perry watched Morgan, who nodded ever so slightly. "We have something we need to discuss. Morgan wasn't completely honest with us about her relationship with Ethan."

"She wasn't honest with anyone," said someone in the shadows.

Quin sat in a chair, arms crossed over her bosom. Jaymie narrowed her eyes. What was *she* doing here? Morgan drove herself the night before.

Morgan shifted and moved, dropping her aunt's hand and getting up. "I'll put on tea."

Miss Perry sighed, and let her go, staring after her with troubled eyes. "Morgan wasn't honest, not with us and not with the police."

"That's never a good idea. It makes them think things. I'm assuming this has to do with her sprained foot?"

"In part, certainly. She didn't jump from the car, Ethan pushed her."

Jaymie's heart thudded. "That's awful," she said, her voice guttural.

"I saw a gun in the glove box and freaked out," Morgan said from the doorway. "We had a horrible argument over it. I said he had to get rid of it. I asked him why he had it."

"Did he answer?"

"He said it was none of my business. And after he . . . after I was hurt he threatened me." Tears ran down her cheeks. "He said if I told anyone, that he'd make sure Aunt Lois would die. I c-couldn't take that chance." She sobbed, hugging herself. "By then I had started to wonder what he was capable of. So I lied, and said he was wonderful. I defended him. I stood up for him. I tried to make sure he was thought of as a good guy. I couldn't let him hurt my aunt."

"But he's dead now."

"And that's the problem," Quin said, leaning forward into the pool of light. "Who's going to believe her if she didn't say it when he was alive? I mean, women can say anything about a guy once he's dead."

Jaymie cast Quin a look. It almost sounded like she was one of those people she spoke of, who wouldn't believe Morgan. "They have no reason to *not* believe her," she replied.

"Quin's right, though. Don't you see?" Morgan said, coming in and perching on the arm of her aunt's chair, her hands squeezed between her knees. "If I tell them the truth now, the police are going to think I killed him!"

"They won't think that!" Jaymie exclaimed, though she heard her own tone, and there was no abundance of conviction. They would most certainly consider her a suspect, especially since she had withheld information after his death, but truthfully, as his significant other she was already on the list.

However, with her hobbling about? How would she get his body on the windy, icy cliffside? "They won't think that," she repeated, and this time her tone rang true. "But you need to go tomorrow to the police and tell them what you know."

"I can't!" she cried. "I'm afraid."

Miss Perry covered her hand. "I'll go with you."

"You don't have to do that, Miss Perry," Quin said in a sweet tone. "I'll take Morgan. She is my bestie, after all."

"No, I'll go with her," Miss Perry insisted. "She can drive now." Her firm tone brooked no refusal.

Morgan gave her a watery smile. "I can't ask you to do that, Aunt Lois."

"Nonsense. It will be thrilling. I've never been to a police station before. I'll make sure my lawyer is there, too. No one will bully you, my dear."

"Rodriguez isn't going to chain her and flog her with a rubber hose, you know," Jaymie said with a smile.

"They have other methods," Quin said darkly. "They'll trick her into saying stuff and before she knows it, she's their number-one suspect."

"That is hardly helpful," Miss Perry snapped.

"Or she'll confess," the woman shouted. "That's what they do, you know. They hold you alone and scared until you confess!" She was trembling, her tone harsh and loud in the quiet room.

"Quin, are you okay?" Morgan said, her tone full of concern.

"I'm fine."

"You don't look quite well."

"I said I'm okay," Quin snapped.

"I don't know you, young lady," Miss Perry said, "but you do have a talent for saying the worst thing at the worst moment."

Quin melted back into the shadows, radiating hurt feelings. She muttered, after a moment, "I have to go to the bathroom." She slumped away, purse over her shoulder.

Morgan went to prepare a tray and brought it in as Jaymie texted Jakob that she would be another hour or so. As they sipped tea, she said to Morgan, "What are you going to tell Rodriguez?"

"This is a good chance to rehearse it," Miss Perry said to her niece.

"No, not rehearse," Jaymie said, alarmed. "If Morgan comes off as rehearsed, they're less likely to believe her."

Miss Perry, affronted, said, "They will believe her because she is telling the truth!"

"The truth she didn't bother to tell them the first time they spoke to her," Quin said as she reentered and took her chair.

"I didn't say *that*," Jaymie said.

"Stop!" Morgan said, one hand up. "I want this over with. You helped me last time, Jaymie. I trust you. When it's all over I need to figure out why I keep attracting losers and scumbag jerks." She took a deep breath. "It all started when Ethan caught up with me at the CVS and told me I was trailing toilet paper on my shoe."

℘ Fourteen ℘

"YOU MUST BE JOKING," JAYMIE EXCLAIMED.

"I *wasn't* trailing toilet paper, of course, but he had my attention. Quin was with me; she knew him and introduced us."

"Where did you know him from?" Jaymie asked Quin.

"Around. You know. Places."

"Ethan said he had to get me to stop because I looked like I was on a mission."

"I don't understand," Jaymie said. "Why did that mean he needed to stop you?"

She shrugged and went on. "I told him I wasn't on a mission, I was on my lunch. He laughed." She smiled but sniffed back tears. "He was the first guy who ever laughed at one of my dumb jokes. He asked me out. I found out we both knew Parker."

"You knew Parker before this?"

"Sure," Morgan said.

"Everyone knows Parker Hellman," Quin said.

"A lot of people knew Ethan, too. Val used to babysit him," Jaymie said.

"I didn't know that," Miss Perry interjected.

Jaymie didn't add Val's honest opinion of Ethan.

"His dad and brothers all moved away," Morgan said. "It's just him and his mom and sister locally. I met his mom and sister. His mother is a sweetheart but . . ." She paused.

"But what?"

"She's a little standoffish," Morgan said, almost apologetically. "I've never met his father and brothers. His sister Olivia seems nice, but she and Ethan don't get along, I don't know why." She frowned. "Ethan's mom said something odd to me. She asked if I was one of Ethan's associates. And she put emphasis on the word *associates*. I asked what she meant, and Ethan gave her a look. She didn't answer me."

So Ethan's mom might know about whatever shady stuff Ethan was up to.

From the shadows, Quin murmured, "His mom is a flake."

Morgan went on with her story. She dated him. He looked like the hero in the Prince of Valhalla series of Nordic romance novels, she said. "Maybe it was lust at first sight, I don't know, but I was smitten."

Jaymie smiled; the Prince of Valhalla series was by her friend Mel Heath. "What drew you together?"

"I'm not sure. He was insistent and pursued me. Maybe that was enough. I was lonely. He was handsome. He could have any girl, and he chose me."

Miss Perry harrumphed.

Jaymie ignored her. "You were living here then?"

She nodded. "He begged me to move in with him. I was swept up," she said.

"That's one way of saying it," Miss Perry said dryly. But she softened it by adding, "Morgan, I've only ever wanted you to be happy, and if that meant moving away from here, I was fine with that."

Moving away from there, leaving an elderly Miss Perry alone. She'd have to return to that thought.

"We found a cute house to rent and moved in together. It was exciting, at first. I felt like I was his whole world, and that's why he couldn't stand us being apart." She wistfully gazed into the distance and whispered, "It was wonderful." She sat up straighter. "At first. But I should have taken more time to get to know him. I didn't see what was coming. I was swept up in the romance, you know? When he would tell another guy to stop looking at me, I thought he was protective. When he'd grab me and kiss me even when I didn't feel like it, I thought he was passionate."

Miss Perry made a derisive noise and Morgan glanced at her aunt. In a defensive tone, she said, "It was kinda sexy, you know, *hot*, like in the books." She colored, pink rising in her cheeks. "Even though he didn't say it, I thought maybe he was so in love with me that he couldn't control his feelings." She blinked. "I've always wanted to be swept off my feet, out of control, passionate, *wild*. Like a romance novel. It got serious real fast. He always wanted to know where I was going and who with."

"And he didn't want you spending time here," Miss Perry said.

"That's not quite true," Morgan said. "He didn't like me staying overnight. He said he missed me too much."

Jaymie sighed, her suspicions confirmed. "Was this around the time that Haskell was away?"

Morgan's brow furrowed.

"What does that have to do with anything?" Quin asked.

Jaymie jumped; she had forgotten Quin was even there. "Humor me."

"I guess it was. Haskell went away . . . when was that, Aunt Lois?"

"He was gone from Thanksgiving to early February," Miss Perry said crisply. "He left when Petty Welch stopped seeing him, and he came back with that barky little pest, Aloysius."

Jaymie smiled at her implication, that the pompous Haskell had, wounded by Petty's irritation with him, purchased a more suitably adoring companion.

"I thought Ethan wanted to be with me. He told me he couldn't stand it when I was out of his sight." Morgan fell silent and gazed into the shadows, her expression revealing. Too late she recognized that none of what she named as his loving behavior meant what she had hoped and thought. Every single one of those behaviors was a control mechanism.

"You were living with him. Did he work?"

"He would go over to Canada all the time on business."

"Did he go with Parker?" Jaymie asked.

"I think so. Sometimes."

"Have you heard back from Parker yet?"

"Not a word."

"Where do you think he is? Last I saw him was down on the river flats staring across to Heartbreak Island."

"I don't know where Parker is. And I don't care."

"What was Ethan's business? What did he do for money?"

"Mooch off of Morgan," Miss Perry said.

"That's not fair!" Quin muttered.

"But it's pretty much true." Morgan hung her head. "He said he was in the middle of a big deal. He had all these plans and he wanted me to be a part of it all. We were going to be rich. I didn't quite understand it, but he started bringing papers home. He asked me to sign something."

"You didn't sign it, did you?"

"I said I would, but I wanted to read it first."

"Okay, and then?"

"I didn't sign it."

"Why not?"

"He took it away. I had hurt his feelings. He said I clearly didn't trust him."

Imagine that, Jaymie thought.

"Things were moving fast and I wasn't sure. He still said we'd be rich. He was going to buy a big house up here on Winding Woods Lane. Or build one in the country. He said I deserved the very best. If I wanted a mansion, he'd build me a mansion. He was going to buy me a three-carat diamond ring, and we'd go places in his helicopter."

"His *helicopter?*" Jaymie exclaimed.

Morgan colored, her cheeks again flaming pink as Quin snorted in laughter. She flashed her friend a look of annoyance. "He dreamed big. I admired that about him!"

"And yet you didn't know what this business was?"

"He said I wouldn't understand, and it would be a waste of time to explain it. We got a joint bank account, and he gave me a bunch of money to put in my account. He must have been successful, or he wouldn't have had so much money!"

Jaymie frowned. It felt hinky, but if he gave her money and didn't take it back . . . "I don't know what to say. It's worrisome that he never explained his business to you."

"But he did."

"He did?"

"Sure. It was something about real estate."

"That clears everything up," Jaymie said. She heard the sarcasm in her voice and hastened to say, "You told us you did know he was involved in something illegal, though."

"But to this day I don't know *what* exactly. I was afraid to ask too many questions," Morgan said.

"At the very least I think that he and Parker were involved in an illegal scheme involving smuggling people across the border. But there had to be something more than that. Ethan threatened your aunt, but he's the one who ended up dead. Think, Morgan. Can you tell me anything else at all?"

"I wish I knew more and could tell you what Ethan was up to,"

Morgan wailed, exasperated with the questions. "Or maybe . . . no, I don't. I wish it would all go away."

"I'll call George tomorrow to see if Parker has been in contact."

"I don't have the energy to worry about Parker," Morgan said. "I'm numb." She shivered. "And scared."

"I understand. Two people are dead," Jaymie said. "I'm scared too."

Miss Perry touched Morgan's shoulder. "I'll be there for you, the way you've always been here for me," she said.

"Thank you, Aunt Lois!"

Jaymie acknowledged what she wouldn't say out loud: maybe Parker was Ethan's killer. A falling-out between business partners? It was possible. Otherwise, why would he not answer the calls about his friend's death? "Morgan, you told me you saw Ethan at the car dealership. Where was he the rest of the day? He had to be somewhere leading up to his death. Where did he go? And with whom?" Morgan had speculated that it was Parker in the car with him, but she hadn't been sure.

"I told you he didn't come home the night before. He said that Parker and he had a business obligation."

"Did he tell you when he'd be back, at least? Were you expecting him that night, or the next day?"

She shrugged. "I told you, he didn't like me asking questions. He was hot and cold. He wanted to know where I was all the time, but he would brush me off if I tried to pin *him* down. It started arguments and he scared me when he was mad. I quit asking."

Jaymie shifted her attention to Quin, who still sat silent in the shadows. "I understand from Morgan that you were talking to someone in Ethan's car?"

"I . . . what?"

Jaymie repeated her question, tagging on, "Who was in the car that Ethan arrived in?"

She frowned and shook her head. "I didn't talk to anyone in the car."

"Quin, you did. I saw you!" Morgan said, staring at her. "And you handed in a package."

"You need to pull it together, girl, because now you're imagining things."

"Maybe you're right," Morgan admitted. "I was distracted and worried about Ethan. We had an emotional conversation."

Quin said, "Oops, that's my phone." She took it out of her purse and stared at a text message, then started tapping away, texting someone.

"Morgan, did you ever notice Parker's red jacket?" Jaymie asked.

Quin looked up, swiftly, but then went back to her text.

"Like what?"

"Like a patch on it that said Crimson Skeleton Riders." Quin made a noise, so Jaymie turned to her. "That's familiar to you?" she asked the other woman.

"I noticed it," she said carefully, still holding her phone. "What's that about? Why do you ask?"

Jaymie wasn't about to tell anyone that the body she found had Parker's red jacket on, or one just like it. "I was curious." She watched Quin for a moment, her suspicions of the woman's behavior heightened, but when Quin got up and headed into the kitchen as she texted, Jaymie turned back to Morgan. "What about you?"

"I guess I saw the patch. I didn't see all that much of Parker. He was off with some new girlfriend, or working, or whatever."

"Did Ethan have the same coat, or one like it?"

"Not that I know of."

Quin, in the hallway, called out, "I gotta get going, Morgan. You coming?"

"Sure. Let me do these dishes up first, though," she said, about the tray.

"I'll take care of that," Jaymie said, following her to the door into the hall. "Quin, about the other person in the car that Ethan was in—"

"Gotta go!" she said over her shoulder, heading toward the front door. "C'mon, Morgan. Time's a-wastin'."

She wouldn't answer. Jaymie considered following and demanding answers, but didn't think it would get her anywhere. She turned and observed the aunt and niece.

"Morgan, you come here and pick me up tomorrow," Miss Perry said. "I'll go to the police station with you."

"I will. My foot *is* getting better and the doctor says I can drive."

She leaned over and kissed her aunt, then straightened. "I'll see you in the morning."

Jaymie said, letting her pass through the doorway, "You'll be okay. The police will figure this out."

"I cared for Ethan, at first, anyway," Morgan said. "But I knew I had to get away from him. I was beginning to think that he wasn't going to let me leave easily. After that episode in the car I was afraid." She glanced at her aunt, and muttered to Jaymie, "Am I horrible for saying Ethan being gone is a bit of a relief?"

"No, not at all. I understand, but it's probably not wise to say that to too many people."

"Will they think I killed Ethan?"

"You'll be okay, Morgan." She pulled the young woman into a hug. "Listen to Miss Perry's lawyer, answer the detective's questions, and go about your business."

• • •

The next morning Georgina had a dentist's appointment, so after feeding the cats as quickly as she could in the still quiet gloom of a gray March morning, Jaymie drove back into Queensville and parked in front of Queensville Fine Antiques. The remaining snow was now soggy. Everything this time of year got thoroughly soaked, including boots.

After seeing the woman off, Jaymie settled at the cash desk with her laptop and a notebook. She worked for a while on organizing her time going forward. There was a lot to do before the Tea with the Queen event in May, and now with the Kitschy Kitchen to think about.

The door opened, triggering the buzzer. A woman entered, glancing around as her eyes adjusted to the interior lighting. Her dark hair was liberally streaked with silver and was wild, the copious split ends suggesting it hadn't been cut in a while. Her eyes were underlined by lilac shaded bags. Strolling around the store, she kept darting glances at Jaymie.

"Can I help you?" Jaymie asked, setting her notebook aside.

The woman approached and examined her carefully. "Are you Jaymie Müller?" Her voice was hoarse, and she coughed into her elbow.

"I am. Can I get you a drink of water."

"No, no, it's okay!" She waved Jaymie away and recovered her breath. "Just a cold. I've been a little run down." Tears glittered in her eyes and her mouth quivered. "I'm so upset. I don't know what to do. I need to talk to someone."

Jaymie eyed her, torn between wanting to help and concern that the woman was having a breakdown. "I'll help if I can. Come and sit," she said, pushing out the guest chair, a high bar stool by the cash desk. "What's your name?"

She perched on the stool and unwrapped a striped crocheted scarf from around her neck, draping it over her lap. Unbuttoning her winter coat, she blinked. "My name is Gabriella Zarcone. I'm Ethan's mother, and I want you to find out who killed my baby boy."

⌀ Fifteen ⌀

STUNNED, JAYMIE BLINKED RAPIDLY AND GAPED. "Uh . . . why are you—"

"Why am I here? I know you found his . . . his b-body." The tears spilled over and it was as if a dam burst. She covered her face with her hands and wept, great gusting sobs that quivered through her slim frame as Jaymie grabbed tissues and handed them to her. Her scarf slipped to the floor, and her purse followed. The unused tissues fluttered to the floor in a white drift.

"I'm deeply sorry, Mrs. Zarcone!" Jaymie scrambled to retrieve the tissues. She awkwardly tucked them into the grieving mother's hands.

"The p-police wouldn't tell me how he was found, b-but I h-heard . . ." She became incoherent and wept, deeply, more heaving sobs.

Jaymie got her a glass of water, setting it down in front of her. After a few moments the woman got herself under control. She mopped her tears with the tissues, drank some water and took in long, shuddering breaths, gradually becoming calmer. "I've been trying to hold it together, but saying the words, saying 'his body' like he's a *thing*, no longer my Ethan, my little . . ." Her voice wobbled again, quavering, thick with tears. *"Oh."*

The sound was a groan, one single syllable moaned on a twisted, clogged sob. She rocked forward and back, like she was trying to soothe herself. "He was the *prettiest* boy! Dark curls, big brown eyes, sweet face, and those cheeks! He would get upset and wave his little fists around, bawling. He was adorable! I c-can't believe he's gone." Tears streamed down her face, but she waved one hand, like she was waving away the emotion. "It's too much. Do you have kids?"

"One daughter."

"And you'd do anything for her, right?"

Jaymie nodded.

"Then you know. You understand." She took a deep breath, letting it out through pursed lips, composing herself. "All I can do for Ethan now is find out who killed him. I've heard about you," she said, her tone almost accusatory, jabbing a finger toward Jaymie.

"You've solved murders before. My daughter, Livie—Olivia—calls you Jaymie Fletcher. Like Jessica Fletcher, you know? She loves *Murder, She Wrote* and *Columbo*, all of those old shows. She watches true crime shows, too, and follows local cases. Murder as entertainment," she said bitterly, tears clogging her voice.

"I don't think of what I've done as entertainment, Mrs. Zarcone, not at all."

"Gabriella, please, not Mrs. Zarcone."

"Gabriella. I like justice. I prefer the truth to lies," Jaymie said earnestly. "I want peace for the victims and their families. I get mixed up in these things accidentally, you know, not on purpose. The police do a great job. I've been lucky to get to the conclusion before them on occasion, right place, right time. If you watch those true crime shows, you'll see how passionate the police are about finding truth and justice for the families of victims. They work hard."

She shrugged off what Jaymie was saying. "That's neither here nor there. Livie said *Mom, she found Ethan and she has solved murders. Why don't you ask for her help?* I said it would be too much. You're a stranger. I couldn't impose, but she asked what was most important to me, and said what did I have to lose?" She looked Jaymie in the eyes. "And she was right, you know? What *do* I have to lose? So here I am asking, will you find out who killed my little boy?"

Jaymie stared at her. She was already trying to figure it out, and here was an opportunity to learn more about Ethan, who was a mystery to her. He was shady and an abuser, according to what Morgan said, and that's all she knew. And yet, to his mother he was her little boy. Did she even know about the darker side of him? Did she care? This could get complicated. She met the other woman's hopeful stare. "I want to say again, the police do an excellent job, truly. I have a lot of confidence in Detective Rodriguez."

She made a face. "Huh! *That man.* He implied Ethan was doing something shady."

"He said that to you?" It didn't sound like Rodriguez.

"Not exactly." One tear trailed down her cheek.

Jaymie wondered, was she sensitive to implications because she knew what her son was mixed up in?

"He doesn't give two shakes about my boy's death. He's not

going to investigate. Not *really*. He'll find a way to blame Ethan. That's what has always happened to my baby. People automatically assume he's in the wrong. Every time he's been in trouble, people assume it's his own fault."

Every time he's been in trouble? "How often was he in trouble? And what *kind* of trouble?"

"Nothing major," she said with a flip of one hand, waving it off. "He's been arrested a couple of times. He took his grandma's car when he was seventeen and she called the cops. I was so mad! My own mother and she ratted him out. Until the day she died she had it in for him. She called him a bad seed. It caused no end of trouble between us, let me tell you."

"I'm sorry that happened," Jaymie said, keeping her tone neutral. "What else did he get in trouble for?"

"Small stuff. He shoplifted when he was in high school, cigarettes and candy bars. Doesn't every kid shoplift? Once he was with some boys who held up a variety store. He got caught up in it, but he didn't *do* anything! No one could prove he had a hand in it. He was just *there*. His father and I had a heck of a time getting him out of that jam, but we did it. It cost us a fortune." She blinked, swiping at the damp tear trail. "It cost me my marriage, in the end. My husband turned against Ethan, said he was done bailing him out. I couldn't stay in a marriage like that."

Jaymie was getting the picture, but it wasn't the one Gabriella Zarcone thought she was painting. "What other trouble was he in?"

"Every single time he's been in trouble, somebody has had it out for him. I don't know why. Take his last girlfriend. She was a real piece of work. Claimed he stole from her and then threatened her. She even said he hit her! He would never hit a woman. He *worshipped* women! What a con artist *she* was!"

"What was her name?"

"Ashley Ledbetter. I liked her at first, but she turned out to be a total liar."

Ledbetter? Jaymie filed that away to consider later. "And all of these people had it in for Ethan."

Gabriella looked away. "I don't want to talk about that."

"You met Morgan, correct?"

"She seems like a nice girl. But Ethan . . . he wasn't sure about her."

128

"Not sure of her? They lived together and were talking about buying a home."

She frowned and her eyebrows pinched together. "Oh, no, he would have told me if they were serious. He tells me—told me—everything."

Jaymie let that pass. "She says that when you met her you asked if she was one of his associates. What did you mean by that?"

"He had so many business deals up in the air. He was talented with money. The last girl he introduced me to was someone he was working with, a skinny girl with a shifty look, so I suppose I thought Morgan was too."

"He has two brothers who moved away?"

"Moved away? Not at all. His brother Luke is a litigation paralegal at Montrose Dickson Law, and Matthew is the mortgage manager at Wolverhampton First Michigan Bank. Why did you think they moved away?"

Because that's what Ethan told Morgan. "I suppose I misunderstood," Jaymie murmured. A more rounded picture of Ethan was emerging, a lifelong liar and scam artist who had his mother fooled. He didn't tell her how serious he and Morgan supposedly were because he didn't want her to interfere, or maybe he knew his mother would be jealous of his new girlfriend. Moms could be possessive of their kids, especially a favorite son. "You have a daughter, too, the one who told you about me."

"My Livie. I'm proud of her. She was twenty-three when she started up her daycare business, and now she has seven people working for her! I wish she'd get busy and have kids of her own instead of taking care of everyone else's."

"Did she get along with Ethan?"

Gabriella blinked. "Not exactly. You know how siblings are. She was impatient."

"Is Ethan the youngest?"

"No, Matthew is the oldest. He's thirty-eight. I was eighteen when I had him. Then Ethan, then Livie and then Luke."

And yet she called Ethan her "baby." "What made Livie impatient with Ethan?"

Gabriella made a face. "She said I did too much for him."

"Valetta Nibley babysat for you back when Ethan was a little kid.

She spoke of you."

"Such a nice girl. It's too bad about her."

"Too bad about her? What do you mean?"

"Oh, you know. There were rumors last fall . . . I heard she was . . ." She shrugged.

"Those rumors were spread by a troubled woman." Jaymie took a breath. "Gabriella, what do you want me to do, exactly? This is a police investigation. I'm no detective, just a citizen who—"

"Who found my son's body," she said, her voice throbbing with pain. "I want you to find out who did this." Trembling, she added, "I won't take no for an answer!"

Jaymie watched her for a moment. Compassion flooded her heart. "I can't promise," she said gently. "I will tell you this: I *am* concerned because I *did* find him. If it helps at all, he looked peaceful, like he went to sleep."

That broke the woman, and she sobbed into her hands. Jaymie waited, handing her tissue when needed, and letting her cry.

"Thank you for that. I was picturing . . ." She shook her head and blew her nose. Jaymie handed her another tissue and she blotted her tears. "I don't know *what* I was picturing. They won't let me see his body yet. He was so beautiful," she said wistfully. "Such a handsome boy. And to end like that . . ."

"He was lucky to have had a mother who loved him so much," Jaymie said.

Gabriella grabbed Jaymie's hand and hugged it to her, then released it. "You understand. I know you do. Find out who did it and then tell me."

"What would you do with that information?"

"Never mind about that. I have to go," she said, buttoning her coat, wrapping the scarf around her neck and slipping off the stool. "I'll be in touch." She plopped a business card on the cash desk and whirled, heading to the door and out, gone in an instant.

The business card read *Gabriella Zarcone*, with her phone number. She was an esthetician at a salon in Wolverhampton.

Jaymie was left feeling restless. Finding two bodies in one day was too much even for her. Their deaths and their bodies found in the same place the same day implied a connection. And where was Parker Hellman? Was he the killer? Or was he another victim, his body so far undiscovered? She was tired of mulling the same questions over in her head with no answers.

Her phone rang. Val!

"I was talking to Brock," Val said. "He did some digging. I knew he could get the answer if I set him on the task."

Jaymie was blank for a moment. "Digging about . . . ?"

"Who is buying Stowe House, of course."

"Oh, right! Who is it?"

"The answer is pretty amazing."

"C'mon, spill it. *Tell* me!"

"Okay, all right," Val said with a chuckle. "Brock couldn't find out through formal channels; none of his real estate friends are talking. But he *did* find out accidentally-on-purpose. He got curious so he cruised by the house. There was a fellow there writing up an estimate for landscaping. He told Brock the guy's name, the one who is buying the house. He's English, a successful music manager from London, England, and his name is—dramatic pause—Fitzroy Jones, brother to Tolly Jones, and according to online sources, former music manager of the Berk Scouse Brothers."

↯ Sixteen ↯

"YOU'RE KIDDING. WOW!" JAYMIE TOOK A DEEP BREATH and let it out. "That is either a weird coincidence or something else."

"Something else. It has to be."

"What are the odds of Tolly Jones's brother coincidentally buying a house in Queensville, the same town where Bog Brewer is *renting* a house?" Jaymie mused. "But why is Bog Brewer hiding that Fitzroy Jones was Tolly's brother?"

"Do you think Bog is our killer?"

"It's possible, I guess, though I don't know what his motive would be," Jaymie said. "He's right there. And he's always out wandering around. It's a chaotic household."

"Or the killer *could* be the new player, Fitzroy Jones," Val said.

"Killing his own brother?"

"Wouldn't be the first time."

"Can't rule him out," Jaymie agreed. "The drama could go back to their interconnected past in music. I know nothing about the man, so I need to find out more, and this new information gives me the perfect excuse. I'll approach Jones about using Stowe House for the Tea with the Queen event."

"You be careful. This is giving me the heebie-jeebies, him being in Queensville and his brother dying."

"I know. I'll be careful, and on *that* note, you'll never guess who visited me this morning." She related the visit by Gabriella Zarcone, and the woman's mission.

"I can't say I'm surprised, given what I know about Gabriella, but I don't like it," Val said. "You're getting a reputation, and the killer is out there. If the wrong person says your name . . ." She left the rest unsaid.

"What puzzles me is, how did Olivia know I found Ethan's body?" Jaymie said. "The news stories didn't say it, and I have to assume the police didn't leak that information when they spoke with her."

"Gossip gets around. So, who do we have as suspects?"

"Bog, for sure. This new guy, Fitzroy Jones. Parker Hellman."

"Anyone else?"

"I generally have a better idea of whodunnit by now, don't I?"

They talked for a few more minutes. Jaymie relayed her conversation with Morgan and Miss Perry from the day before, and how they were talking to the police today. She trusted Val completely and knew that would go no further.

As she hung up, Georgina drifted in smelling of gin and happiness—a midday liquid brunch at the Queensville Inn must have followed the dentist's appointment, an alcoholic pain reliever—and she cheerily, brusquely shooed Jaymie away and took her throne, the seat behind the cash desk. Liquor made some people argumentative, but for sour Georgina, liquor made her positively sunny. She wasn't drunk this time, just squiffy, as she would put it. Tipsy, as Jaymie would say. It would wear off quickly and she'd be back to her usual demeanor.

Jaymie had her own luncheon plans with a certain nonagenarian at the Queensville Inn, so she headed there and parked. Mrs. Stubbs had company at her table in the restaurant when Jaymie arrived. Mrs. Bellwood and Miss Frump were avidly discussing the bodies on the river as Mabel Bloomsbury smiled and drank her tea. Jaymie sighed, knowing the questions would come. And they did.

But Mrs. Stubbs, to whom everyone listened, put up one hand and said loudly, "Now, girls, Jaymie does not need to be badgered. She has had a rough few days and will enjoy lunch in peace, and then we will speak of what I invited you here to discuss, how we can help her put on the best Tea with the Queen event Queensville has ever seen. Put your thinking caps on, girls, she's going to need a lot of help. We'll show Haskell Lockland just how wrong he's been. Now . . . let's order!"

Jaymie ordered roasted cauliflower soup and a cheese tea biscuit. It was delicious, as always. After their dishes were removed, Mrs. Stubbs started the conversation about the tea event. Mrs. Stubbs and Mabel Bloomsbury had been conniving, and the elder lady had a list prepared of people who had promised help in the past and could now be counted on to carry on.

"I think you'll find it comprehensive," Mrs. Stubbs said, sliding the list to her, a foolscap sheet covered in a spidery, crabbed hand.

Jaymie glanced at it. Mrs. Stubbs had put herself on top. Mrs. Bellwood, Bill Waterman, Ms. Frump and Mabel Bloomsbury followed, but there were others, with phone numbers listed, and an annotation about their past involvement. Jaymie knew most of the names because she had been helping at the event since she was a teenager, but this was better than her memory, for sure. There were also names of women, and a few men, she did not recognize.

She had put together a separate list of donor companies, corporate entities or businesses that had donated cold hard cash in the past and might be persuaded to do so again in future. Jaymie quailed at the thought of having to go, hat in hand, begging for a donation. When she expressed that fear, Mrs. Stubbs dismissed it.

"You, my dear girl, are far more persuasive than you think yourself." She reached out one arthritis-crabbed hand and poked a long fingernail at Val's name, at the top of the list. "Practice on her. Ask for a donation from the pharmacy, and move on to the next easiest, the Emporium, and so on. I'll set up a meeting with Lyle," she said of her son, who owned and operated the Queensville Inn. "He can offer a candlelit dinner for two as a prize for a drawing at the tea event. And he'll pitch in money; I'll see to that. You can do this."

It was a productive meeting because of Mrs. Stubbs's ruthless ability as a clubwoman of historic local fame to keep people on track, but inevitably the questions afterward returned to the murder. Mabel Bloomsbury excused herself, but then the two other women — locally known affectionately as the Snoop Sisters after reuniting following years of enmity, and now sharing duties as Queen Victoria at the Tea with the Queen event — were avid crime fanatics.

Jaymie evaded most questions and gave only vague answers. Finally, after she flatly refused to talk about it, the two departed, eager to get on with the bossy business of recruiting others to help with the tea event.

"Now that Mabel and those two busybodies are gone we can talk." Mrs. Stubbs leaned back in her mobility chair and planted her elbows on the arms, lacing her arthritic fingers together. She fixed her with a gimlet stare that bored into Jaymie's troubled soul. "I can tell there is something on your mind."

Jaymie half smiled and drank the last cold dregs of her tea. "I suppose I can tell you what I won't tell anyone else but Val and Jakob," she remarked. "I appreciate that more than you'll ever know.

To have someone to confide in, what I've seen, what I've felt . . . it means a lot."

Mrs. Stubbs, eyes watering, reached over and patted Jaymie's hand. "Now, now, let's not descend into maudlin sentimentality. Tell me what you need to say."

Talking to Mrs. Stubbs was better than talking to herself, Jaymie always found. She rambled through what she had seen, heard, and witnessed, withholding, of course, details the detective wouldn't want her talking about, like the nature of Tolly's deadly wound. She then went back through it, organizing it logically.

Ethan had been in trouble his whole life, a cheat and a scam artist who blamed everyone around him, aided and abetted by his mother, she told Mrs. Stubbs. He never took responsibility for the trouble he was in and had never paid the price, slipping through the cracks with the help of parents who bailed him out time and again, despite the cost to themselves. He could also be violent, at times, judging by the complaints of his last girlfriend and the injury inflicted on Morgan. "He lurched from scrape to scrape and his mother kept bailing him out of trouble. Her marriage died because of it."

"She should have left him in jail once or twice. It would have taught him a lesson," Mrs. Stubbs said.

"Would it have, though? Some people never learn. It's like a kink in their personality that nothing is their own fault. They blame it on others, or circumstances, or that the world has it out for them. Some people are exactly the opposite; *every* misfortune is their fault, they think. I don't know what would have straightened him out, or if *anything* would, but it's too late to wonder now. All we can do is find out who killed him and why."

"Oh, is *that* all?" the elder lady said with a smile. "Of course, if anyone can do it, you can, my dear."

Jaymie smiled and put her hand over her friend's. Mrs. Stubbs's faith was touching, but this felt out of her league and out of her solving. "I can't figure out how it all hangs together. Ethan was pushing some kind of real estate deal, but no one knows what it was. And what does that have to do with Tolly Jones's death?"

"Maybe the real estate deal wasn't his alone. Maybe there were others involved."

Jaymie's eyes widened. "Other than Parker Hellman, even. Or maybe he was tangled up in something else entirely."

"Investigate like you always do. Figure out the threads that wind through different people's lives, how they tie together, how they break. Ask questions."

"Asking questions is generally where I get in trouble. I'll have to be careful." She sighed. "And I can't forget there *is* an outside chance that the deaths of Tolly Jones and Ethan Zarcone are *not* related. Ethan was the kind of guy who made enemies. For now, I'm thinking the two murders are connected, but I'll keep an eye out for any information that tells me otherwise."

"So, you are officially on the case?" Mrs. Stubbs said with a smile.

Jaymie shrugged. "Not officially," she said. "I can't help but try to figure it out. Darn that detective, though! I can't get a read on the man. I wish Detective Vestry was here."

"Never thought to hear you say that," Mrs. Stubbs said.

"Morgan was trying to get a hold of Parker when she couldn't find Ethan. Has anyone heard from him lately, I wonder?"

"Do you think he killed the two men?"

"I consider Parker Hellman a person of interest, I suppose." Jaymie smiled. "I'm starting to talk like the police, aren't I?" She sobered. "I hope he's not another victim. I wish I knew where he was."

"I know a thing or two about that young man from George. He has an instinct for self-preservation. Parker gets himself into scrapes, and then slithers out of them like he's a greased pig. Unlike Ethan, he never had family that would bail him out, except for George once or twice, so he managed on his own."

"You don't think he's the killer?"

"I hope not. Tell me more about this odd English couple living next to Lois."

"He's English, but she's not. I can't get a handle on Bog Brewer's behavior. He and Duckie keep clashing; they have a volatile relationship. He's desperately worried about someone named Alf, whoever that is. The only Alf I know is the old TV character, and ALF stands for Alien Life Form."

Mrs. Stubbs chuckled, which turned into a cough. "Maybe that's it."

"And why the coyness over admitting that Fitzroy Jones was in his house? It's all so odd. I don't know if whatever Bog is hiding is connected with the murders or something else entirely."

"You said yourself that the two murders may not have been done by the same perpetrator, which means you could have two murderers," Mrs. Stubbs said. "Maybe one of them is Ethan."

"I suppose Ethan could have killed Tolly, and then someone retaliated by killing Ethan."

"Not necessarily retaliation, maybe cleaning up loose ends," Mrs. Stubbs said with a wave of one hand.

"Loose ends!" Jaymie shuddered. "That's cold-blooded."

"When you're as old as I am, your blood does run cold."

They talked a few moments longer, about Haskell and Hoagie, Heidi and the veterinarian, the cats, and the identity of the new owner of Stowe House. Then Jaymie had to go. Mrs. Stubbs drove her motorized wheelchair to the door and waved goodbye. Jaymie did up her coat as she walked to the parking lot.

She sat in her SUV letting it warm up for a long minute while deciding what to do. A bird feeder on the snowy lawn outside Mrs. Stubbs's suite had attracted a bunch of twittering sparrows and juncos. Birds of a feather . . . maybe she could kill two birds with one stone. What a gruesome saying *that* was! She must track down Fitzroy Jones. The place to start *that* search was with Bog Brewer.

• • •

Winding Woods Lane was quiet this time of day, early afternoon. She parked on the street and then remembered what she had intended to do and would now. She hadn't thought of telling the police about the shopping bag of stuff in the wood storage box. But first . . . she got out her phone and dialed. "George! How are you? How is Florida?"

"Great. Nice and warm. I've been fishing most every day. Everything okay with the cats?"

She told him about Sadie and Hoagie.

"You're doing okay if you can get Sadie a home and Haskell helping out. What else is up?"

She explained about the bodies she had found, as he listened in shocked silence punctuated on occasion by exclamations of surprise.

"Holy mackerel! I bin outta touch!" he exclaimed.

"But there's something else worrying me, George. First . . . can you think of any reason there would be a shopping bag of stuff left in the storage bin?" She explained what she had found, and how.

He growled. *"Parker!* It's *got* to be him, using it to store stuff for some reason. He's the only one other than Bonnie and me and Miss Perry who has a key, or who has had access to a key, anyway. I told you I had Parker take care of the cats over Christmas. He returned the key to me, but I'll bet he made a copy. I'll call him and make him give it back."

Right after he made a copy of the copy, she thought. "Never mind that for now, George. It was an odd assortment of stuff," she said, thinking it through as she spoke. "There were granola bars and a wool hat and other survival stuff." What you might need if you came ashore illegally. Was it there for Tolly Jones, but he was murdered before retrieving it? Parker *must* be the human smuggler. He had probably moved the tongs, and then forgot to place them back in the deck box when he put the bag of supplies in. If that was true, then it certainly meant he didn't kill Tolly Jones, or why would he put the bag of supplies there? "Have you spoken to Parker since you've been down there?"

"Nope. I don't talk to him unless I have to."

"Was he close with Ethan Zarcone?"

"Sure. They were kids together and lately had some business, but I don't know what it was. I never liked that fellow and I told Parker I didn't trust the guy."

"Why didn't you like Ethan?"

"Don't mean to speak ill of the dead, but Ethan Zarcone was sneaky. He always got Parker to do his dirty work for him."

"What do you mean?"

"Look, this is God's honest truth: Ethan and some fellows stuck up a store once. The guys he was with got in big trouble, but the Zarcones put up their house, everything they owned, hired a great lawyer and got Ethan's charges dismissed. The other two guys weren't so lucky."

That was quite a different tale than the one Gabriella spun about her feckless son. Only one story could be true. "What does that have to do with Parker?"

"He was supposed to be there, promised his best buddy, Ethan, but he took *my* car without permission, crashed it, and was stuck on the side of the road when the stick-up happened. If it wasn't for that, Parker would have gone to jail with the other two guys. But did he learn? No, he did *not*. He still palled around with Ethan. I got no use for that guy. He was always bound for a bad end."

"George, you know that red parka Parker wears?"

"Sure thing."

"Do you know what the patch means?"

"Patch?"

"The black patch on his red parka . . . it has a red skull on it."

"Oh, *that*. Yeah, I asked him about it. Motorbike gang, Crimson Skull or Crimson Skeleton Riders, one or the other, led by a guy named Rider or Raider, or some such tomfoolery. I figure it's like all the guys who wear Harley-Davidson T-shirts that wouldn't know a Super Glide from a Knucklehead." He paused, then said, "Parker told me he hung around with a couple members for a while. I told him to watch his back. He's the kinda guy can't help mouthing off and getting himself in trouble."

"But a biker gang?" She knew some fellows who rode motorcycles, but there hadn't been official bike gangs locally. "Around *here*?"

"Not Queensville, more Wolverhampton way. Just a few guys who were trying to start a chapter of some English biker club. So I heard, anyway. Can't say I know more than that."

An *English* biker club. Two Englishmen, one of them dead, and an English biker gang. A big fight started by bikers at Shooters the very night there was suspicious activity that Miss Perry called in to the police. Time to call Clutch Roth, who knew all there was to know about biker activity locally and beyond. "If you do hear from Parker, tell him he needs to call the police. They want to talk to him." About why he was down on the flats looking over toward the island. And about a certain red parka.

She got out of the SUV, walked down to the Brewer residence, and rang the doorbell. No answer. She banged on the door and rang the bell again and again. Thumping music was coming from somewhere. After a few more minutes Duckie opened the door, sleepy and out of sorts. Her blonde hair was a frowsy mess, with a ponytail elastic caught in the tangle and mascara smeared under her eyes.

"Whatdya want?" she asked.

"Is Bog here?"

"In his studio," she said.

"May I speak with him?"

"Help yourself." She wandered off, leaving Jaymie standing on the doorstep peering in.

Probably the closest to an invitation she was going to get. Jaymie stepped in, closed the door behind her, and stood, uncertainly, wondering what to do next. Duckie had disappeared from view. Bog's presence was implied by the raucous music.

She took off her coat and boots and left them by the door, then advanced into the house, padding silently in stocking feet. She had never been inside before. It was bigger than Miss Perry's or Haskell's, and cavernous. It appeared that the Zanes had modernized it considerably from what it was at one time. The floors were polished marble, white with jagged streaks of black and gray. A staircase curved away to the left, with glass railings, and above, the second floor had a gallery lined with the same glass panels. A door was closing; that must have been where Duckie disappeared to, perhaps back to bed.

The walls were covered in pearl gray wallpaper with a pattern in a faint sheen, and they were punctuated with niches, each holding a Grecian-style urn decorated in cavorting classical figures. If they were real they'd be worth a fortune. The foyer opened to a huge living space with a view of the landscaped backyard, now glistening with a blanket of snow and ice, through the floor-to-ceiling uncurtained windows. Three snow white sofas made a U shape, pointed toward a black marble fireplace in which no fire blazed. Framed gold records were mounted above the fireplace.

The music was louder. Duckie said he was in the studio. She wound through a dining room and a gleaming kitchen in which pizza boxes formed a tower on the counter. Past that was a more modest staircase down, and the echo of music got louder. She descended and found a corridor lined with several doors.

Upon one was affixed a brass plate labeled *Studio*. Jaymie

banged on the door. It took five more tries, and waiting for a pause in the thumping music, before she heard a shout ordering her to *stop the bloody knocking and come on in*. A haze of pot smoke hung in the air, and the lights were low. As her eyes got accustomed to the dark, she saw that one wall was lined with shelves holding amplifiers, speakers, mixing boards, a keyboard, and other equipment.

Bog reclined on a sofa, head on the armrest, puffing a joint, cell phone in his other hand. He opened his red-rimmed eyes and . blinked. "Oh, you. What d'you want?"

"I'd like to talk, if you don't mind?"

"Grab a throne. Wanta puff?" He held out the joint, squinting at her as he let loose a stream of smoke from his mouth.

"No, thank you." She coughed. "Could we go upstairs to the living room?" He nodded and she turned and exited, ascending to await him.

After a few minutes he joined her, slouching back on one of the white sofas. He looked depressed. With Tolly's death, no matter if they were estranged in some way, Bog had lost a friend. Sometimes we don't know how a loss like that will hit until it happens, Jaymie thought. "I'm sorry that you lost an old bandmate," she said. "Were you two close?"

"We were bruvvers, more like. Once, anyway."

"I asked you if Fitzroy Jones was Tolly's brother, and you didn't answer. But I think he is. And I find it weird that he's here, in Queensville, and intending to stay. Why didn't you tell me about it? What are you hiding?"

"You don't arf demand answers, do ya?" He examined her through half-closed eyes. He glanced at his phone, then threw it down on the table, sat up with sudden vigor, squared his shoulders and said, "Awright, I'll tell ya. Fitz Jones were manager to the Berk Scouse Brothers back in the day, yersee, an' when 'is bruvver Tolly got in trouble, 'e turned 'im in. I 'ate the dude. 'E's a right proper arse."

"Could he have killed Tolly?"

Bog reared back, eyes wide. "Nah, nah! 'At's not whut I said, wuzzit? You better not go spoutin' that to the rozzers," he said, shaking his tobacco-stained finger in Jaymie's face.

Frustrated, she stared at him. The guy seemed utterly panicked, but why? "Well, *someone* killed Tolly Jones yards from your home. He was clearly coming to see you. I don't know why he had to see you face-to-face, but there it is. Did he die because of it?"

"I din't . . . that ain't . . ." Bog stared, shaking his head as one tear leaked out of his left eye and ran down his cheek. He repositioned the cell phone, checking it, then pushing it away. "I dunno. 'E were 'is own worst enemy. We mightn't of seen eye ter eye, but I know the old blighter only ever wanted to 'elp." He squinted at her. "Mebbe I oughter talk to you."

"You can tell me anything. I'll listen."

"But you're also a pal to the rozzers, and I ain't ready to talk to them 'bout anythink." He shook his head vigorously. "Nah. I fink you oughter go. Those bloody coppers 'ave already bin 'ere, snoopin' 'round. Don't need no more o' that." He heaved himself out of his sofa and stomped to the door, holding it open while she followed, put on her boots and coat and headed out.

She was about to say one last thing when his cell phone rang. He stiffened, looked back at the living area, then slammed the door in her face. What was he worried about?

℘ **Seventeen** ℘

LOST IN THOUGHT, JAYMIE DROVE TO DOWNTOWN QUEENSVILLE and parked near Stowe House, then got out of her SUV. She strolled over and stood for a moment on the road, examining the house, which was vacant and had been for a couple of years, with no one willing to buy it from Daniel Collins. There had been a couple of close calls and once it was even under contract, but ultimately every potential sale fell through.

Stowe House, like the Leighton home a few blocks away, was a Queen Anne, but much larger than Jaymie's more modest abode. It was a mansion built by one of Queensville's most prominent citizens, Lazarus Stowe, in 1882 to replace a smaller home. Typical of its style, it had multiple cupolas, a sweeping porch with a large rounded section to the left front, and a widow's walk at the peak of the turreted section. In spring the sloping broad lawn would be brilliant emerald green, but currently, with the weather warming, the snowy expanse was showing patches of vegetation and slick ponds of ice and water in low points.

A pickup truck pulled in behind her. Jaymie examined it. *Windows-R-Us* was emblazoned on the side. A guy in jeans and a heavy parka and wool cap got out, clutching a clipboard, paper fluttering in the breeze. He glanced at her, then strode through the open wrought iron gate, carefully picking his way up the icy stone walk toward the house. He disappeared around the side, looking up at the windows and making notes on his clipboard as he went.

A luxury rental car pulled up behind the truck and out got Fitzroy Jones. Aha! She raced toward him. "Mr. Jones! *Mr. Jones!*" Maybe he was hard of hearing. She shouted louder, *"Mr. Jones!"*

He stopped, turned, and eyed her. "Ms. Müller. That's your name, correct? Haskell told me about you." He sounded faintly disapproving.

She examined him closely, trying to see a resemblance to his brother. Maybe the dagger tattoo beside his eye and the Jolly Roger tattoo on his neck were faint memorials of his rock-and-roll past as band manager. She'd forgive him his bad mood. She'd be angry too if she'd lost a sibling. "Call me Jaymie. I'm sorry about your brother.

I wonder how it happened. Did you hear from him in the days before . . . before his death?"

"Before you found his body, you mean? Say what you mean, lass."

She smiled. His accent was as English as Bog's, but more genteel. Why was that, she wondered? Different lifestyles, she would imagine. "I can't help but wonder what was he doing sneaking across the border and coming to Queensville?"

He eyed her. "Dunno."

"Was he coming to see you? You were here buying this house. Or was he coming to see his old friend and bandmate, Bog Brewer?"

The window guy had completely circled the house and was walking toward them, perhaps to consult with the new owner. Jones glanced at her, then back toward the window contractor.

She was not ready to let it go. "I've heard because of an old drug smuggling conviction Tolly wasn't allowed in the United States," she said, trying to elicit a reply. "Why would he come here then? And *how* did he get here? Were you in touch with him in the days before his death? Was he coming here to meet you, or Bog Brewer?" she repeated.

He began to edge away. "I'm not sure I should be speaking with you, young lady. Especially about police business."

She followed him. "It's odd. Why would he come to the States when he wasn't allowed? If he wanted to see you, you could have gone to Canada, right? So why come to the U.S.?"

Jones firmed his lips. "Maybe business between him and Bog. Those two had a bad falling-out years ago."

Aha! "A personal tiff?"

"Business. They fought like cats and dogs over who wrote songs, or who got the rights to them. It got right narsty, I must say."

"But why would Tolly come to talk to Bog about *that*? Wasn't that all in the past?"

The window guy waited, shifting from foot to foot, impatient. Jones glanced at him, then at Jaymie. "Miss, I wish I knew what my brother was doing 'ere. Unfinished business? Maybe. I'm good with Bog. We've mended fences."

"That's not what he said."

Jones shrugged. "He hasn't always been an upright type. He was a right proper barsterd, pardon my French, when they were bandmates. Who's dead and who's alive, eh?"

"You think Bog killed him?"

"Dunno, do I? He's got some right dangerous friends, though, that's all I know."

"Bog has dangerous friends? Like who?"

"I gotta go. Business." He turned away.

"*About* that, Mr. Jones?" The man turned back to her, exasperated impatience on his lean face. "I'm assuming, then, based on this," she said, fluttering her hand at the window salesman, "that you've bought Stowe House?"

"What business is that of yours?"

"I'm getting to that. So, you *have* bought it. It's funny, no real estate agents locally know anything about it."

"Didn't go through a dealer, did I?" he said haughtily. "Bought it direct from the owner, bloke in California, cash deal."

"You've spoken directly to Daniel Collins?"

"You know him?" Jones said, his wayward eyebrows climbing up his forehead. "Didn't know anyone in town did."

She smiled. "I actually dated him before I married my husband. Tell Daniel I said hi."

He nodded and turned away again.

"Mr. Jones! I wasn't finished."

He turned back and this time his irritation was evident. "What *is* it, Ms. Müller?"

"I'll be quick, I promise," she said, moving a few paces toward him so she didn't have to shout. "Every year Queensville celebrates the Canadian holiday called Victoria Day. You know, celebrating Queen Victoria's birthday. She's why our town is called Queensville, a tribute to our cross-border connections. We hold an event that supports our local historic society. It's called Tea with the Queen, and it takes place here on the lawn of Stowe House," she said. "It's a kind of reenactment, with a local playing Queen Victoria."

He stared. "You Americans are an odd lot."

"I was hoping you'd agree to let us continue hosting it here. At least for this year."

"When is this?" he said.

"The weekend before the Memorial Day weekend."

"Which is . . . ?"

"Oh, sorry, Memorial Day weekend is the last weekend in May. We hold the tea event on the Victoria Day weekend, which is the weekend before." She was overexplaining as usual, but that's what happened when she got flustered.

He nodded curtly. "I'll be 'aving work done on the place, but as long as it doesn't interfere, I don't see why not."

"Do you have a phone number, Mr. Jones?"

He sighed with exaggerated patience. He took from his jacket pocket a silver case and handed her a card. "My business phone. If you'll excuse me . . . ?" He gave a mock bow, and whirled on his heel, walking away, accompanied by the window salesman.

As she got back in her SUV, another truck pulled up, a roofing company. He was going all out. Landscaping, windows, roofing. The paint on the porch and railing and around the windows was blistering and peeling, so it was good that someone was going to take care of the place before it fell apart.

As she started her SUV, she wondered: last time she had seen him, he was arguing with Ethan Zarcone in the parking lot after the historic society meeting. Too bad she hadn't thought to ask what that argument was about. It was odd that both Jones's brother and the guy he was arguing with were dead. Coincidence?

Or was Fitzroy Jones the next victim?

• • •

Jakob and Jocie helped her feed the cats that evening. She left them petting the cats and doling out treats while she spoke briefly with Miss Perry, who was in a blue mood and anxious about Morgan. Their conversation at the police station had gone all right, she said, with her lawyer by their side, though Morgan had worried that taking a lawyer with them made her look guilty. Miss Perry was now second-guessing her insistence on his presence, wondering if it painted Morgan in a suspicious light.

The detective had asked a lot of questions, and Morgan had told him about Ethan having a gun in the car, their quarrel, and him pushing her from the car, resulting in her injury. After that, questions became more pointed, Miss Perry said. Did Morgan tell anyone about this at the time? Quinley Gustafson, she admitted. *That's what girlfriends do,* Morgan had said, *tell each other things they can't tell anyone else.*

"Since when can she not tell me?" Miss Perry sniffed, hurt and angry.

"Maybe she was ashamed."

"Why? It was his problem, not hers."

"She didn't want to worry you. She loves you a lot." Jaymie told her she'd be back the next day.

The Müllers returned to the Queensville house. Jocie went up to bed, and Jakob lit a fire in the parlor fireplace. They snuggled together on the sofa, talking quietly, as Hoppy snored in his basket by the fire. Lilibet was upstairs with Jocie. Jakob held her close and let her worry and fuss and reason through as much as she could and offered input when asked, but even after the conversation none of it made sense to her. "It's impossible to figure any of this out without knowing where people were at the time in question."

"True, but shady people are not going to confess their shady movements," he said with a chuckle that resonated through his chest, where her cheek rested.

"But I have so *many* questions!" She told him about meeting Fitzroy Jones and the upshot, that he had bought Stowe House, and that they'd be allowed to have the Tea with the Queen event there.

"Something to celebrate," he said softly, and kissed her. "I'm happy for you."

"I'm relieved. I don't know what I'd do if he had said no. But I wonder, was Fitzroy Jones in Queensville that day? Did he kill Tolly, and if so, *why* would he kill his brother? He implied that Bog might be involved, that there was bad blood between them. Is that true? Or is he lying? Did Fitzroy Jones kill Ethan? I saw them arguing at the historic society meeting. Not really arguing, more like a discussion. Was Parker involved? Did *Parker* kill Ethan? If not, why is he missing?" She paused and twisted, looking into Jakob's soft brown eyes. "Or is Parker dead too?"

"I wish I knew, *liebling.*"

"And is Fitzroy Jones in danger? Should I have said something to him?"

"Maybe if you get a good night's sleep answers will come to you in your dreams." He kissed the top of her head and smoothed back her hair from her face, then kissed her lips. "Time for bed. You need a good night's sleep. You go up and I'll make sure the fire is safe."

"I'll try, but no promises." She carried Hoppy up to bed.

• • •

She slept poorly and rose more tired than when she went to bed. Sometimes, she had learned, if she went about her day-to-day business, things came to her: solutions; information; ideas. She ferried Jocie and two of her friends to school, then set about knocking items off her to-do list, taking care of business first before going out to feed the cats.

The rice pudding had turned out wonderful, and the pictures were perfect. She had gotten better at that aspect of her food column, "Vintage Eats." She edited the copy to go with it, and emailed it to Nan, at the *Wolverhampton Weekly Howler*. Nan had called several times, but Jaymie was avoiding her. The newspaperwoman was trying to wheedle Jaymie into agreeing to be interviewed for a piece on the murders. There was a constant tension there, Jaymie found, between her insistence that she was just a food columnist and Nan pressuring her to give them the inside scoop on the crimes she had helped the police solve.

She would mute her cell phone for a few hours. She should be focusing on the Tea with the Queen event, but the Kitschy Kitchen called a siren song that today, at least, she would heed. She headed on foot down to the ferry and across to Heartbreak Island. She had a favor to ask from an old friend.

The Johnsonville–Heartbreak Island–Queensville Ferry ran daily, three hundred and sixty-five-ish days a year—more daily runs in summer than winter—weather permitting. It carried passengers on the three-stop run, but also cars and freight, supplying the island inhabitants, some of whom lived there year-round. In winter there were occasional times when the river iced up and travel was impossible. A few years before an ice floe damaged the ferry and it was out of commission for a couple of weeks, but usually the stoppage was a matter of days. Islanders were careful and kept a good amount of everything they needed.

Today, with the temperature hovering above thirty-two, what ice there had been was breaking up. Chunks floated on the choppy river as a sleety rain pelted the boat. Jaymie retreated into the shelter of the ferry cabin, taking one of the molded plastic seats bolted to the floor in rows. The voyage only took a few minutes. She disembarked on the other side after the sole car going over had driven off. Thankfully the rain was brief and stopped as she walked along the dock and up the slope into the island portion of Queensville.

She had texted her college friend Rachel—once financial whiz, now baker—that she was coming over and would check on a little problem at Rosetree Cottage, which her old friend was renting through the winter. She would then head to Tansy's Tarts to speak with Rachel about her project, though she hadn't told her what it was about yet.

The problem at the cottage was the toilet running. It was an easy one to solve for Jaymie, who was intimately familiar with the cottage plumbing. She bent the wire arm and the float mechanism performed much better. Still, she sent a text to the local plumber to contact Rachel. It was time to replace that mechanism, she had noted, because the drain flapper was getting old. May as well modernize the toilet innards.

That vital task out of the way, she was on to the pleasant part of the day!

Tansy Woodrow's shop, Tansy's Tarts, was a bakeshop on the American side of the island. Her specialty was butter tarts, the recipe a secret that had been handed down from her Canadian grandmother. When you bit into a Tansy Woodrow butter tart, the filling gushed like liquid heaven, sweet and buttery, golden perfection crusted with buttery flaky delectability. The shop itself took up much of the main floor of a white two-story frame structure with a big pink-and-white-striped awning over the front window and door with Tansy's shop name in golden script. Beyond the shop was the bakery at the back. Tansy and her hubby, Sherm, lived in an upstairs apartment and had a deck out back from which they could see over the narrow canal to the Canadian side of the island.

They had hired Rachel Kimball, Jaymie's college friend, and in the months that followed she had taken over the business end of the shop, as well as the baking. Tansy had divulged to Rachel the recipe for her indulgent butter tarts, telling her that she must not, on pain of death, share it. Rachel had expanded the bakery's product line to other treats that were bringing new customers. There wasn't much in the way of restaurants on the island, other than the Ice House, so she also sold sandwiches using her home-baked bread and rolls, as well as wraps and quiches.

She had hired an assistant. When Jaymie entered there was a bright young fellow in neat khakis and a pink-and-white-striped golf shirt serving at the counter. He was cherubic and plump, clean-shaven with curly sandy hair neatly combed to one side. He had pink cheeks and a smile that glowed with charm. The shop was lined with antique bakery cases, white porcelain and chrome, with huge glass expanses. On the wall behind, wire shelves were laden, this early in the day, with tarts and cupcakes and other assorted baked goods. The bakery cases held wrapped sandwiches and the quiche of the day. Pink-and-white-striped boxes with *Tansy's Tarts* inscribed in turquoise and gold script—Rachel's new design—were piled to one side, ready to be filled with goodies.

Locals were lined up to order, but the young fellow, who knew her by sight, called for Rachel, who came out from the back room. She discarded her gloves and came through the pass-through. They hugged, then took a table near the front window.

After assuring her that the plumbing problem had been temporarily solved, but that a plumber would be contacting her to install a new mechanism in the toilet, Jaymie said, "I hadn't expected this on such a gray day, but you're busy!" Three customers left, but two more entered.

"We are hopping!" Rachel said, looking around with pride.

The tart shop was supposed to be a temporary job until she decided in what direction she wanted to take her culinary career, but she had settled in, and according to their last conversation, she coyly admitted she was dating an islander. If all went according to her new plan, she'd find a place to live on the island so the Leighton family could rent out the cottage in the spring, summer and fall months, as they usually did.

"Winter sales are *way* up. They never used to make much from November to April so they had started closing up for the season after Thanksgiving."

"They weren't sure about having you keep the shop open over winter."

"I told them I thought there was a year-round market. They were mostly concerned that they wouldn't be able to go south, but when I said I'd take care of the store they grudgingly said yes and . . . voilà! Tansy is thrilled, and Sherm has been hinting at a partnership, if I want it."

"I'm impressed, Rach. It's only been a few months but you've done wonders. I've got news of my own!" Jaymie then told her about the Kitschy Kitchen.

Rachel squealed excitedly and grabbed her friend's hands across the table. "That couldn't be more perfect for you. And Valetta is an ideal partner. How is it going to work with your other obligations?"

"You and I are alike in some ways; we both like being busy. Weren't we in every club in school? Mel said we were busybodies, but I always said we were just bodies who liked to keep busy." They laughed together. "That leads me to my next question." Jaymie then explained what they wanted from Rachel: exclusive access to Tansy's Tarts in Queensville. The chef from the Queensville Inn had been trying to duplicate the recipe for years but hadn't matched it yet. Having Tansy's Tarts to serve at the Kitschy Kitchen — with a suitable markup — would guarantee customers who couldn't always get out to the island for the addictive treat.

Her cherubic face was pensive. She was dressed in brand-new chef whites, with a hairnet over her springy dark pink-tipped (the color of the tips changed from turquoise to pink to purple, depending on her mood) curls. "I'd say yes right away, but Tansy is prickly about her tarts."

"It's a closely guarded secret," Jaymie agreed.

"It's not just that. She figures it's the exclusivity that makes them desirable. I'll ask her." The husband and wife were in Florida, so she'd call them.

"Half of Queensville seems to be in Florida," Jaymie said. "Including George Hellman. If that wasn't so, I'd never be tangled up in the whole mess that's going on."

"I heard about the stuff going down in Queensville. Girl, you found *another* body?"

"*Two* bodies, within twelve hours." Jaymie sighed, holding up two fingers and waggling them. "I don't mean to be flippant, but it's so weird." She glanced around to be sure no one else was too close, then explained the circumstances, in low tones. "It's not like I go out of my way, it just happens!" she finally said. Which led her thoughts in another direction. "Say, maybe you, being an islander now, can tell me, is there ever any odd business going on over here?"

"Odd business?"

Jaymie hesitated, but then explained what she meant, what she had gleaned from chatter about smuggling of all sorts, including human.

Rachel leaned over the table, pitching her voice even lower. "I *have* heard about people who come over by ferry to the Canadian side, and then sneak across the border. Someone on the U.S. side takes them to shore. Nobody will admit knowing who is doing it, but it must be an islander with a boat."

That was exactly how Jaymie had speculated Tolly Jones arrived on the west shore of the St. Clair River. "I've heard that in the past," she admitted and explained what all she had learned so far. "From her upstairs window Miss Perry has been using her binoculars to spy on what goes on. She saw lights down on the riverbank the night before all of this went down. I can't help but wonder if it's all related."

"You mean these murders are connected to Heartbreak Island?"

"Maybe. I wish I knew more. Maybe someone on the island knows or saw something. Rachel, do you know a guy named Parker Hellman?"

Rachel blinked. "Of course I *know* him. Didn't I tell you? I'm dating him."

⚘ Eighteen ⚘

"YOU'RE *WHAT*?" PEOPLE AT A TABLE BY THE COUNTER TURNED. Jaymie toned her voice down. "You're *dating* Parker Hellman?"

At the surprise in Jaymie's voice, Rachel cocked her head and frowned. "I told you I was dating an islander."

"Rach, you never said his name!"

"Are you sure? I thought when you mentioned his uncle, George, that—"

"I'm sure you didn't tell me his name. Do you know where he is?"

Her cheeks colored. "Not exactly."

"What do you mean, *not exactly*?"

"He said he had stuff to take care of."

Stuff to take care of. Taken in a certain light that sounded ominous. "When did you last see him?"

"A week ago."

"When did you last talk to him? Has he called you?"

"Not since I saw him last. He was supposed to call me today, but it's early yet. Let me check to see if he's tried to call or text." She dashed back to the bakery and came back, checking her phone. "That's weird," she said.

"What's weird?"

"Parker texted me. He said he can't explain right now, but he's had to take off for a few more days. He'll get in touch next week."

So he was alive, but not home and not planning to come home. Jaymie tried not to let her skepticism and worry show on her face, but Rachel examined her, her own expression showing concern. She handed over her phone without comment. The text read, *Babe, somethings come up. Gotta go somewhere. Explain later. Talk next week.*

Let me guess what's come up, Jaymie thought; Ethan's death. And Tolly Jones's death, maybe after being brought over to Queensville by a human smuggler. "I only met Parker with his Uncle George. What is he like?"

Rachel cocked her head slightly and examined her friend. "I've only known him a couple of months. I met him at the Ice House's New Year's Eve party. He's sweet. A little shy, I'd say."

"What does he do for a job?"

"He *was* a custodian at Wolverhampton General, but they were cutting back staff so he's at loose ends right now. Jaymie, why all this interest in Parker?"

Parker had not featured in the *Howler* articles about the murders, so there was no reason she'd know there was a connection. "Did you ever meet Ethan Zarcone?"

"I did, once," Rachel replied. "Parker introduced me. I didn't like him at all. He was smarmy, like he thought he was so smooth that I ought to warm to him immediately. I didn't. He was too sure of himself." She shrugged. "Ethan was the kind of guy who thought he was making a great first impression exactly as he was making a bad first impression, you know?"

"Not self-aware," Jaymie said. "I met him and agree."

"He pulled Parker away—we were at a party—and kept hold of him for a long while, talking. I asked Parker what was up, but he kind of shrugged and said that Ethan was bent out of shape over something unimportant."

"No other hints?"

"Not a one. I was surprised to hear Ethan was one of the two who died. I texted Parker asking if he'd heard, and telling him I was sorry, because I knew they were friends, but he never answered." She frowned again and knit her brows. "That's odd, I guess, that he never answered. And now he's blowing me off. What exactly happened, Jaymie? To Ethan, I mean."

"I found him, but I don't know how he died."

"Jaymie, where is this going?" she asked with a worried expression. "Do you think I ought to call the police? I still don't get what Parker has to do with any of this, but *you* seem worried, and that worries *me*. I've known Parker a hot minute; I've known you since we were eighteen." She leaned over the table and said urgently, "I don't know what to do. *Tell* me!"

Jaymie felt her friend's worry and urgency, and wished she had better advice. "Let me think about it. But I do know that Parker shouldn't be hiding out. He should contact the police right away."

At that moment a familiar figure strode into the tart shop, and Jaymie felt a surge of relief. It was as if she asked the universe to send her a message, and in had walked former Queensville police department chief Horace Ledbetter. She jumped up and greeted him.

"Chief, am I glad to see you!" She gave him a quick hug.

"Jaymie, good to see you. Rachel, taking a break?"

"Break time is over," she said with a smile. "Now that my favorite customer is here. I'll have your order ready to go in a few minutes, Horace. Why don't you sit with Jaymie a minute and catch up? I'm sure you two have a lot to discuss. Maybe he'll be able to tell me how to handle that little problem," she said with a significant look at the chief.

He shrugged off his parka and hung it up. They sat at the table while Rachel brought the chief a coffee and Jaymie tea. The two had met years before when Jaymie was new to crime. The now retired Chief Ledbetter and his wife were building an A-frame kit house on the island, but there had been snags and construction would not be done until late spring. He came to check on the site frequently, which was why he was there today, having used his own little boat to reach the island. His other purpose, of course, was to pick up an order of Tansy's butter tarts for his wife's book club meeting.

They chatted, then he said, "You'd like to pick my brain about the bodies you found. Why don't you say it out loud?"

She smiled. "I do have questions. I hear Detective Rodriguez and you had a chat about me, and my penchant for sticking my nose where it doesn't belong."

"Ah, at the retirees' dinner. Now, I didn't say that to him. He didn't say I did, did he?"

"No, no, he didn't. He said you had talked about me, and that it was interesting."

Ledbetter chuckled. "He's a fascinating fellow. New to our local PD. It was smart of him to come to the retirees' dinner. They don't all do that."

Jaymie smiled, then sobered and said, "You know this island now, and the people on it. When you were police chief, had you ever heard of smuggling from Canada?"

"You mean drugs?"

"I mean humans, those who can't get across the border any other way than illegally."

He regarded her calmly, but one brow lifted. "What are you saying, Jaymie? Do you think Ethan was involved in getting Jones over the border illegally?"

"A reasonable assumption."

"How do you figure that?"

She thought about it and frowned into her tea mug. "First, it doesn't seem likely that two deaths in the same place on the same day aren't related."

"Okay. But I don't think I follow your reasoning completely."

"I'll tell you what I think. I know Parker has a small boat. I think he is the smuggler and brought Tolly Jones over." She told the chief about seeing him on the flats gazing over toward the island. "But he wouldn't have been in it alone. I heard that he and Ethan were business partners, so was that the business they were in, smuggling people over the border? If so, it's too much of a coincidence that Ethan died right there, on the bluff overlooking the river."

"I'm sure there's more on your mind."

"Was the second death—Ethan's—a *result* of the first death? Did someone kill Ethan because they *thought* he killed Tolly Jones? He's the type who would brag that the human smuggling was all his show. What if the wrong person heard him brag? I'm conjecturing at this point." She considered Fitzroy Jones and told Chief Ledbetter what she had seen and what she wondered. "It makes a certain kind of sense for Fitzroy Jones to kill Ethan if he thought that Ethan killed his brother, Tolly."

"You have, so far, a whole lot of *what-ifs* and *maybes*," the chief said.

"I know," she groaned. "Believe me, I get that it's a whole lotta nothing so far." She glanced around and made sure Rachel wasn't close by, then leaned across the table. "Chief, Rachel has been dating Parker. I'm sure the police are looking for him, but she doesn't know where he is, I'm positive. Should she go to the police, or stay out of it?"

"I don't know Rachel that well. You know her *very* well. What do *you* think she should do?"

Jaymie stared out the window, watching an older couple, bundled up in parkas and mittens, stroll by. "I don't know."

"Unless she knows where he is, I don't know what she could offer the police at this point, any more so than his other friends and family. I would tell her that, if I were you." He watched her for a moment. "I don't like to see you so worried. Maybe this time leave it up to the police. This involves some nasty folk. You don't want to be in the middle of trouble among them."

"I don't intend to get in the middle of it."

"You never do."

"But I would like to help, if I can," she said.

"Why?"

"I'm worried about Morgan Perry, who was Ethan's girlfriend. And finding both bodies is part of it." She examined him. "I know how Tolly died, or I assume I do. His head was bashed in. But Ethan's body appeared uninjured, no blood, no vomit, no other indications. Was he drugged? Is *that* how he died?"

He stared at her, twisting his lips. "Don't say this to another living soul, and I mean nobody, not Valetta Nibley, Jakob or your friend Mrs. Stubbs." He looked directly into her eyes. "Promise?"

"I promise."

"I don't mean that flippantly," he said, his direct stare riveted on her. "It's important. Telling you is against everything I believe in, but you have this astonishing ability to see to the heart of the mystery. If they could teach that at police academy, we'd have no more cold cases. I'm being facetious, but just barely."

"I wish it were true, Chief, that I see to the heart of the mystery," she said, her voice faltering. "In truth, I feel my way through until it comes together. I'll take whatever I learn straight to the police."

He nodded. "I believe you, kid. Now, do you *promise* not to tell another soul what I am about to tell you?"

She took in a deep breath and held her hand over her heart. "Chief, I would never betray your trust. I promise not to breathe a word of this to anyone."

He nodded, then said, "Exogenous insulin."

"What is that?"

"An injection of insulin."

"You can kill people with insulin?"

"You can. The ME found the puncture mark on Ethan Zarcone in post and suspected something was up, so she did a few tests at the injection site. Insulin is usually concentrated at the puncture wound."

"How long would it take to die?"

"Depends on the dosage, but it wouldn't be immediate."

"The killer would have to stick around, waiting for him to die. How awful! How *would* he die?" she asked, feeling breathless and queasy.

"Seizures. Unconsciousness. Then death."

"Quickly?"

"Like I said, it would depend on the dose. A big enough dose? Quickly enough. Not immediate, but soon."

Rachel emerged from the back with a bakery box in a shopping bag. "You two done with your chat?"

"I suppose so," Jaymie said, feeling faint. The steamy sweetness of the air in the bakery was nauseating her. "Are you on your way to the building site, Chief?"

"I am."

"Can I walk with you?"

"Sure. I'm up for a little company."

"Good." She had one more question for him that she didn't want to ask with others listening. She said goodbye to Rachel, telling her she didn't think there was any point in calling the police about Parker unless she learned where he was. She also received assurances that her friend would be checking in with Tansy and Sherm about tarts for the Kitschy Kitchen—Chief Ledbetter cast her a questioning glance—and they hugged goodbye.

The two strolled on the river road toward his building site as she explained her new venture with Val and Violet Nibley. He was enthused, saying his wife would be among the Kitschy Kitchen's first customers. His niece would likely enjoy it too.

"Your niece?"

He glanced over at her. "You *know* that my niece, Ashley, dated Ethan Zarcone for a while."

"I wasn't sure Ashley Ledbetter was related to you, but I *was* going to ask. Who told you that I heard the name in connection to Ethan?"

"No one had to tell me. As soon as you mentioned Ethan Zarcone I figured you probably heard Ashley's surname in connection to him. It isn't that common around here and you're no dummy."

"I spoke with Ethan's mom, but I'd prefer to hear from you what went down between them, if you don't mind." She jammed her hands in her coat pockets and glanced sideways up at him as they walked. "I had concerns about Morgan dating Ethan."

"He's dead, but he won't be mourned. Not by me, and not by anyone who got burned by him."

"Burned?"

"Let me tell you what I know about Ethan Zarcone."

The chief's talk took them the rest of the way to his building site.

Ashley was his younger brother's daughter. After a nasty divorce, she had moved away from Toledo, Ohio, the previous autumn and was staying with the Ledbetters trying to figure out what she wanted to do. She was a quiet girl, so it came as a surprise to them that she got a job at Shooters, the dive bar on the highway between Queensville and Wolverhampton. It was there that she met and started dating the gregarious Ethan Zarcone.

"I know the place, and I know some of the people that go there," Jaymie said, thinking of Clutch Roth. "And of course I know Johnny Stanko, who works there sometimes. You've met him; he's a good guy."

He nodded. "I know Johnny, Clutch, and a few of the others. I don't give a hoot who Ashley dates, as long as they're good to her. And there are a hundred guys that hang out at that bar I'd prefer to see her with. We didn't know she was dating anyone for a few weeks. I think she felt something off even then, or she'd have told us about him. But she didn't. We didn't know she'd moved in with him until it was a done deal. She moved out of our house and in with Ethan while we were away one weekend."

"You're close."

"I'm her godfather. Ashley is like a daughter to me. My wife and I were both hurt that Ashley didn't feel she could tell us what was going on."

"What happened, Chief?"

"The short story? A few weeks after she moved in with him he hit her so hard she fell against a radiator and it knocked her out. We got a call from the hospital and rushed to see her. She wouldn't tell us what happened at first, but I could see in her eyes she was scared and ashamed." His voice was a low growl. "Scum like that . . . makes me so mad that someone could hurt her and make her feel like it was her fault!"

"I'm so sorry."

"I should have seen it coming. I knew what rough shape she was in after her divorce, how unhappy and uncertain. But I thought all she needed was time, and at first, when she got the job, she was happy."

"You said the short story. Is there a long story?"

He frowned. "There's more, but I don't know it all. He was pressuring her to do something, she wouldn't tell me what."

Jaymie made an alarmed noise.

"No, nothing like *that*. Not drugs or anything sexual. This was about his business. He wanted to bring her into it, she said, wanted her to sign some papers, but she was reluctant and that's when he got mean. *That's* when he started threatening her."

"But you don't know more than that?"

"Nope."

"She didn't go back to him?"

"She never had a chance. He dumped her, so she slunk back to Toledo. He told her he'd found someone else."

"Morgan Perry," Jaymie said. "Didn't Ashley charge him?"

"I wanted her to, but she wouldn't. She wouldn't even admit what happened to the police. She was ashamed, I guess, and wanted a clean break. I said she had to make him pay, but if she charged him she'd have to see him in court, she said, and that scared her. She wanted to go home to Ohio and move on with her life."

"Morgan ended up with a badly sprained foot from him. And yet to hear his mother tell it, he was a misunderstood angel."

"All I got to say is, with his track record, it's a surprise he wasn't murdered earlier."

Jaymie nodded. "So . . . insulin as a murder weapon. You'd have to have a source, right?"

"Sure. They will be looking for someone with access to insulin. There's your killer, right there, or at least an accessory. An unwitting accessory, even."

"Would that necessarily be true? Aren't there other sources of insulin?"

He nodded, frowning. "You can get it OTC, I've heard, but it's an older type. The detectives will be checking. But you know what I think? I think there are a host of fathers and brothers who had it out

160

for Ethan. *Cherchez le family,* if you ask me."

Jaymie disagreed. This did not feel like a crime of passion, an angry father or sister or mom. It felt clinical. Just business.

⚘ Nineteen ⚘

ON THE MAINLAND, SHE RETURNED TO THE LEIGHTON FAMILY HOME.
After a week there was a mountain of laundry, as well as
vacuuming, sweeping, dusting, all manner of tidying to bring the
house back up to Becca's finicky standards before her sister arrived
back from Canada. But first she put a call through to Clutch Roth
and left him a message.

As she was doing dishes, he called back. She grabbed her cup of
tea and sat at the kitchen trestle table. Clutch was a good guy, a
friend who had suffered the pain of losing a beloved daughter. He
was vigilant for violence against everyone, but particularly against
women. They chatted for a few minutes. Then she asked him how he
was doing.

"All right, I s'pose. Mad as hell at some folk."

"Oh? Why?"

"Trouble at Shooters."

"I heard there was a brawl there the other night. What was that
about?"

"Don't know, that's the problem. Couple of good old boys got
themselves in some trouble mouthing off to new guys," he drawled.
"Normally the bouncer can calm 'em down, but he'd been drinking,
it seems, though he denies it. He was too drunk or stoned to help, so
it got outta hand. Anyway, you asked some questions."

He told her he had met Ethan at Shooters. "He was a braggart
and a blowhard. Didn't know he was an abuser, though. We woulda
had words if I'd known that."

"Did you know Ashley Ledbetter?"

"Sure. Quiet little gal, sweet-natured. Came in one night with
Quin and next thing you know, she's got a job at Shooters. Niece of
Chief Ledbetter. I kept an eye on her. She did well. Then I saw she
was going out with Zarcone—s'pose Quin introduced them—but I
never knew he hurt her."

"Quin. You mean Quinley Gustafson?"

"The very one. Skinny little gal who comes in to Shooters all the
time."

How odd; Quin introduced Ethan first to Ashley, and then she made friends with Morgan. And Quin was with Morgan when she met Ethan, and introduced them to each other. Quin was likely the woman that Ethan had introduced to his mother as an associate. She seemed to be everywhere in this mess. "Clutch, the real reason I called was to find out what you know about a bike gang called the Crimson Skeleton Riders. I've come across a jacket with their patch on it."

"Uh-huh. I know of 'em. British dudes trying to establish a chapter here. They're led by a guy named Raider Dobbs, a skinny English guy, greasy long hair, always dresses in black denim. He collects Triumph Bonnevilles and drives one around like it's something special. He's nasty, I've heard, and you know I keep my ears and eyes open."

"How long has he been here in Queensville?"

"Not long. Coupla months? Matter of fact, it was some of his guys who got into it at the bar."

"The night the police had to be called."

"Yup. I still can't explain why the bouncer was out of it. He swears he didn't have but a single beer."

"Clutch, could he have been drugged?"

"Roofied?" Clutch went silent, then said, "I never woulda thought it. I'll talk to him. Maybe I've been judging him wrong."

"What started the fight?"

"Word is, one of Dobbs's crew insulted a waitress."

"Huh. Was Dobbs there? Did he get involved?"

"He wasn't there that night. He's a shady character, in and out whenever he feels like it. He was off starting a chapter in another town, I heard."

"Are the guys who started the fight connected in any way to Ethan Zarcone or Parker Hellman?"

He was silent for a long moment, then said, "I'm not sure about that but I'll tell you who they *are* associated with, though, and that is the same Quinley Gustafson we were talking about. She's the head guy's old lady."

"Raider Dobbs?"

"Yup, one and the same. Heard tell she's his woman."

• • •

After the housework was done she showered and had lunch, all while trying to figure out the tangle of this murder investigation. Her conversation with Ethan's mother looped through her mind. Why had Ethan implied that his siblings had all moved away?

Unless one or more of his siblings knew about his dirty dealings?

Gabriella had given her a reason to approach them, so she investigated and found that Olivia Zarcone's daycare was called Little Hands Big Hearts. The law firm of Montrose Dickson was on a street off the main thoroughfare in Wolverhampton, and she already knew where Wolverhampton First Michigan bank was.

She dressed carefully in leggings, boots, a sweater, scarf and her best coat, a dark green faux-fur-trimmed swing coat her mother-in-law had passed on to her as "too dressy for myself." She had enough time, she figured, to talk to all three Zarcone siblings, and then go pick up Jocie from school.

Olivia first. She found the daycare, three rooms in an industrial parkette on the outskirts of town. It had a large, fenced playground, with brightly colored plastic equipment currently buried in heaps of snow. There were some older tots in a circle in the snowy fenced playground playing Duck Duck Goose. Jaymie approached the fence and asked one of the two young workers about Olivia Zarcone, saying she was a friend of Olivia's mother, Gabriella. The young woman called Olivia, and Jaymie was directed to a door, was buzzed in and followed directions down a hallway plastered with messy bright art, past noisy rooms of kids.

Olivia's office was a haven of calm organization. She was at a desk working on a laptop. She stood, leaning across the desk to shake hands. Jaymie shed her coat and sat in a chair opposite the young woman. They exchanged pleasantries. Olivia Zarcone was dark-eyed with short dark hair swept back from her pale oval face. She wore large dark glasses, and a cowl-neck red tunic sweater over black yoga pants. Despite the casual dress—well-suited, likely, for getting down on the floor and playing with little kids—she was a businesswomen through and through and got right to the point. "I'm so glad my mom came to you. I hope you can help."

Jaymie cautioned her that she could not truly investigate, that that was the police's job, and reiterated her support for and faith in the police.

"Don't be shy, Jaymie. You're kinda famous around here, you know." She smiled, faintly, but quickly sobered. "Our own Miss Marple–Nancy Drew mashup."

"I'm so sorry for your loss. Were you and your brother close?"

"Not really. He was a pain in the neck most of the time and gave Mom all kinds of trouble. But still, he was my brother." A shadow of pain flitted across her expression, and she took a deep breath. "I did love him. I wished he would do better, though."

"I have a question. My name wasn't in the news reports as the one who found your brother's body. How did you find out about it?"

"That's kind of an odd story. I overheard it."

"I beg your pardon?"

"Uh-huh. The other night I was at a bar having a drink with a friend. She knew I was upset about Ethan and wanted to cheer me up, so she took me out. Two people passing our table were arguing and I heard my brother's name."

"Okay."

"I was about to go ask them what they knew, when the woman—"

"A woman?"

"Yeah, it was a woman and a man. I know I've seen her before, but I'm not sure where. Anyway, that's when I heard her say some snoopy broad found Ethan, and then she said your name."

"Snoopy broad?"

Her cheeks colored. "Sorry, but that's what she said."

"What did they look like?"

"They were leaving the bar and it was dark. A woman and a man, that's all I saw. He was wearing leathers and she had on a jacket too small for how cold it was. I was taken aback and I hesitated, not sure what I'd want to say to them. I followed after a few seconds, but they got on a motorcycle and roared off."

"What bar was this?"

"Shooters, down on the highway. A dive bar my friend likes. She flirts with the biker dudes, and it's usually surprisingly safe in there."

"I know a couple of people who work there," Jaymie said. "So then you told your mother about me?"

Olivia nodded, took a deep breath and said, "What I want is

peace for my mother, but she's never going to have that until whoever killed Ethan goes to jail. I thought maybe she could enlist your help. I hope I didn't overstep?"

Not sure how to answer that, Jaymie didn't and instead asked her about Ethan. As the woman spoke it became clear that Olivia did not share her mother's rosy view of him. He always took the easy way out, she said. He had a temper. He didn't share, as a child.

Jaymie eyed her quizzically and Olivia smiled. "Here's what I can tell you as a childcare expert," Olivia said. "No child shares naturally; it has to be taught. But should kids be *made* to share? Are we setting kids up to fail by expecting them to willingly give up a favorite toy? And do we risk teaching them that they aren't allowed to have feelings about ownership? Feelings about what they want for themselves? Or is it important that kids learn to share so they know that thinking of others is important in society?"

"I don't know," Jaymie admitted. "I got my daughter ready-made at eight, and she's pretty terrific about sharing."

"I think there is a balance to be found, but with Ethan, Mom never found it. We had to share with him, but he didn't have to share with us."

Aha, so there was a point to the rant. "Why is that?"

"My brother spent a lot of time in hospitals with gastric issues as a kid, so Mom spoiled him when he was home. He had special food that was expensive, so we never got any of it. We weren't allowed to hit him back if he hit us. He learned that he was untouchable, you know? And to Mom, he was."

"Sounds like you've put a lot of thought into this."

"I went to college for early childhood education. I thought I was going to be a teacher, but I like being my own boss." She waved her hands around. "This is all mine. I've worked hard for it. But I *have* thought a lot over the years about Ethan's upbringing, and how it was different from mine and Luke's and Matt's."

"Your brothers."

"Yes. Are you going to go see them?"

"Should I?"

"You should."

"Why? Do you think it's possible that his murder, if that's what it was, was committed by someone in his life? Like, a friend?" She was specifically thinking of Parker Hellman.

"A good question to which I don't know the answer."

"Do you know any of his friends?"

"My brothers may. I'll text them and make sure they'll see you." She picked up her phone and rapidly tapped a text. "In many ways, Ethan grew up like an only child," she said as she tapped away. "Mom protected him so much. He was always with her, while the rest of us were on our own."

"You said he was sick, gastric issues. Were any of the rest of you sick?"

Olivia looked at her oddly. "Why?"

Jaymie shrugged, and carefully picked through the minefield of knowing too much. "Getting a full picture, I suppose. I mean, my parents were older, so I dealt with a lot growing up. My older sister had to take medication for a long time, and my dad became diabetic, dependent on insulin," she said, crossing her fingers as she casually lied. "Any of that in your family, you or your brothers?"

"Gosh, no. He was the only one sick, *ever*. Other than a few colds and flus and earaches, I mean. My mom . . . well, you've met her. She is the picture of health. And Ethan grew out of his stomach issues."

"But you blame how he turned out on his childhood illness?"

"Not exactly his illness, but because he was shielded from the consequences of being a little jerk. It didn't have to be that way just because he had a condition. He grew up to be a crook and kept pushing the boundaries. I warned Mom if she kept bailing him out of trouble he'd go too far one day, and that's what happened." She set her phone aside.

"Tell me what you mean."

She sighed. "I don't know how to explain it except to say, I miss who he *could* have become. He was smart and funny."

"But . . . ?"

"But he got in a lot of trouble as a teenager and in his twenties. Mom and Dad argued about him all the time. That's what broke them up. I thought lately that he'd smartened up. *Now* I think he figured out how not to get caught."

"What do you think he was up to?"

"I don't know exactly."

She asked Olivia about the possibility that he was working with Parker Hellman to smuggle people over the border.

"That's not his style," she said promptly. "Too much risk and work for too little reward. He said only suckers think small."

"But if he didn't do the actual work? If he left it to someone else?"

"Mmm, okay, I can see him thinking he was a hotshot, making secret plans and letting a minion carry it out. Someone like Parker."

"You know Parker?"

"Sure, I've met him once or twice. He was the kind of guy Ethan would have recruited, someone easy to push around. I know my brother had *some* scheme going, the little sneak. But smuggling would have been a side hustle if he was involved. He had a real estate thing he was working on. I knew him too well to think it was on the level."

Jaymie thought back to the first time she saw him, talking to Haskell Lockland, a deal he was trying to get the town to get involved in. Real estate deals seemed to come up a lot in any conversation about him. He tried to get Ashley involved, and the same with Morgan. What *was* the deal, or deals, Ethan was working on?

Olivia, when pressed, repeated that she didn't know. "But it was crooked, I'll guarantee it," she said. "Matt or Luke might know."

"One more question: why did Ethan lie about your brothers moving away from town?"

"Did he do that?"

Jaymie nodded.

"Interesting, but I don't know why he'd say that. Lying was second nature to Ethan."

Jaymie drove to the center of Wolverhampton and parked on a side street. The law firm of Montrose Dickson was in an old yellow-brick industrial building repurposed into cool loft housing on the two upper floors and offices on the main floor and mezzanine. She was buzzed in when she gave her name and said she was coming to see Luke Zarcone on a private family matter. A receptionist showed her into a small boardroom. The walls were exposed yellow brick with modern paintings mounted. It was furnished with steel and canvas chairs.

A man entered and glanced around, catching sight of her. He introduced himself as Luke Zarcone, reached over the table and shook her hand, but appeared in a hurry, ostentatiously checking the time on his phone. He sat in a chair at the end of the glass table, again glancing down at the phone in his hand, then up at her, expectantly. Jaymie saw the likeness to Ethan. He was a good-looking guy, dark-haired, dark-eyed, dressed in suit slacks and a dress shirt, no tie, with a two-day growth of beard on his chiseled jawline. "Olivia texted me and said I ought to see you," he admitted.

"I'm so sorry for your loss," she said. "Were you and your brother close?"

"If you've talked to Olivia I'm sure she's already filled you in on the tortured familial dynamic," he said with a rueful smile. "The Zarcone psychologist at work, dissecting our little family drama."

Sarcasm; interesting. And with a shade of belittlement. "I'd like your take on that family dynamic."

"Like I said, I'm sure Olivia has told you all about our coddled brother, Mama's little teddy bear. A teddy bear with fangs, if you ask me. He always blamed me for breaking or losing things. He never once took ownership of problems."

She was surprised at how frank he was. "I met your mother. She's protective of his memory."

"That's putting it mildly. Ethan could get in any kind of trouble, but Mom would give an excuse, even when he was a grown man and should have known better." He grimaced. "That sounds like I was jealous of him. Maybe I was, a little. He sucked the life out of the family and killed Mom and Dad's marriage. That's what Dad says, anyway."

"Where is your dad?"

"He moved for his job. He lives in San Fran. We—meaning Matt and Olivia and I; Ethan can never be bothered with dear old Dad so he stays here with Mom—fly west at Thanksgiving."

"Did you know that Ethan told people you and your older brother had moved away from town?"

It was news to him. "Huh. I wonder why?"

"Do you know what Ethan was up to lately? Your mother wants—not surprisingly, I think—to know who murdered him. And she wants justice. Surely your brother deserves that?"

"Of course he does," Luke said, sweeping his dark locks off his wide forehead. He was silent after that.

"Do you know what he was up to lately?"

"Nope. And I don't care."

"Do you know Parker Hellman? He and Ethan were friends, and possibly had a business venture together. I was wondering if—"

"I do *not* know Parker Hellman!"

"Okay, all right," Jaymie said, frowning.

"Don't mind me if I sound irritated. I had a two-hour meeting with the police and we went over all of this. I told them what I know, which isn't much. I don't know Parker Hellman, I don't know any of Ethan's friends. I didn't even know he was dating again after that disaster with Ashley."

"You met Ashley?"

He nodded. "Nice girl, sweet, kinda shy. I felt sorry for her. She looked scared of Ethan, and I know what a jerk my brother could be. He almost hit my mom once. I would have plowed him for it if he did, but he pulled back. Mom made all kinds of excuses, and I swore after that day I would wash my hands clean of Ethan. If she was going to let him get away with crap like that, I was not going to get between them."

He did sound jealous.

"I'm not surprised he's come to a bad end. I'm sorry, but none of it was my business, and I stayed out of it. I try to stay out of *all* of Ethan's business, family and otherwise. I'm only talking to you because Olivia asked, and says Mom wants me to. You're better off talking to Matt. He was always trying to help Ethan. I think he felt a responsibility as the oldest."

"I *will* be talking to Matthew." She regarded him for a moment. "Olivia thinks Ethan may have been involved in a property scam. Do you know anything about that?"

"Again, talk to Matt. He's the expert in that field."

"Oh?"

"Sure. He's a mortgage guy at the bank."

• • •

The Wolverhampton First Michigan Bank was a new building of pale stone, steel gray angles and glass, on a corner three blocks from the heart of town. Matt was willing to give Jaymie a few minutes if she came immediately, he had texted in reply to her query. She hustled directly there after leaving Montrose Dickson. She walked into the bank and saw, past the row of glassed teller windows, a glass-walled office. A portly fellow seated at a desk in the office beckoned to her.

She strode along the carpeted floor past the tellers and entered the office. "Matt Zarcone?"

"That's me," he said, standing, He gestured to a chair across from his desk then sat, settling his suit over his belly and shifting his shoulders. He was a big fellow, his face broad, his jowls and chins making the transition from head to shoulders one column of flesh. The family good looks, in him, had become a self-satisfied portliness. He was a handsome man, his bulk commanding the room. "Olivia told me she sent Mom to talk to *you* about Ethan's murder?"

His tone was incredulous, and Jaymie felt a prickle of doubt about how much help Matt would be with that attitude of skepticism. "What exactly did she tell you?"

"That you're some kind of local true crime fanatic, like she is, and that you solve murders as a hobby."

Jaymie winced. That was the worst possible construct to put on what she had done for the last few years. She'd bet, though, that wasn't what Olivia said, it was what Matt heard. Interesting. She was sensing waves of hostility from him that made her question his reactions. "I don't go out of my way looking for mysteries to solve, it just happens. In this case I found Ethan. Your mother came to me and asked for my help."

"Don't misunderstand me. I want whoever killed my brother to be caught and nailed to the wall, but at the same time, I don't want my mother taken advantage of. Don't you have a podcast?"

"No, I do not."

"I thought I heard about you on a true crime podcast?"

"I don't run that," Jaymie replied, keeping her tone even. Lately a local true crime podcaster had started covering some of the murders she had helped the police with. It wasn't exactly flattering to her at times, she understood. She refused to listen. Val was right; she was getting a reputation, not her intent in the least.

"Matt, like I said, your mother came to *me*. I felt the least I could do is take her pain seriously. Your brother *was* murdered."

He threaded his hands together over his stomach and sat back. "I've already talked to the police about it, at length, ad nauseam, end of story. What can you do about any of it that the police aren't already doing?" He paused. "Except maybe interfere with the investigation?"

The only way around the armor of his distrust was to ignore it. "Were you close to your brother?"

The question surprised him. He sat, blinking a moment. His expression changed, his eyes misty. "Ethan and I were probably closer than the others. I was his big brother. He was my first sibling." He cleared his throat, his eyes glistening. "I remember a time, before he got sick, when he followed me around."

"I am sorry," Jaymie said.

"That was a long time ago. Things have changed and we haven't been that close in the last few . . . *several* years. I missed him long before he was murdered." He met her gaze and sat up straight. "All in the past. If Mom and Olivia want this, I'll oblige. How can I help?"

"I want you to know I have a great deal of respect for the police. They are good at what they do, and I'm sure they'll find the killer."

"Unless you find him first."

"Sure."

"Isn't that interference with the police?"

"Not at all. I'd never interfere with their work. I didn't intend to get involved, but I can't ignore your mother's plea. Anything I figure out or find out I will take directly to the police, you have my word on it. Let's say that I generally go down byroads the police don't have access to. Sometimes they seem unconnected. Occasionally I get lucky."

He nodded.

"I first met your brother at a heritage meeting. He was waiting to talk to the heritage society president about a scheme he had for empty historic homes in Queensville."

"What kind of scheme?"

"I wish I knew. Your brother Luke said you would be more likely to know, as a mortgage specialist?"

Matthew's face twisted in perplexity. "Why does that mean I'd know anything? I can't imagine what Ethan had in mind. Like I said, we haven't been close for some time now."

"Your siblings both say whatever it was, it was likely crooked."

His face reddened from his thick neck, the color spread to his cheeks. "That is uncalled for."

"I didn't say it, they did," Jaymie pointed out.

"They don't remember the Ethan I recall."

"I get that, but they were speaking of him as he is today . . . or was."

"I don't know what he had planned."

A colleague came to his door. "Matt, your three o'clock is here and waiting," she said, indicating a man who paced outside the office.

"We're done here, I believe, Ms. Müller?"

"One more question. Ethan told at least one person that both you and Luke had moved away, that you didn't live here anymore. Do you know why?"

He frowned. "Not in the slightest. Maybe your source is wrong. Ethan would never have said that." He stood and held out his hand and they shook. "I'm sorry I can't be more helpful, but you probably know more about whatever scheme he had in mind than I do."

More helpful? He hadn't been any help. Jaymie buttoned her coat and slung her purse over her shoulder, then leaned over and took one of his cards, slipping it into her purse. "Thank you for giving me your time," she said. "You have my number. I'd appreciate any help you can give. For your mother's sake."

Jaymie exited as Matt's client turned. It was Fitzroy Jones. Ignoring Jaymie, he strode past her into Matt's office and the two men shook hands, then sat down opposite each other.

Interesting, but maybe not surprising. Jones was buying Stowe House, and to do that he would likely need to go through a mortgage specialist.

Or would he? Didn't he say he was buying the property outright?

Yes, yes, he did. He said he was paying cash.

If that was true, then why was he coming to see a mortgage specialist? This was not the time to demand answers. She had learned that information is power, but that to get information, one needed to be prepared. She exited the bank and stood shivering in the breeze on the sidewalk. *That* was a question for a real estate agent, so next time she spoke of it, she'd have information to back her up. She got out her phone, sent a quick text to Val, then put her phone away.

Time to go pick up Jocie, then head off to feed the cats early.

❦ Twenty ❦

DINNER HAD BEEN EATEN AND DISHES WASHED. Jaymie stood at the kitchen counter packing a large container. Jocie snuck closer and snatched a heart-shaped cookie. "Hey!" Jaymie exclaimed, laughing. "Now I have an uneven number of cookies for the girls." It was Friday night and she was in town, so she was getting together with friends for a "girlfriend party."

"What is a girlfriend party?" Jocie asked, climbing up on a stool and spraying cookie crumbs as she enthusiastically munched. Jaymie pinched her soft cheek, but Jocie swatted her hand away with an exaggerated "Mo-om!"

Jaymie laughed. At first her stepdaughter had called her Mama, but lately she had been Mom, often with that exaggerated two syllable pronunciation. She finished her packing, carefully placing wax paper between layers of cookies coated with pink and red icing. "It's a party for girlfriends." She had written goofy messages on the cookies, making them look like the old-fashioned heart-shaped candies: BFF Forever; Love U; Bestie; Girlz Rule. Silly fun for grown-up friends, and a reason to break out the heart-shaped cookie cutters that otherwise were only used for Valentine's Day.

She pushed the plastic lid on, making sure it sealed. "Boys and girls, men and women, there's nothing wrong with mixed parties, but guys like a boys' night out sometimes—like your dad's getaway last weekend with his brother and friend—and girls and women should get together sometimes so they can talk. So we started having girlfriend parties. It's a fun way of celebrating the girlfriends in our lives. Even when we have boyfriends and husbands and kids, we don't want to forget those female relationships that give us strength."

Jocie's cute face lit up. "I'm going to a sleepover tomorrow night at Peyton's. Gemma and Noor and Mia are all coming. Can my friends and I make *that* a girlfriend party sleepover?"

"You sure can! Check with them. We don't want to hijack Peyton's party if they've got plans. But if they say okay, and I check with her mom or dad, I've still got cookie dough in the fridge. We'll roll it out and bake cookies tomorrow for you to take."

Tonight's party was at Bernie's house and would feature

nonalcoholic drinks—everyone had a reason to stay sober lately—snacks and some rousing rounds of girl power karaoke ballads. Lots of Beyoncé and Britney, Christina and T-Swift, and some throwback girl power like the Supremes and Wilson Phillips. Jaymie had Becca's *Control* CD, Janet Jackson at her finest, in her purse. That should start the party off on the retro right foot.

As she carried her container of cookies up the walk at Bernie's place, her phone chimed. She waited until she had entered—Bernie was in the kitchen at the oven and sang out to take the snacks down to the basement rec room—and shed her boots and coat before checking her text.

It was Val, asking her to call. She sat down on a bench in the hall and called. "What's up? Do you have an answer to my question from earlier?" she asked her friend. "Are you on your way?"

"Yes, I have an answer to your question from both Brock and Greg," Val said, naming her brother and her friend, both real estate agents. "But no, I'm not on my way yet. I have a visitor," she said, sounding vexed and perplexed.

"A visitor. Who?"

Her voice softened to a whisper. "It's Judy Jones, Tolly's widow. She was the one calling his cell phone, the one whose message you heard." She raised her voice to normal volume. "She's come over from Canada and wants to meet you."

"Oh."

It was awkward, no two ways about that, given that they were supposed to be having a party to celebrate girlfriends. "I'll call you back," Jaymie said.

She asked Bernie what to do. When the off-duty police officer heard about Judy Jones, she had one question: would the woman be going to the police station to talk to the detectives about her husband's death? Jaymie texted the question to Val, who replied *yes*, Judy had spoken to Detective Rodriguez on the phone and had an appointment with him the next morning. She had checked into the Queensville Inn, but after chatting in the dining room with an elderly diner, Mrs. Martha Stubbs, and hearing Val and Jaymie's names, she had tracked down Val's business number and called it. Val checked the pharmacy number often, in case a customer needed her, and, recognizing the name, had called her back.

Bernie chewed her lip for a moment and eyed Jaymie.

"Given your position on the police force, I completely understand if you're not comfortable with this," Jaymie said. "I can go over to Val's instead. Would you prefer that?"

"It's just going to be you, me, Heidi and Val. Tell Val to bring Judy along." She knew Heidi well enough to know that their empathetic friend would most definitely agree.

That was how the evening changed from a girlfriend party to not-quite-a-wake for an old rocker and his devastated widow.

Val arrived after Heidi, who had been swiftly brought up to speed on the shift in the evening's priorities by Bernie. She ushered the teary Judy Jones into the house and helped her off with her parka. Instead of descending to the rec room, where the party decorations were a little too festive, they stayed in Bernie's mid-century modern living room, the décor featuring the clean lines and muted colors of mid-century, without the worst starburst-ugly-wallpaper excesses of that period. A sofa in olive green nubby fabric lined the far wall, with an amoeba-shaped two-level coffee table in front of it. Two walnut and tan leatherette chairs faced the sofa. Jaymie sat in one, and Bernie in the other, while Val and Heidi flanked the grieving widow on the sofa.

Judy Jones was English, plump, her hair a frowsy white and her skin blotchy from the weather and her emotion. She wore black wool trousers and a heavy long cardigan over a T-shirt that said *Rock On.* Around her neck hung a silver pendant on a long chain; she often touched it like a talisman. Parked in the middle of the sofa, cradling in her hand a gin and tonic that had been mixed at the elegant 1960s bar cabinet Bernie had bought at an auction, she looked around, slightly bewildered. "This is like a classy version of me mum's lounge, when I was a kid."

Bernie smiled. "I'll take that as a compliment. That's kind of what I was going for."

"I'm so sorry for your loss, Mrs. Jones," Jaymie said, as Bernie darted back to the kitchen to take her brie crostini out of the oven.

"Judy, please." The woman's eyes filled, and Val handed her a tissue. "I don't know what I'll do without me Tolly. He were everything to me."

"How long have you been married?" Val asked, as Heidi took

Judy's hand and cradled it in hers. Heidi was empathetic, and her eyes filled with tears for the woman.

"Married? Oh, going on thirty years, I guess. Let's see . . . twenty-nine, yes. But we've been together a lot longer." She related how they met in England when he was with the band. "He was a wild man back then, but I loved him enough to forgive a lot. Don't know how long I would have lasted if he 'adn't straightened out, though." She stuck by him after the band broke up. He had frittered away the money he had earned in the Berk Scouse Brothers band, so he did odd jobs and worked as a truck driver when he could, or as a bartender and occasional deejay at an English-style pub when they moved to London, Ontario. She worked as a janitor and they were superintendents of apartment buildings, through the years.

He had always claimed to have been cheated, though, saying he was owed money. Tolly and Bog had a falling-out over the writing credits, rights and income from the songs the band had made famous.

"Judy, he wasn't allowed into the States, so why was he coming over to Queensville?" Jaymie asked. "We can't figure that out."

"He was coming to warn Bog."

"*Warn* him? About what?"

"That the Crimson Skeleton Riders were out to get 'im, and they'd use any means possible."

"I don't understand."

Judy's eyes shimmered with tears. "I don't know a lot. Tolly was that scared. He wouldn't talk about them, not to me, anyway. I overheard 'im talking on the phone. I know that back in the nineties my 'usband owed them a lot of money. My poor Tolly was an addict back then, you see—he's been clean for years, but it was too late in some ways—so he paid his bills to his dealer by smuggling drugs across the border."

"Which he got caught doing, which is why he wasn't allowed in the States," Bernie filled in, pulling oven gloves off.

Judy nodded. "We lived in Canada, up near Pickering, then moved to London."

"I have family there," Jaymie said.

Judy's gaze flicked to her and she nodded, but continued speaking. "He did time in the U.S., and then was deported to

Canada—we were both naturalized citizens by then—and finished his time in a Canadian jail. He's been out years now, clean the whole time. He could never go back to the States, not without his record being expunged, I think they call it? Which takes a lot of money to be able to hire a lawyer."

"Why didn't he send Bog Brewer a letter or an email?" Val asked.

"He tried, but Bog wouldn't talk to him, letters came back unopened, and we think he dumped the emails unopened too. Their fights back in the eighties were epic battles. They both had an 'orrible temper."

"Why not email him from an anonymous address?"

The woman shrugged. "Didn't think of that. He couldn't wait no more. He had to warn Bog."

"Couldn't he go through someone else?"

She shrugged.

It was immaterial now, so Jaymie dropped it. "I still don't understand, why were these people after Bog, if Tolly was the one who owed them money?"

She shrugged again in helpless ignorance. "Don't know. Tolly thought Bog knew about these biker guys froom someone in 'is family. Tolly heard Bog was gonna testify against one of them Riders in court, back in England. Don't know what about. Then Tolly heard from someone that the Riders was gonna kidnap Bog's son, Alf—"

"Alf? Alf is the name of Bog's son?"

"Sure. Alf Brewer, short for Alfred, y'see."

Jaymie's mind was spinning. That was the Alf Bog kept mentioning. She hadn't made the connection between Alf, Alfred and . . . oh! Fred! It was starting to make sense. "Where is Alf now?"

Judy shrugged. "Don't know. Gone underground, probably, if he's smart."

"Or maybe he's already been kidnapped." That would explain Bog's odd behavior; his anger, the tension between him and Duckie, his depression.

"Maybe. Tolly wanted to come over and warn Bog. He was hoping to prevent it from 'appening. They was best of mates a long time ago, and he felt like he should warn him."

"He was taking an awful chance, though, coming over the border the way he did." It cost him his life, she didn't say out loud.

The bad guys must have gotten word that Tolly was coming.

"Don't I know it," Judy said, her tone bitter. "I warned 'im, didn't I? I told 'im Bog wouldn't give him the time of day, so why should he help him? That sounds bad, but poor Tolly had tried over the years. Instead, he died. How *did* he die?" she asked Jaymie, sobbing. Heidi handed her a tissue, and she dabbed at her eyes. "No one will tell me."

Jaymie exchanged a look with Bernie, who shook her head. She nodded back. However much she sympathized with the widow, what did she really know about her? And she had promised not to hinder the investigation. "I'm sorry, but we can't discuss that. I'd encourage you to talk to Detective Rodriguez about it tomorrow. If anyone can answer your questions, it's him." If he would.

"My poor darling!" she cried, mopping the tears with a sodden tissue that Heidi replaced, taking the wet one in two fingers and depositing it in a nearby trash can. Val had gotten a couple more tissues for the woman, because it was clear she was going to need them. She blew her nose, but this time rose and deposited the tissue herself. "Tolly thought if he could meet Bog in person, they could sort things out. He 'oped that after warning Bog about Alf bein' in danger, that he could then talk about the writing credits."

Ah, that was the real reason he snuck over the border, Jaymie thought.

"He thought Bog would appreciate the warning, and Tolly could borrow some money to finish paying off the Riders so they'd stop hounding him—"

"He *still* owed the bikers money? After all these years?"

"They're like the mob," she said bitterly. "Interest adds up, and before you know it the debt is ten times what it was, and who you gonna complain to?"

"Why didn't Tolly get his brother to loan it to him?" Jaymie asked. "As a matter of fact, why didn't he get Fitzroy to talk to Bog?"

"What do you mean?" Judy said, staring at her, perplexed. "Fitz is in England, and Bog won't talk to him, either. How could he help?"

"Fitzroy is right here in Queensville," Jaymie explained. "And I've seen him at Bog's, so I know they've been talking. Wasn't Tolly in touch with his own brother?" Remembering what Bog had said about the brothers, she tagged on, "I know they had a falling-out years ago."

"They mended fences and talked on the phone every few days. Tolly did ask Fitz to intercede, especially with the whole copyright issue, but Fitz said it was impossible, that Bog wouldn't take his calls neither. But you say Fitz is in town? *Here?* And he's seen Bog? That's not . . ."

Jaymie waited a moment, but the woman didn't finish her sentence. "I've seen him at Bog's house," she repeated. "Tolly *could* have talked to his brother and gotten him to talk to Bog. Maybe he didn't want you to worry, so he didn't tell you everything. Fitzroy appears to have a lot of money. He's buying an expensive home in Queensville for cash. He could have given Tolly money, surely, to help him pay off the Riders."

Judy stayed silent, her eyes wide and her mouth gaping as she stared at the far wall over Jaymie's head. Finally, she said slowly, her voice trembling, "Whoever that guy is, the fellow you say you've seen with Bog, he can't be Fitzroy Jones."

"What? Why do you say that?"

"Describe him to me."

"He's tall, six foot and skinny, with a narrow face and acne scars. He has a dagger tattoo by his left eye. His hair is thin."

"And long?"

"No, not at all," Jaymie said.

She said stubbornly, "Hair can be cut. That is *not* Fitz. It's someone else."

Jaymie saw fear on her face. The woman's breath had accelerated, and she sat up straight, clutching a tissue in both hands, tearing it to pieces. "Judy, I'm guessing that you know who this is, the guy you say is pretending to be Fitzroy Jones. First, how do you know it's not him, and who do you think it is?"

"It's not Fitz, 'cause Fitz is laid up in 'ospital in England with a broken pelvis. Some goon jumped 'im."

Jaymie gasped and uttered a word that might have been *sugar* but wasn't.

"I'd bet my last pound that the man pretending to be Fitz is Raider Dobbs, 'ead man of the Crimson Skeleton Riders."

• • •

The revelation sent Jaymie for a loop. While they ate the delicious foods they had all prepared—the heart-shaped cookies with the funny messages were excruciatingly inappropriate given the sober sadness of poor Judy Jones, but the woman ate readily enough— Jaymie tried to reason through all she had thought and wondered about with this new knowledge. Judy, weary after her long drive from London, Ontario, was ready to go back to the Queensville Inn, so Heidi offered to take her.

Bernie was cleaning up, steadfastly refusing any help, so Jaymie took that moment alone with Val to ask about what Brock and Greg said about why the faux Fitzroy Jones would be talking to a mortgage specialist if the Stowe House sale was for cash.

"Both Brock and Greg had the same answer. Even if this guy bought Stowe House for cash, he might go to a bank and take out a mortgage, using the equity as collateral to fund renovations."

"Oh. Good point," Jaymie said. "He had a window guy there when I saw him, and he mentioned major renovations, including roofing, landscaping." She sighed and shook her head. "I'm going to have to think this all over now. If this is Raider Dobbs, why is he buying a house in Queensville? And why bother with renovations? That indicates a long-term commitment that seems out of keeping with a biker gang trying to gain a toehold. I mean, what if it doesn't work? Won't he leave, then?"

"I have a thought about that. You say Clutch and others have said that the Crimson Skeleton Riders are trying to start a chapter here. Don't gangs have a lot of money they need to launder? And isn't property a good way to launder money?"

"True, and yet . . . it's weird. If you are a criminal organization, would you choose to splash around a lot of money on the fanciest house in town, especially the house that no one else wants to buy? It's been on the market for years, so the sale will cause all kinds of curiosity. Wouldn't you be more discreet? What is it about Stowe House that makes it a good buy for him?"

"I don't have answers. Do you still have Daniel's number? Why don't you ask him about the purchase? Maybe he knows Dobbs. Wouldn't the guy have to buy the house under his real name?"

"We don't know for sure yet that this guy *is* Raider Dobbs," Jaymie demurred. "We're taking Judy's word for it."

"And Daniel might have that info. All the more reason to text him."

"Val, what the heck would I even *say* to Daniel?" She had dated the multimillionaire for a while, but things got complicated, they broke up, and he was now married with a child. "I mean, would I say *'Hi, Daniel, I know we haven't spoken in years but I want to know if you're selling Stowe House to a biker gang?'* That sounds crazy."

"Be honest," Val said sensibly. "Tell him what you've witnessed, what you fear, and tell him you wanted to make sure he was up to date on it all. Then ask him what he knows about the buyer. Frame it as concern from a friend. Do it now, before you chicken out!"

"Buk, buk, buk, *bagawk!*" Jaymie said, with a dispirited flapping of her elbows.

Bernie ducked her head around the corner and stared. Jaymie gave her a chagrined look. Their hostess disappeared and the sound of the sink draining signaled she was almost done with her cleaning.

"C'mon, Jaymie. How are you going to know unless you ask?"

"Okay, okay." She got out her phone, found Daniel's number, and tapped out a message. "It'll be, uh . . . seven p.m. there." She hit send.

• • •

Jakob was in bed reading when Jaymie got home, but he set his book aside and invited her into the warm circle of his arms. She shivered and cuddled up to him, then told him about her odd night. She finished with telling him about the text to Daniel. "I thought tech types were right on top of their phones. I thought he'd text right back, but zip, zero, zilch, nada, so far."

"Give him time. Doesn't he have a kid? Maybe he's actually spending time with his wife and child."

"Yeah, maybe."

He kissed her good night and they turned out the lights.

✄ Twenty-one ✄

SHE HAD A RESTLESS NIGHT, STILL TROUBLED BY THE DEATHS, and on a more trivial front, knowing how busy the next few days would be, as they moved all their stuff back to the cabin after a week in town. Daniel hadn't yet answered her query.

Jaymie had dug out boxes of kitchen utensils she wanted to go through for the historic house and the Kitschy Kitchen. She knew she had some neat tongs but hadn't found them yet. Jakob was going to take the boxes to their cabin so she could sort them at her leisure. He would then drop in to his parents' place.

Jaymie and Jocie took Hoppy for a long walk. The weather had warmed and as the sun rose, it turned the sky radiant with pinks and peaches, promising a warmer day. You would almost think spring was on its way, by the bare pavement and sidewalks, but it was wise to not be taken in by a Michigan almost-spring day, which could turn back into winter in a flash.

When they got back Jaymie called Peyton's mom. Everyone was happy to make it a girlfriend party and sleepover, so Jaymie showed her daughter how to roll out the cookie dough. They spent the early part of the morning baking the cookies, frosting and decorating them, and packing them in containers. Jaymie roped her daughter into helping her finish the cleaning that needed to be done before Becca and Kevin reclaimed the house the next day.

They went together to feed the cats. Perhaps because she was feeding them later in the morning than usual, the big tomcat waited near the path down to the river, watching as the food was doled out. He was, as far as one could tell, one of the last unfixed males, besides the other skinny one. She had asked Dr. Kasimo how they were going to catch him. The answer was a trap, of course, but it would be difficult for many reasons. In winter it could be dangerous to trap a cat that might be stuck in the device for hours, not able to seek shelter. The project would have to wait for more settled weather.

Jaymie unlocked the bin, extracted the tongs, and removed the bedding from the last of the shelters that still had them. She and Jocie then pitched in clean straw. As Jaymie filled bowls and organized the feeding stations, making sure that all cats got equal access to the soft food, Jocie held Jaymie's phone and checked all the pictures with the cat names. They saw most of them.

But the whole time Jaymie kept glancing over to where she had found Ethan's body, trying to figure out the tangled murder mysteries that plagued her town. Was a British biker gang really poised to take over Wolverhampton and Queensville? Why had Ethan been murdered? Tolly she could imagine, given how he had angered the bikers, but what had Ethan done? And to die by an insulin overdose; how diabolical a method, a silent killing. But to do it you had to have access to the drug, enough of it to kill a man. And you had to have time enough for it to work, according to the chief.

When they emerged from behind the houses it was to find Morgan arriving at Miss Perry's, again with Quinley Gustafson.

Jaymie eyed the woman with interest. Clutch had said that Quin was Raider Dobbs's woman. Where better to find the truth? She hadn't been going to, but she accepted her friend's invitation to have tea. While Morgan and Jocie entertained Miss Perry, Jaymie joined Quin in the kitchen, where Jaymie had volunteered Morgan's friend to fill a treat tray.

"I've been talking to a few friends and acquaintances and discovered, to my surprise, that you introduced Ethan Zarcone to his latest girlfriends, both Ashley Ledbetter *and* Morgan," Jaymie said, moving so she could see the woman's face. "What a coincidence!"

Quin eyed her, but said nothing, filling the kettle and peering at the stove, figuring out how to turn on an element.

"And how odd that of the three of them, Ashley wound up in the hospital because of Ethan, who beat her, Morgan was thrown from a car in the middle of the street and sprained her ankle, and then Ethan ended up murdered."

Quin turned to face Jaymie, one hand on her hip, which was cocked to one side. "Why don't you ask what you want to know, Miss Goody Two Shoes, instead of making stupid comments?"

"What business were you in with Ethan?"

"I don't know what you mean."

"You know more than you've ever said. I think the police should talk to you."

"Ethan and I were friends, sure, but—"

"Friends? You were helping him with the biker gang connection, weren't you? I know a guy who hangs out at Shooters and he says you were there all the time. That's how I know you introduced Ethan to Ashley Ledbetter."

"So what?"

"And Ethan introduced you to his mother as a business partner. In what business?"

The kettle whistled and she whirled, rattled. She clattered about, putting the box of cookies on the platter and filling the teapot. Her hands were shaking.

"What business, Quin? Was it Parker's people-smuggling business, or whatever Ethan had cooked up concerning properties in Queensville?" No answer. Jaymie regarded her and considered how to continue. This woman had information, she was sure of it. What would make her give it up? She was wary about accusing the woman of being the bike gang leader's girlfriend, treading carefully before revealing all she knew. "Quin, if you don't talk to me, then I'm going to *have* to give your name to the police as a person of interest in Ethan's death."

Quin swore furiously, slammed down the box of cookies, and turned, thrusting her face in Jaymie's. "*Do* it. Go ahead," she hissed, spittle flying into Jaymie's face. "*Do it.*" She backed off and said, in a more reasonable tone, "I wouldn't advise it, but hey, you do you. Do what you want, and live with the consequences, I always say." She grabbed the tray, sloshing tea, and shoved past Jaymie, departing the room.

Do what you want and live with the consequences. That sounded like a threat, and with Quin's connections, it was a threat with fangs. She hadn't even gotten to her meatiest question: was Raider Dobbs the man pretending to be Fitzroy Jones? If so, why the deception?

Jaymie took in a shaky breath as she thought it through. Quin was the most likely killer, though she would have needed help. Maybe Parker Hellman was her assistant, delivering to her the victims. First Tolly Jones, and then Parker's good buddy, Ethan Zarcone. But why? She could not connect a motive to any of them.

She still had more questions than answers. What was the property swindle Ethan was involved in? What was the smuggling business Parker was involved in? Were the two tied together? And how?

And why did people die?

It had been the stupid impulse of the moment, with a soupçon of frustration added in, to threaten Quin with the police. Of all the rules she had learned in the last few years, the most vital was that if you poke the bear, it comes after you.

Never poke the bear.

Should she warn Morgan about her new "friend"? That was a difficult call. She joined the group. As they all sat together, Jaymie's mind raced as she tried to decide what to do. Poor Morgan had been through so much, and this was yet another betrayal coming her way. But the girl was far too trusting, and, if Jaymie was being honest, too transparent. The problem was, if Jaymie warned Morgan now, the young woman would never be able to keep a poker face around Quin. That would cause real problems. Given the stumble Jaymie had already had with Quin, she needed to get Morgan alone to warn her.

After tea and chat, with no sign that Morgan or Quin were going anywhere, Jaymie guided Jocie out to the car and helped her in, trying to decide how to rectify what she may have inadvertently done.

She was out of her depth. She'd been in some sticky situations, but never one quite like this. Detective Rodriguez should be her first phone call. A police cruiser drove by slowly, and she waved to the officers inside.

As Jocie buckled her seat belt, Jaymie climbed into the driver's seat and considered her dilemma. Wasn't Quin's reaction all the confirmation she needed? The woman would not be so hostile if Jaymie hadn't hit a nerve.

She looked down at Bog and Duckie's house, undecided. Quin and Morgan emerged from Miss Perry's house. Quin glared at her with squinted eyes. Morgan, unaware, waved at her, got in the car, pulled out of the drive and drove away. Darn it! What to do? This indecisiveness was making her crazy. It had to stop. She needed to solve this thing and make sure no one else got hurt.

Jaymie climbed back out and went to her daughter's side door. "Jocie, would you go back in and check on Miss Perry again? I don't know if Morgan cleaned up the teapot and tray and I don't want Miss Perry to be left to do it alone."

"I can do it." Jocie, unbuckling her belt, paused, eyeing Jaymie with suspicion. "What are *you* going to be doing?"

"I'll be talking to an acquaintance."

"And you don't think it's the kind of talk I should hear," Jocie said, as Bog emerged in his boxer shorts to grab a package from his step. She climbed down out of the SUV. "Got it."

"You, young lady, are too clever for your own good."

As Jocie entered Miss Perry's home, Jaymie stomped down to Bog's house. "You and I have to talk," she said, taking his arm, turning him, and marching him back into the house.

They stood in the entry, she still holding his arm, afraid he'd bolt.

Bog tossed the package aside and eyed her warily. "Whatdya want wiv me?"

"I want to know what's going on."

He stared, irresolute and shifty, but didn't speak.

"Bog, I know that Tolly was coming over to warn you about your son being kidnapped by a biker gang back in England. I know the leader of that gang, Raider Dobbs, is here, in Queensville, pretending to be Fitzroy Jones. He, or at least his gang members, have already kidnapped your son. I also know that Dobbs is up to some shady financial business to do with a local historic house, though I don't know what that's all about yet." She paused and stared at him as he trembled. She took her shot in the dark. "And I know he is behind the killing of Tolly Jones and Ethan Zarcone."

He stared at her, his bloodshot eyes wide with fear. "'Ow'd you get all that?"

"Last night I spoke with Judy Jones." His whole body jolted at the name. "Yes, she's here, in Queensville. She told me what she knows, including that Fitzroy Jones is laid up in a hospital back in England with a broken pelvis given to him by some biker gang brutes."

His eyes filled with water and he whimpered.

"And today she will be talking to Detective Rodriguez. Why are you protecting them, given that they've kidnapped your son and are holding him ransom?"

"You don't understand, I carn't . . ." Tears streamed down his face.

She pitied him, but his silence was not helping. "Bog, talk to me," she urged. "I have friends on the police—"

"Nah, nah! No rozzers," he shouted, pulling himself loose and backing away. "I never trusted 'em, never will. You go to them, an' I swear ta God you're signin' a death warrant on me lad."

"Bog, listen to me. You *have* to talk to someone. And didn't you hear me? Judy Jones is already talking to them, right this minute, likely. What do those guys want from you? What have they told you to do, before they release your son?" Her phone, in her pocket, was pinging and ringing, but she could not let this go. Bog needed to talk to her and let her help, if she could. One way or another, she was going to the police with all of this information to back up Judy Jones's tale.

"I ain't talkin' to you," he said. His eyes were bloodshot and he quivered. "And I ain't trustin' no rozzers. Get out of me 'ouse, now."

She eyed him sadly. He was not the trailblazing rocker he once was. He may have misspent his youth with drugs and alcohol, but now he was an old man who loved his son and was desperately afraid for him. She both pitied him and was irritated by his stubbornness. "Bog, I'm on your side," she said more softly. "These guys are dangerous, you know that better than anyone. I don't know for sure who killed Tolly and Ethan, but if Dobbs did, the police will get him. Your best bet to ensure your son is rescued is to get their help."

He swore and turned away, saying, over his shoulder, "Not talkin' ta rozzers. You can show yerself out."

• • •

She took Jocie home, sending her upstairs to get packed for her sleepover while she read her texts. The first text was a reply, finally, from Daniel. He apologized for the delay, and then said why he was slow responding. He had been checking with his business team, which was handling the sale of Stowe House. It *was* sold, pending some legalities. He had been confused by her text because the name she gave had not matched what he remembered of the buyer.

Neither Fitzroy Jones nor Raider Dobbs had bought the house.

"*What?*" Jaymie exclaimed involuntarily. What was he saying?

It had been purchased, Daniel wrote, by a gentleman by the name of Nigel Charles Dudley, an online personality.

Oh. Wow.

Jaymie found the fellow's video channel. He posted charming videos from his elegant Beacon Hill brownstone, which he had painstakingly renovated into a showcase for his antique collection. He presented afternoon tea, quirky cooking videos, housekeeping tips, and musical interludes during which he played the piano while his husband, a prominent entertainment lawyer, sang tenor opera pieces.

And indeed he was *not* Fitzroy Jones, nor was he Raider Dobbs. He was as American as Apple Pandowdy.

Huh. If it was true that he had bought Stowe House, it appeared Dudley would be the kind of owner the town would appreciate, someone who knew how to care for a heritage property and had the money to do it right. And she couldn't help thinking that he might be persuaded to let them go ahead with the Tea with the Queen event on his lawn.

However . . . back to the problem at hand. She stared out the back window, wondering what it all meant. She was puzzled why Raider Dobbs/Fitzroy Jones was speaking with a mortgage manager at the Wolverhampton bank. Unless . . . Jaymie was suddenly hit with a thought. Oh. *Oh!* Maybe Ethan's brother Matt was involved in what seemed to be some kind of scam, though Jaymie didn't understand it in the slightest. The plot was getting more complicated the more she discovered.

It was time to call the detective with all that she had learned and suspected. The Matt Zarcone–Raider Dobbs connection might turn out to be more important than she even knew. Rodriguez was, surprisingly, in, and she told him all she had discovered over the last few days, about Judy Jones—he didn't confirm that he had spoken to her, but she assumed he had by his apparent familiarity with Jaymie's information—and finally, the confrontation with Quinley Gustafson. "I understand from Clutch Roth that Quin is Raider Dobbs's girlfriend. Supposedly." She explained what else she thought, about why she suspected Quin of being the killer. "I'm afraid I may have put my foot in it, Detective. I tried to get her to talk to me, but instead she gave me the hint that I'd better keep my nose out of it, if I knew what was good for me."

"Did she actually threaten you?"

Jaymie thought back to the conversation, and admitted, "Not really."

"What did she say *exactly*? Please be precise." Jaymie repeated what Quin had said—that Jaymie should do what she wanted and reap the consequences—and he harrumphed after it. "Not an actionable threat, I'm afraid."

Jaymie shivered. "You don't think . . . Detective, should I be scared?"

"We're way past that, Ms. Müller. Stay as far away from these people as you can. I'm going to try to arrange protection for you, but the department is stretched thin right now."

"I saw a cruiser drive past Miss Perry's house."

"We're doing that as often as possible. Until this is over, don't go anywhere alone."

"I won't, Detective."

"Promise."

"I promise. I mean, I can't say I won't walk down my street alone, or go to the store, but I won't go to feed the cats alone."

He grumbled, but it was enough to satisfy him.

She had missed a call from Jakob while on the phone with the detective, so she called him back, but he didn't answer.

Odd.

If she wasn't going out to feed the cats alone tonight, she'd have to wait until Jakob came home. But until then, she could not stop living. She had responsibilities.

She leashed Hoppy and together they walked Jocie down to her friend's house in twilight, the sky an ominous bruised purple. She kept looking over her shoulder as her little dog bounded along, barking randomly at noises and movements in the shadows. It got dark early in March, and it was becoming icy again. The warmth of the brilliant day had darkened to a frigid evening, with a cold wind that swept down the town street. All the meltwater was now freezing into slick patches of ice, which they had to pick their way around with difficulty, as Jocie carried her pillow and duffel bag, and Jaymie carried the cookies and held Hoppy's leash.

Once there she stood in the foyer and smiled at the girls' excitement at the cute cookies, and the girlfriend party decorations the mom had scrambled together at the last moment, mostly old Valentine décor. A string of hearts down the stairs to the basement had girl power messages on them saying "You go, girl!" and "Girlz Rule!" Jocie's friends were already there, and they crowded around Hoppy, petting the happy three-legged dog, who turned and waggled his rear end to each new cooing girl. Finally, she managed to break Hoppy away from the adoration. Jaymie waved goodbye, but Jocie was already heading for the rec room with her girlfriends.

Jaymie got home, locked up tight, and unhooked Hoppy from his leash. He started up the stairs in his own, unique, three-legged manner. Lilibet would be curled up on Jocie's bed so he would probably join the little cat in a cuddle puddle to snooze. Jakob was still not home. She called him again, starting to panic. Winter in Michigan meant icy roads and uncertain weather. It was all too possible that he had slid off the road into a ditch.

Where *was* he?

Promising herself she'd give it another half hour before calling his parents, she tidied up Jocie's room. It looked like a tornado had whirled through it, but the animals were indeed curled up together on her bed. She was heading back downstairs when her phone rang. It was Jakob! "Thank goodness!" she gasped into it. "I was starting to worry."

"I'm sorry, hon, but I didn't want to text. Don't worry, I'm fine. But Mom had a dizzy spell and fainted."

"What?"

"It's okay, it's all right. She keeps wanting to clean the tops of her cupboards, so I was doing it for her. She was sitting in a chair in the kitchen when she got lightheaded. She wouldn't let me take her to the hospital. I stuck around because I was worried. Papa was too, though he wouldn't say so out loud. Then she fainted and slumped down, hitting her head."

"Oh, *no*! Jakob, I'm so sorry," Jaymie said, staring out the kitchen window into the dark backyard. "Is she going to be okay?"

"I don't think it's serious, at least I hope not. We called an ambulance and they took her away, but she was saying the whole time that it was too much fuss, and that they shouldn't be bothering. You know what she's like. But I have to take Dad to Wolverhampton General to see her, or he's going to worry himself into a fit." Jakob's father's driver's license had been suspended until the effects of new medication had been worked out. "Wait . . . I've got another call coming through. It's the hospital. I'll call you right back."

A few minutes later he called again. "They think the light-headedness might be a side effect of her new blood pressure meds. They let me talk to her, and she sounded great, but she doesn't want the grandchildren worried until she can talk to them herself."

"Okay, I understand. I won't call Jocie. You take your dad to the hospital. Be careful on the roads. Jocie is at her party so she's good until tomorrow morning."

"Have you been out to feed the cats yet?"

"Uh . . . no." She wasn't sure, with all his current worries, how much to tell him about all she had learned that day. It could wait, she decided. "I'm going to go out there now, but it's dark, so I won't do it alone. I'll get Morgan to meet me there, now that her foot has healed enough to drive." She needed to warn Morgan about Quin anyway, or she wouldn't sleep, so this was a way to see her face-to-face.

"*Promise* me you'll wait until Morgan meets you at Miss Perry's house before you get out of your car? If it wasn't for having to take Papa to the hospital—"

"Jakob, don't worry about me. I'll be fine. You take care of your parents. I love you."

"I love you too."

"I wish I could hug you," she whispered into the phone. "I'll meet you at the hospital as soon as I can."

"No, hon, don't. The weather is going to be crappy."

"What?"

"Didn't you hear? I was watching a weather report. We have a storm on the way."

She dashed to the back window and flicked back the curtain. Well, *that* had changed in a hurry! The first flakes of snow were drifting down. Uh-oh. Michigan storms could start like a pretty dream and descend into an icy nightmare in a hurry. Her breathing came faster. She hated driving in rotten weather.

But she had no choice. She had to go or she'd worry all night. "I didn't know. I'd better get out to feed those poor cats before the weather closes in. But I could still come to the hospital."

"Jaymie, honey, as much as I wish you were with me, *please* don't go out on the highway tonight. If you go now I'm sure you'll be okay driving to Winding Woods, but just there and back, okay? And text me as soon as you get home safely. I'll come back to Queensville the moment I can. Dieter has to stay on the farm to look after the animals," he said about his oldest brother, who lived in a suite over the garage at his parents'. "But Helmut is on his way back from a farm conference in Kalamazoo. Sonya said he should be back sometime tonight and will meet us at the hospital."

"If he gets through the weather."

"If he gets through the weather," Jakob agreed.

"Okay. I would rather be with you, but I don't want you to worry more than you already are."

"I'll be home before morning, I promise."

"I'll see you then. I miss you already. Let me know later how your mother is doing. Tell her I love her."

"I will, *liebchen*," he whispered. "Papa is ready to go. He's standing here with his coat on and tapping his boot. I have to load his walker in the truck and get a move on."

"Tell him I love him."

"I will. Love you. You *promise* me you'll wait for Morgan? And that you'll text me when you get home?"

"I promise. Cross my heart."

℘ Twenty-two ℘

JAYMIE CALLED MORGAN. "HOW ARE YOU?" SHE ASKED.

"Tired."

Oh, dear. "I have a big favor to ask, Morgan. I have to go out and feed the cats. There's a storm coming in, and I don't want them to go without in case the roads are closed tomorrow. But I promised Jakob that I wouldn't do it alone." She explained briefly what was going on with Jakob's family, and why he wasn't there to go with her.

There was silence on the other end of the line.

"Morgan, will you meet me there?"

"At the cat colony. On an icy Saturday night. Jaymie, I already have my pj's on."

There was a whine in her voice, but Jaymie held fast. She had promised Jakob not to go alone, and she would not. Plus, she was determined to have a chat with Morgan about Quin. They needed to confront some cold hard truths about the woman. She stayed silent.

A heavy sigh. "Okay. I'll meet you there."

"You know I wouldn't ask if it wasn't necessary. I'm heading out now. I'll wait outside of Miss Perry's house until you get there." There was a noise in the background, a banging sound, and a tinkle. Jaymie said, "What was that?"

"I don't know," Morgan replied. "I'd better get going if I'm going. I have to get dressed and then I'll leave right away."

Jaymie donned her parka and heavy boots, made sure Hoppy and Lilibet were comfy, then headed out. The rising wind buffeted her as she walked down the path toward the parking lane. It was getting cold again, midwinter icy and mean, even though it was the Ides of March. She got in her SUV and started it up, cranking the heat. She texted Morgan to be sure the girl hadn't gone to bed. Morgan texted back *on my way wait for me at the cat place start without me and I'll meet you there.*

Sheesh, cat place? Could she not spell *colony*? Jaymie backed out of the parking spot and drove slowly through Queensville as the wind strengthened, a sleety snow slanting across the windshield as she took River Road and turned on to Winding Woods Lane. It was miserable! She parked in front of Miss Perry's place to wait for Morgan. She hoped the girl didn't take too long. The weather was

195

getting worse and worse, and she still had to drive home through it, as did Morgan. But at least Morgan could stay at Miss Perry's if it got too bad.

She tuned in to a weather report on the radio. Blizzard conditions expected overnight. Don't drive unless you must. She took up her phone and found the weather app. Wind warnings. Local airport shut down. Don't drive unless you have to. She hoped Helmut could get home to his family. Her mind wandered to Jakob and the Müllers, hoping everything was all right. She typed a text to ask, but then didn't send it. He'd call her when he knew. She tapped her thumbs on the steering wheel and checked her rearview mirror. No headlights, no Morgan.

She texted her again. No answer. Morgan should have been here by now if she left when she said she was leaving, Jaymie thought, worried. If she waited too long, it would be that much harder to feed the cats in a blizzard. She didn't want the poor pusses to be out in the wind trying to eat.

Darn! She was second-guessing her decision to call Morgan. She was worried, she had to admit.

No, she was *not* going to give into fretting. To heck with it. In her last text Morgan said she *was* coming, to meet her at the cat colony and start without her, so Jaymie wouldn't be out there alone for long. No hit man or attacker was going to be fool enough to brave a Michigan snowstorm. And how would they even know she was there? Jaymie glanced around, but there was no car parked nearby.

She went to Miss Perry's house. The woman invited her in so they stood in the warmth of the front hall. Jaymie didn't want to go further into the house with wet boots on. "Morgan said she'd meet me out at the cat colony, but the weather is getting worse. Maybe, given her injured foot, she shouldn't try to walk across that icy patch out back."

Miss Perry, a worried expression on her lined face, shook her head. "That girl! I swear she'd try the patience of a saint. If she started out when you say she did, she should be here by now."

Jaymie didn't want to raise the possibility she had been fretting about, of an accident or car trouble. She explained, though, her own reasons for hurrying. Her mother-in-law was at the hospital, and she was worried, despite Jakob's reassuring words. She wanted to be home in case she was needed.

"You go on, then. I'll keep an eye out front for Morgan," Miss Perry said.

"Okay. I'm going around." She peered out the door, but no Morgan. "I don't know what to think. Maybe she got tied up at home. Maybe I should text her and tell her to go back."

"You let that girl make her own decisions. If it's too dangerous to drive, she'll figure that out. She needs to start using that noggin. Maybe that's what happened—she started out, but the weather is too bad so she turned back. You'll get a text any minute saying that."

"Okay. I won't see you again before I leave. You stay safe and warm; it's getting nasty. You've got my cell number. Call me, even if it's while I'm still out back, if you hear from Morgan, okay?"

The woman nodded. Despite her irritation with her great-niece, she loved Morgan fiercely and appeared extremely concerned.

Jaymie carefully picked her way past icy patches and returned to the car. She unloaded the canned food from the back of her SUV as Haskell drove up. He got out of his car and stared down the road. "Did you see some lunatic speeding along here? A guy in a black car . . . big thing, like a tank! Driving it like it was stolen!"

"No, I was in Miss Perry's house. I just came back out to get the cat food."

"He's gonna kill someone," he grumbled, pulling his coat collar up around his reddening ears. He turned back and eyed her and her full bags. "You're not going out there in this blizzard to feed those cats, are you?"

"They still need to eat, especially in this weather. How is Hoagie doing?"

Haskell's patrician face was transformed by a fatuous expression as he jammed his gloved hands deep in his pockets. "You would not believe it. I think that cat must be a super-intelligent purebred, and not some mutt of a feline. He is so clever!" While Jaymie moved from foot to foot, and the snow started blowing sideways harder, he explained all that Hoagie had "learned" to do, and what a gentleman he was. He scratched on a scratching post! He used a litter box and covered up his poop! "And you wouldn't credit it, but he and Aloysius have become fast friends. I didn't know it was possible for a cat and dog to bond, but my little Aloysius refuses to sleep anywhere but with Hoagie, in the big cat bed."

"You bought a cat bed?"

"I did. The best plush cat bed money can buy. Hoagie took to it immediately. Dr. Kasimo says he has never seen anything like it. I guarantee you, that cat once had a pampered life, and is now remembering the little luxuries to which he was once accustomed. He especially likes sliced chicken livers and a little filet."

Jaymie stared up at him in amusement. There was no cat lover like a new convert! Imagine, a cat using a cat scratching post and a litter box. No one had ever heard of cats doing such *amazing* things. Soon, Hoagie would have a new name—something pretentious like William Hogarth II—and would be a purebred Himalayan prince. She shivered and pulled up her parka hood. "Haskell, I have to get moving. I want to take care of the cats before this storm gets worse. I don't want to be stuck at Miss Perry's overnight." Maybe he'd offer to help.

But he turned away and, with a jaunty wave, headed toward his walk. "So long, then! It's time for Hoagie's treats. Be careful out there."

Grumbling, Jaymie gave herself a good talking to as she focused the beam of her flashlight along the dark icy path around Miss Perry's house. She had volunteered for this knowing what March weather in Michigan was like. And who else was more reliable than she was? How would they have fared if it had been left to the disappearing Parker? Those poor cats would have starved.

Well, no. Miss Perry wouldn't have allowed that.

She looked up against the wind, her eyelashes becoming frosted with the sleety snow, as she rounded the corner of Miss Perry's house. Why had she not asked Haskell to help? She should have, instead of expecting him to offer and being mad when he didn't. New resolution: *if you want something, ask for it.*

She headed out on a diagonal across the snowy expanse toward the cat colony, slow going with the weight of the bags and the difficulty of the terrain, and needing to balance the flashlight. She couldn't help her mind returning to the mystery of Ethan and Tolly's deaths and tried to figure out Parker's part in everything. Ethan's partner, certainly, and likely in hiding after what happened to Zarcone.

Unless he was the killer, or an accessory.

But no. Jaymie thought back to what she had heard about Parker. The guy was loyal to a fault, everyone acknowledged that. He would *never* kill Ethan, nor would he help someone else do it.

If he would just come forward he could help the police a great deal because he doubtlessly had inside information to offer. Of course he'd probably end up in jail for human smuggling, but maybe he could cut a deal.

Gosh, this wind. She could hardly see with the snow blowing and the parka hood up. She almost dropped the flashlight as she juggled the bags. Darn it, her phone was ringing, but it would have to go to voicemail, because she did not have enough hands.

The awful notion that Parker was dead could not be discounted. She sincerely hoped not. As fecklessly and stupidly as Parker had behaved, Rachel seemed to care for him, and she wished no one ill. She considered what she had thought of earlier, a possible solution to who had provided the instrument of Ethan's death. It made sense, but oh, she did not want to think it true!

And yet . . . as she trudged, she thought and reasoned. It made sense, what she was thinking. Someone likely supplied insulin to kill Ethan. If Morgan would just get there she could answer one question Jaymie had: was Quin an insulin-dependent diabetic? Is that what she meant by "calibrating her meter"? And why she had to occasionally absent herself?

And is that what she was doing, while Morgan spoke to Ethan at the car dealership hours after Tolly's body was found? Was Quin providing insulin to Ethan's killer? Surely not. She wouldn't, would she? Knowing how it would affect Morgan?

Who knew how that woman's mind worked? Who else was in the car that day, Parker? Raider? Someone else?

She finally reached the colony. There were few cats around, their eyes flashing in the beam of the light. She had no desire to be out in this monstrous weather any longer than necessary, so she peeled off her gloves and set to work, swiftly emptying bowls, throwing dirty ones into waiting bags, filling others with kibble. All that was left was her last task, the canned food. Some cats were circling but skittish, racing away, bellies close to the ground, but hungry enough for the good stuff that they crept closer again. The big bruiser, the unfixed male, paced uneasily, his big head turning this way and that, his glowering glare shooting into the distance, at some perceived enemy. Occasionally he arched his back and hissed, growling uneasily. A cat like that, an unfixed tom, probably saw enemies everywhere. The other cats watched him as they ate, heads popping up and glancing his way, wary and alert.

A herring gull shrieked in the distance. She straightened as the tom paced toward her and the dish of food she had set down. A gull? In this weather, and this time of night? That couldn't be right. The tom gulped down the food, grumbling uneasily as a smaller cat crouched nearby, hoping for scraps.

She heard the noise again, and this time it was clear that the sound was not a gull, but a scream drifting on the wind and the snow toward her. *Help. Help!*

She froze in place, quivering. A rush of terror, that history was repeating itself, washed through her.

Help. Hel . . . ! It was a woman, the last shriek strangled off. Her heart pounded, the urge to rush to someone's aid thrumming in her veins. As the big tom wolfed down his chow she dropped the bag of canned food, watched by a score of glittering eyes around her, and fished in her pocket for her phone, her fingers freezing to numbness and clumsy from the cold.

She tried to navigate the device, her fingers stiff. It was being stubbornly slow to wake up. "Come on, come *on!*" she muttered, as the shriek again cut the sound of the wind.

A beam of light cut through the dark, and the sound of voices coming up to the cliff drifted and wavered on the frigid wind. She played her own flashlight beam toward it, and saw, to her horror, Morgan, in pink flannel pajamas, being half shoved, half carried by the formerly elegant faux Fitzroy Jones, Raider Dobbs, accompanied by Quinley Gustafson, who stumbled along beside him like a frightened toddler, into some trouble way too deep to fathom.

"Stop it right there, you feckin' harpy," the biker yelled. "Drop yer phone right now and listen, or yer mate 'ere gets it."

Jaymie saw the knife. He held the blade to Morgan's neck and she whimpered, her eyes wide, as Jaymie's flashlight beam glinted dully on the slim brilliant cutting edge of the otherwise black blade.

Yoga breathing—in through the nose, out through pursed lips.

She did not drop her cell phone. "Raider Dobbs," she said with what calm she could muster as he got closer. They were mere feet away. Quin held a flashlight, illuminating the scene.

"'At's me. Now, behave or this daft wench gets a new smile." He made a wretched movement as if to slice her throat. "Drop yer phone."

She was focused solely on the perpetrators, ignoring Morgan as she tried to navigate this dangerous moment. She could not waver, could not let this moment devolve into murder. Morgan needed Jaymie to be at her best, and so she *must* ignore her friend's whimpering and sobbing. She turned her attention to the other woman. "Quin, I see you've thrown your lot in with this criminal, your new boyfriend. Life behind bars an appealing fate for you?"

Quin, not looking as confident as she had earlier, moaned but didn't reply. She was shuddering with cold, poorly dressed for the weather in a short bomber-style puffy jacket, skinny jeans, Adidas and no gloves. She clutched the flashlight with quivering bare hands.

"Smarten up! He's using you," Jaymie said harshly. So this was the noise she heard in the background at Morgan's place, the two of them breaking in. And the texts on Morgan's phone had informed them Jaymie would be a sitting duck for the man's predation. "Quin, don't be a fool. Raider Dobbs is going to dispose of you when he's done here. You'll be next."

"Don't talk to 'er," the fellow roared. "She's 'most as useless as this tart."

Morgan groaned with fear and Jaymie met her gaze. The terror glazing her eyes was heartbreaking. They were at the tipping point. Jaymie had been through this too many times and there was a cold dark core at the center of her now that she retreated to. This was the moment when things could resolve or get much worse. She must focus to keep that latter fate from claiming poor Morgan.

Her one asset in this moment was that she had been through this before and survived. "What do you want, Raider?" Jaymie asked.

"Tell me what you've gone and done, you stupid slag. What didya tell the rozzer? I know yer talked to 'im, the greasy sonuva . . . 'ere, keep that cat back!" The unfixed tom was circling him, and he kicked one booted foot at it. "An' drop yer feckin' phone now or I swear, there'll be blood!"

Anger built in the pit of her stomach, and the insults and cat kicking were the end. "What good will it do telling you what I said in my *long* conversation with Detective Rodriguez?"

"I talked to him too, you know," Morgan squeaked. "I . . . I—"

His rugged face twisted in fury. "Shut yer trap, you dirty little . . ." A stream of filthy expletives streamed from him then as his rigid self-control began to break down.

"This hasn't gone your way, has it, Raider?" she taunted. That tipping point that she had been trying to navigate was teetering. Poor Morgan was sliding down in his grasp, unable to keep her footing in slippers on the icy snow, and the knife cut her, ribbons of scarlet coursing down her neck, soaking into the pink flannel. She had to distract him. Keep him talking. "Raider. *Raider!* I'm nosy, you know that. What was the plan here? I know about the human smuggling part of the plot, but I still don't understand why you pretended to buy a house in Queensville."

He just shook his head, watching her. He was trying to figure out how to resolve this situation, Jaymie thought. She had to keep him off balance, make him talk about something, anything! "Raider, why did you leave Ethan's body on the bluff? It was a really stupid move, so it had to have some meaning. Was it a message or . . . what?"

He grabbed Morgan against him harder, hefting her up. "'At was so that fecker Bog would know we wuz not foolin'. 'E'd think Tolly was a one-off, y'see, but that berk Zarcone . . . 'at was a warning he oughta listened to." Morgan shifted and tried to get away and he grunted, then pressed the point of the knife in. She cried out in pain. "Listen 'ere, time ta move this along. Throw yer phone down and foller me, or she gets it in the throat!" He pressed the knife. Morgan sobbed.

"Raider, don't hurt Morgan!" Jaymie cried, reaching out one hand. *"Please!"*

In a blindly fast and chaotic series of actions, Quin lunged at Raider, her flailing causing the knife to slew sideways, cutting the sleeve of her parka, feathers pouring from the slash and flying up in the wind as blood poured from her cut arm. As Raider flailed, falling backward, his grip on Morgan failed and she wrenched away. Jaymie couldn't see it all happening, but she trained her flashlight beam on the scene just as the big tom cat, with a wild and eerie shriek, launched himself at Raider and attached himself to the biker's face, biting down on the flesh of his cheek as the man screamed in terror and pain, blood flooding his eyes. Morgan staggered sideways and fell into the snow. In that moment too, sirens wailed, lights flared and illuminated the expanse, snow falling sideways in the beams of light from officers who surrounded and took control.

Bernie was one of the responding officers. She efficiently nailed Raider Dobbs with one booted foot as he tried to scuttle away, kneeling on his back and cuffing his hands as the tom scooted away into the dark. By the light of Bernie's big police flashlight Jaymie could see Dobbs's blood from his feline wounds seeped into the snow in blots like a pink Rorschach. Jaymie started toward Morgan but a sturdy police officer had raced to her side and helped her to her feet. She stared up at him crying, pretty and bewildered, disheveled and adorable in snow-coated pink pajamas that were beginning to shade red at the collar with the stream of blood from a superficial wound on her neck. She shivered and he put one arm around her, helping her limp away, around the house and into the dark, toward the warmth of a patrol car until the paramedics arrived.

Another officer had Quin cuffed even as blood stained her slashed puffer jacket. Jaymie stared at her and said, "You tried to help Morgan. You may have even saved her life."

The woman shuddered, whimpered and nodded.

"I *will* tell the police what you did, Quin," she said, now certain of her theories. "But I'll also tell them you tried to help Morgan in the end."

She wept and wailed. "I didn't know he was going to try to kill Morgan! She was so nice to me, the only girlfriend I've ever had, and I couldn't . . ." The officer led her away as her voice still trailed on the wind. "I didn't know, I swear it, I didn't know Raider was going to kill people. I tried to warn you off, Jaymie. I *tried*! I was so scared of him by then, but . . ." Her voice died out.

Quin was rewriting the record of her behavior, Jaymie thought, the little bit of cynicism she allowed herself percolating to the surface. Good luck with that, because she *did* know someone was going to die but didn't care until the next victim was supposed to be Morgan.

Rodriguez was there a few minutes later, hunched in his wool trench coat, hands jammed deep in the pockets. By the glare of a police tripod light swiftly set up, he eyed her. "Ms. Müller. We meet again. I know there is a lot to go over. We'll need a preliminary statement, but we won't keep you out in this weather long."

"Can I go to Miss Perry? She'll be dying to know what's going on."

"Oh, she knows," he said with a wry chuckle. "Who do you think called us?"

She laughed as the snow suddenly, in one of those weird Michigander shifts in weather temperament, stopped, abruptly, as if it had done its job and could now dissipate. "Her and her binoculars!"

"You can go see her after we talk."

She followed him out to the road and they sat in his car with the heater on. She watched out the window as Haskell, bundled in a parka she had never seen him wear, bounded around, getting in the way and talking to anyone who would listen. The enclosed space in Rodriquez's car smelled of a lavender air freshener and fast food. Rodriguez cranked the heat and directed the stream at Jaymie, warming her until she stopped shivering.

It had occurred to her that the car Haskell saw racing down the road had probably delivered Morgan, Quin and Raider. Maybe they had watched her go in to talk to Miss Perry, and used that time to drag Morgan around to the back. Raider planned to use the young woman to lure Jaymie toward the cliff overlooking the river. That meant there was another accomplice, hopefully one of his gang and not Parker. It was a hastily and poorly planned denouement to end what had been a carefully orchestrated and tightly controlled plot before this night.

That was probably because Jaymie had gotten in Dobbs's way, with her questions and snooping. Quin would have reported Jaymie's rash questioning earlier in the day. Jaymie told the detective about her night, including what Raider had said about the placement of Ethan's body, and finishing with her surmises about why he held Morgan over the edge of the sloping path down to the river. He had been trying to lure Jaymie, so he could kill her down there and dispose of her body.

"I'm not stupid enough now to go toward that kind of danger. At least not without help." She watched the scene outside the car, finally warm again, but still quivering, her body vibrating like a struck tuning fork. "I was *trying* to get my phone to work—darned cold weather made it slow as molasses—when he must have realized I wasn't going to be stupid enough to go toward the screams."

"And that's when he came up the path and you saw them?"

She glanced over at him and nodded. "And saw the danger to Morgan." She finished her tale then fell silent, staring again out at the scene beyond the car. It was a blaze of headlights, flashing light bars atop cruisers, and more lights on ambulances parked willy-nilly around the street. Haskell was now talking to the paramedics, who had finished bandaging Morgan and were loading her into the back of the ambulance to take her to the hospital in Wolverhampton. "I have to go to the hospital," she said suddenly.

Alarmed, Rodriguez said, "Did he hurt you?"

"No, but my mother-in-law is in the hospital, and my father-in-law is there and my husband . . . I want to see my husband." She sobbed and her breath caught, her eyes tearing up. "I *have* to see my husband. He's the o-o-only one who will help me stop sh-shivering."

He regarded her and gently said, "We'll make sure you get there, Jaymie, police escort all the way."

She wept softly for a minute, then mopped her face with the tissue he handed her. "Quin tried to help at the last minute, you know," she said to him, her voice thick. She cleared her throat. "I will give her that. She may have saved Morgan's life."

"Don't waste too much gratitude on her," he said grimly. "It was her insulin that killed Ethan Zarcone."

"I had figured that part out. I recalled her talking about recalibrating her monitor, and she had a little bag she was always putting back in her purse after trips to the restroom. I assume it held her insulin and needles. I was hoping I was wrong."

He was silent. She looked at him and realized what she had said.

"You were right to tell me about all of that, though it seems almost miraculous that you made that leap, that connection." He watched her carefully. "You couldn't possibly know that in post the ME found a puncture in Zarcone's groin."

Jaymie guiltily looked away. She wasn't about to admit to Rodriguez that the chief had told her about the needle mark. Maybe he had already figured it out. She hoped Chief Ledbetter didn't get in trouble.

"You remember you told me what Morgan had said to you, about seeing Quin pass something to someone in the car?" Rodriguez continued.

"Quin told her she was imagining things, and Morgan folded."

"I believe Quin was handing her insulin kit and syringes to Raider, who was driving the car. That is some nerve to give a killer the weapon practically in front of the intended victim. Zarcone was killed with a massive dose of insulin."

She nodded without comment.

He glanced at her, and then away. "When we patted him down we found that he had the kit with him tonight. That was going to be your fate, Jaymie."

She gasped and shuddered. "Thank God for mean cats and Quin's last-minute heroics!"

"Heroics that wouldn't have been necessary if she hadn't helped Dobbs and his crew from the beginning. Morgan would likely have disappeared." He cleared his throat. "So don't pity Quin and what is about to happen to her. When it came down to it, if her efforts to save Morgan hadn't worked, she would ultimately have gone along with Raider."

"Or died herself," Jaymie said.

"Or died herself," the detective agreed. "There is no way out with people like Raider Dobbs."

℘ **Twenty-three** ℘

THIRTY MINUTES LATER JAYMIE GOT TO THE HOSPITAL and found her husband. "Jakob! Oh, Jakob!" Jaymie fell into his open arms.

He buried his face in her neck and held her close, then kissed her cheek, his lips warm against her skin. "They told me what happened. Morgan came in by ambulance. I wish I was there to protect you!" He pressed his forehead to hers and whispered, "Oh, my love, what you have been through!"

He guided her to a sofa in a nook near the elevator. Long minutes followed of kisses, hugs, whispered words of nonsensical comfort. Finally, she extricated herself and stared up into his beautiful brown eyes. "How is your mother?"

"She's good," he said with a deep, relieved sigh. "It *was* her medication. They're figuring out how to get it all balanced. Papa is sitting with her now."

"It's too late to call Jocie. I have to go home, though, and let poor Hoppy out."

"Hey, you two lovebirds." It was Helmut, Jakob's brother.

"You made it through the storm!" Jakob said as he stood. The two men greeted each other in the restrained Müller manner, with hearty handshakes.

"Yeah, I don't know what all the fuss is about," he said with a puzzled frown. "Papa said the same thing. But I drove all that way and didn't go through a single snowstorm."

Such is the wildly unpredictable winter weather of Michigan. It had calmed, so Jakob and Jaymie were able to drive home to Queensville. She let Hoppy out into the fresh snow, he bounded about, piddled, and came right back in. Jaymie's bed had never felt so soft and warm as it was that night as she lay in her husband's arms.

• • •

A lovely Sunday morning together was all the refreshment Jaymie needed to sing her way through her morning tasks. Becca called, and after expressing alarm and shock at what Jaymie told her, she relayed her own news: they were going to be a couple of days late.

London was socked in by a late winter snowstorm of epic proportions from Lake Huron streamers, bands of snow that came off the lake and often targeted London. Once a pattern like that settled in over the city it could dump several feet of snow before it was done. So there was no hurry for the Müllers to exit the Queensville house.

Jakob was walking down to pick up Jocie from her friends' sleepover, which had been a huge success. With their sudden free time, not needing to be out of the house, they were going to stroll over to the Queensville Inn and have Sunday brunch with Mrs. Stubbs. But before that, while Jakob retrieved their daughter, Jaymie had a multitude of tasks to take care of, not the least of which was to feed the cat colony and check in with Miss Perry.

Another trip out there and the routine she was by now used to. The cats circled, hungry and happy to be fed the good stuff, all uneasiness gone after the events of the night before. She gave them extra, doling out canned food in generous amounts. Her phone chimed, and she took it out, checking her messages. Sure, *now* it worked easily outdoors!

It was Rachel texting *call me*. She finished what she was doing, then found a spot in the weak March sun to stand, overlooking the sparkling St. Clair River toward the island, as she turned her back on the view and instead watched the cats gobbling the canned food. Hero, her new name for the tom, was there, eating his fill. She wondered if Raider's skin and blood were still under his claws.

The two friends caught up on what had happened the night before, which Rachel had heard from Chief Ledbetter. Then she said, "I have news. Parker called."

Jaymie gasped. "Seriously? What did he say? What did *you* say?"

"I told him to get his butt back to Queensville from wherever he was, and to check in with the police, or he could stay gone."

"But what did he tell you?"

He had been in the business of smuggling people over the border, he told her, people who, for one reason or another, were not allowed into the United States. Or, as in the case of Raider Dobbs, who simply had their own reasons for not wanting it to be known they had crossed into the U.S.. Dobbs had crossed in early January. Parker had never known the full story. Ethan always told him to shut up and do as Dobbs—"Mr. Bigshot," Parker called him—told them to do. He had since learned that Dobbs had a beef to settle with the Brewer men.

Zarcone had been complaining that Mr. Bigshot wasn't doing what he promised, cutting them in on the bigger deals he was planning, Parker told Rachel. Such complaints would not have gone down well with Dobbs. Though they'd never know the full truth, given Ethan's cocky personality he had likely threatened the gangster with exposure, and that led to his murder. One must watch who one threatened. Ethan was not a killer. Raider Dobbs was.

Jaymie filled in what *she* knew, that Bog was in trouble with the Crimson Skeleton Riders, Dobbs's gang, and his son had been kidnapped because of it. Dobbs likely saw it as a twofer: he could make Bog pay for whatever he had done *and* settle Tolly's longstanding drug debt. If they couldn't get the money from one member of Berk Scouse Brothers, they'd get it from another. Dobbs and his gang had threatened Bog Brewer, who had money enough to ransom his son and pay Tolly's outstanding debt.

"Parker did bring over that guy, Tolly Jones, the one who ended up murdered," Rachel said. But he didn't know Tolly was murdered until he talked to Ethan. Ethan sounded scared, he said, and put him off, saying he'd call him that night, but of course he died. "Parker panicked when he heard about it and took off."

"Parker has a lot of explaining to do," Jaymie said.

"He does indeed, and some of it is to me," she said, her tone grim. "He swears he didn't think it through. He was just doing what Ethan told him to do. He didn't know the people he was bringing over were dangerous."

"Do you believe him?"

"It doesn't matter if I do or not, it's the police he has to answer to. I don't trust him now. He's not who I thought he was."

"I'm sorry, Rach."

"I'll be okay. We weren't serious, you know. Or at least I wasn't. I've only known him a couple of months." Rachel said she had to go, as the shop was getting super busy. "Oh, one more thing. Tansy will let you serve Tansy's butter tarts to folks at the Kitschy Kitchen. Not to sell in half dozens, but to *serve*. At least to start. I'd be happy to do other tea treats too, scones, squares, Napoleons, Victoria sponge . . .

lots of wonderful baked goods!"

"Oh, Rachel, *thank* you!"

Once she was done feeding the cats, Jaymie checked in with Miss Perry, standing in the front hall and talking to the woman, who leaned on her walker. "I don't think I can ever thank you enough for calling the police."

"I was worried when Morgan didn't show up!" the woman said, looking tired but satisfied. "But you can thank Haskell. He called me and said that from his second-floor study he saw someone with a flashlight on the slope beyond the cliff, and I knew *that* wasn't right. You'd *never* go down there in that weather. So I called the police and told them there was going to be a murder at the cat colony where two bodies had been already found if they didn't get there in three minutes." She smiled in satisfaction. "There was a cruiser nearby, so they beat my deadline."

"What if it had been a mistake?" Jaymie said, bemused.

"Then they would have written me off as a batty old woman."

"Miss Perry! You put yourself at risk of not being believed in future."

"Young lady, I am in my nineties, and like my cousin have earned the right to do exactly what I want without lectures from children."

Jaymie laughed and left, wanting to get home. But as she packed her stuff in the car, she saw Bog Brewer pacing in front of his house in boots and a housecoat flapping in the wind, yelling into a cell phone. There was much she still wanted to know.

He looked up as she approached and, with tears in his eyes, waved the phone around. "Just got orf wi' me son and his sweet'art."

"He's been found?"

"Aye. 'Cause o' you, I bin told. That arse, Raider Dobbs . . . 'is mates back 'ome let Alf go and ratted Dobbs out," he said. With a keening wail, Bog lunged at her and wrapped her in a bear hug so hard Jaymie couldn't breathe. "'E's safe, all 'cause o' you! Alfie's girl is gonna 'ave a sprog. I'm gonna be a grandad! We're packin' up and 'eadin' back 'ome next week."

Once he finally let go of her so she could breathe, she congratulated him. She left him smiling and prancing in the new snow like a gibbering but happy idiot. Duckie came out and danced around with him as Berk Scouse Brothers songs blared from the open door. Jaymie smiled all the way back to the house.

Val met them at the Queensville Inn for brunch. They gathered, awaiting Mrs. Stubbs, who Jocie had gone to fetch. Jakob strolled over to the far side of the room to talk to an acquaintance. Val leaned across the table and demanded the whole story. Jaymie told it as succinctly as she could. She then told her friend about the morning call from Rachel, her conversation with Bog, and that their new shop was going to be able to serve the most delicious treats this side of the U.S.-Canada border, Tansy's Tarts butter tarts.

"You've crowned the whole tale with the most important part," Val joked. "But I also have some news for you, something Brock told me in confidence. I know a lot more now about what was going on with Stowe House. Raider Dobbs was pulling a con of some sophistication. Brock and I did a little research."

"Do tell," Jaymie replied.

"It's called property title theft." Val explained. Con artists sought out specific vacant or rental properties, ones that were not watched over closely. "According to Brock, there is a two-step process to property title theft, first, stealing an identity—"

"That of Fitzroy Jones, in this case, which is why once Tolly Jones came to the U.S., he had to die—"

"Right, because Tolly would have exposed the fake Fitzroy immediately, whereas Bog knew he *had* to go along with the ruse or endanger his son."

"Ah, yes, and that is what caused all the tension between Bog and his wife. I'll bet she wanted to go to the police, but he was afraid to."

"Dobbs stole Fitzroy's identity," Val said. "And then posed as a legitimate purchaser. He had the fake paperwork with Daniel's forged signature showing he had bought the house for cash. Dobbs had learned that of all the houses available for sale in Queensville, Stowe House was the best bet because Daniel Collins hadn't been back to check on his property in more than a year. He had a property manager, but that guy was gone to Florida with half of the rest of Michigan."

"But he didn't know that I know Daniel quite well and have his cell number. He looked surprised when I told the fake Fitzroy that I once dated a millionaire."

"Right you are! He went to the bank to take out a mortgage on the property, saying that though he had bought the property outright, he still needed the mortgage money for renovations he was planning. That is a vast oversimplification of what happened, and I don't pretend to understand the whole mechanism, but you get the drift. It is a common occurrence for people to borrow against equity for renovation money."

"It all makes sense." Jaymie drank the last dregs of her coffee and sat back. "So does this mean that Matt Zarcone was *not* in on it?"

Val shrugged. "Why don't you ask his mother?" She nodded over at the door, where Gabriella Zarcone stood, glanced around.

Jaymie crossed the room and said hello. The woman whirled.

"I was looking for you. Your . . . whoever that odd woman is that works at your sister's shop?"

"You mean Georgina?" Jaymie stifled a chuckle. "She's not odd, she's just English."

"She told me you were here. Can we talk?"

Jaymie led her to a dimly lit alcove beyond the dining room. They sat on a bench, the sounds of the restaurant a soft babble in the background. "How are you doing?" Jaymie asked her.

"A little better," the woman said. She sniffed and took a tissue out of her purse. "This cold is hanging on, I don't know why. I never get sick, but right now it seems I'm sick all the time."

"Maybe it's how your grief is coming out? It's lowering your immune system," Jaymie suggested gently. "I don't mean to be presumptuous, Gabriella, but you've been through an awful time. Maybe you should get grief counseling or join a group for mothers who have lost children to violent crime. I know Ethan wasn't a child—"

"But he was *my* child," she said. "Olivia suggested the same thing. I'll think about it."

They spoke for a few minutes. Gabriella expressed how relieved she was that the killer had been arrested. "I can't believe that witch Quin was involved. She was supposed to be Ethan's friend, his business associate, he told me."

In a business that was illegal, Jaymie thought, but didn't say. No point in rubbing salt in an open wound. The detective had speculated in their interview that Ethan was trying to get Raider Dobbs to cut him in on the real estate con, but Dobbs was not having it.

"I have something else to thank you for, though. In bringing this all to light you may have saved my Matthew from a big mistake. He told me this in confidence, and said I could say it to you but no one else. That fellow — I don't know what to call him —"

"Raider Dobbs?"

Gabriella nodded. "He came in to the bank and was trying to get a mortgage on that historic home in the middle of Queensville, do you know it?"

"I do," Jaymie said. "Stowe House." She explained her connection and how she knew what Dobbs was up to.

"Matt was examining the paperwork. It appeared real, he says. He would have done a few more background checks, but if it all looked good, he *may* have issued the huge renovation loan — a quarter of a million dollars — to that killer if he hadn't been exposed in the nick of time."

"What the guy was doing is called property title theft. I didn't know about it until now. So, Matt didn't know Dobbs before that?"

"Not in the slightest. Matthew said the guy told him . . ." She looked away into a dark corner. Her voice clogged, she murmured, "The guy told Matthew he knew Ethan as a business acquaintance. Ethan had told him to go to his brother, he said, and that Ethan would vouch for him. I don't know if it's true."

Jaymie saw the difficulty. If it was true, then Ethan was willing to cheat his own brother by sending a con man to abuse his trust. "What do *you* think?"

"I don't know. It has become evident to me lately that I had rose-tinted glasses on when it came to Ethan. He was far from perfect, but still, he was my boy." She stared into Jaymie's eyes, her own watery, glittering with unshed tears. "I'll never stop loving him, or missing him," she said with a trace of defiance. "I'm grateful that his killer is behind bars."

• • •

Brunch was delicious and fun. But it was Sunday, and that was family day. After walking Hoppy, Jaymie sat with Jocie, who did her homework at the table in the kitchen.

"Mom?"

"Yes, baby?" Jaymie said, looking up from her laptop. She was writing the copy for her next "Vintage Eats" column.

"Remember we were talking about how the cat colony was going to have to be moved? That the cats that could be adopted should, but that there might be some that would never be adopted?"

"I do."

"I have an idea." Her pretty brown eyes held a serious expression. "I read about a program called Working Cats."

"Working cats? What does that mean?"

"It's for cats that are too wild to adopt, the ones that wouldn't be happy living in a house. It adopts them out to farmers and stable owners. The cats earn their keep hunting mice and rats, while the humans give them food and a warm place to live." She paused.

"And you know someone who could help?" Jaymie had a feeling where this was going.

"I was thinking of Emma and Dani," she said. "I know Emma would be interested and will help us find farmers who will give feral kitties a home."

"You've really thought this through. That is a fabulous idea."

"Mrs. Stubbs said she'd teach me to crochet, and that I can start with something small, like catnip mice for Lilibet! Oma has a patch of catnip near the house and dries some every fall. I could use that. I was thinking, maybe I can make enough and sell them and raise money to help support the cat colony as we get the Working Cats program going!"

Jaymie smiled, a little teary eyed. "Sweetie, you're a marvel. Hey, I have an idea! There is a whole bunch of wild colored balls of yarn at the Knit Knack Shack. I was going to donate them to a local agency, but maybe you can take a few and use them to crochet the catnip mice! Once you're done with your homework, why don't you write up a proposal. We'll compose an email to Emma and Dani. Do you want to go out with me and feed the cats!"

"Can I?" Jocie bounced in her seat.

"You can. Let's get ready."

⚥ Twenty-four ⚥

THERE WAS MOST DEFINITELY A THAW GOING ON, JAYMIE THOUGHT as she emerged from Queensville Fine Antiques into spring-like sunshine after having a morning coffee there with Becca. Most of the snow was gone now, with puddles remaining in low spots and on the roads. The sunshine was getting stronger; you could feel the warmth when you turned your face up to it.

It was late March. Becca and Kevin had been back for a week. Everyone was getting together for a little party with the Müller family in another couple of days. Val and her beau were coming, and so was Heidi and her handsome veterinarian, Dr. Kasimo, who Jocie had a giant crush on. Jakob's parents were both doing a lot better, but would not be coming to the party, preferring to stick close to home for the time being.

Spring Break was almost upon them. Jaymie, Jakob and Jocie would be driving down to Boca Raton to spend a week with Jaymie's parents.

She was just putting her hand on the car door when her phone chimed. It was a text from Brock. *Jaymie, meet me at Stowe House.*

Okay, that was odd. A text, from Brock? She knew the name of the real owner of Stowe House, of course, but she had been a little shy to approach him. So she had asked Brock his opinion on the best way to ask permission to hold the tea event there. He hadn't replied to her query yet. Maybe he had news.

She drove over to Stowe House. Brock was standing on the porch with Daniel Collins and a gentleman Jaymie immediately recognized as Nigel Charles Dudley. As she walked along the path toward them she examined the gentleman closely. He wore a navy pea coat with a blue and green tartan scarf knotted at the neck, and shiny black boots. He was older, with silvery sandy hair, probably in his sixties, but fit and square-shouldered, with bright blue eyes, his gaze darting to all the windows and gingerbread of the house. His expression was of absolute delight.

After introductions all around, Dudley asked if he could speak to her for a moment.

When she assented, he took her arm and strolled along the porch with her, looking out over the enormous swath of lawn. He released her as he turned and said, "I understand you're coordinating an event normally held here every Victoria Day."

"You know of the holiday weekend?"

"My dear, I am a transplanted Canadian. From Toronto. Well, Hamilton, but no American except those in Buffalo knows where Hamilton is, so I say Toronto."

She explained the Tea with the Queen event, and what it supported, and how important Stowe House was. She spoke of her own Canadian ties, and how much she enjoyed serving at the tea. She talked about the Dickens Days festival every December. He listened with rapt attention and sparkling blue eyes.

"That sounds magnificent," he said, clasping his hands to his chest. "I would adore it if you would continue the tradition at Stowe House. I won't say indefinitely, but *maybe* indefinitely."

"Oh, thank you, sir! I mean, Mr. Dudley!"

"Call me Nigel. We're going to have to work together." He turned and surveyed the house with a critical glare. "The crook who tried to steal the title was right about one thing, there is much that needs to be done before then." He half turned back, gazing at her over his shoulder. "I do have one proviso. I hope it won't be a sticking point."

She felt a qualm. What was he going to ask for? "And that is . . . ?"

"I would like to be master of ceremonies." He fully turned toward her and took her hands in his own. "I want to dress up as Prince Albert, and escort Queen Vicky."

"Uh, our Queen Victoria is definitely the queen when she is, like, eighty. You're a little young for her, and she was a widow for a long time by that point. Prince Albert only lived to be . . ." She saw the trap of trying to guess his age, and stopped, letting the sentence linger unfinished.

"I know, I know. I'm *far* too old to be Prince Albert." He smiled, his eyes sparkling with good humor. "However, as long as I don a dashing mustache, will anyone care about historical accuracy?"

Jaymie grinned. "Gosh, no! I see you already have us pegged as the most historically inaccurate event on the face of the earth. Nobody will care, not in the slightest."

"Then that's settled. I shall be master of ceremonies, opening and closing the event. May I meet my queen?"

"Oh, you'll meet them," Jaymie said, eyes wide.

"Them?"

"Yes, *them*. There are *two* Queens Victoria. It's a long story, which I will tell you if you'll join me for tea at the Queensville Inn. I'll make arrangements and you can meet your queens, as well as Mrs. Stubbs, who is my most important supporter. They'll all love you."

"Good. That, too, is settled, and tea sounds divine. I'm going to be here a few days. Can we meet to begin strategizing the event? Our styles of organizing may be different. I'm devotedly hands-on, and I . . ." He faltered. "I *desperately* need something to occupy me."

She frowned. He sounded sad. "Perfect. Mr. . . . uh, Nigel. I don't mind saying I will take all the help you can give me."

He eyed her with one raised brow. "Are you willing to appear on my little video show online as we make our plans?"

"We can talk about that," she said with a smile.

They descended from the porch, looked up at Stowe House, and at the same time sighed in happiness. Jaymie glanced at her new partner in the tea event. "This is going to be fun."

✄ Vintage Eats ✄

by Jaymie Leighton Müller

Sometimes simple is simply the best.

Do you need a dessert recipe that is fit for all ages, easy to make, with few and on-hand ingredients? Then rice pudding, like its cousin bread pudding, will come to your rescue.

I found this recipe in my grandmother's handwriting from when she was a new bride. The page was spotted with splashes of vanilla and butter, so I know she made this a lot, and I think I even remember it, the smell of spicy and sugary goodness filling the kitchen! I've altered it slightly, because at the last minute I discovered I didn't have any raisins in the kitchen I happened to be cooking in, which was not my country cabin kitchen.

Old-Fashioned Baked Rice Pudding

Makes: Many servings! Great for a family potluck.
Prep time: fifteen minutes
Cooking time: one hour

1–1½ cups sugar (add the larger amount if you prefer it sweeter)
¼ teaspoon nutmeg
½ teaspoon cinnamon
3 large eggs
2 tablespoons butter, melted
1 teaspoon vanilla extract
½ teaspoon salt
2 cups whole milk
3 cups cooked rice (I used jasmine rice, a fragrant long-grain rice, for this pudding, as the long-grain rices hold their structure best. You can experiment. Basmati would hold up well, while arborio and other short-grain rices would make a thicker pudding, with less rice structure. Probably not what you're going for.)
¾ cup dried cranberries (This was my emergency substitute. Traditionally, you would use raisins, but I didn't have any, and I did have dried cranberries left from Christmas baking.)

Preheat oven to 325 degrees. Grease a three-quart/liter casserole dish or a nine-by-thirteen-inch baking dish with butter and set aside.

Whisk sugar, nutmeg, and cinnamon together and set aside.

In a large mixing bowl, add eggs and beat well. A fork will do, or a wire whisk. Add the sugar, nutmeg and cinnamon mixture and whisk again. Add melted butter, vanilla, and salt and whisk until smooth.

Add ½ cup of the whole milk and whisk, then the remaining milk, and whisk again until blended. Stir in the rice and dried cranberries and pour into the prepared casserole or baking dish.

Bake for 30 minutes, then stir from the bottom to distribute fruit and rice evenly throughout the pudding. Bake for another 30 minutes *or until set*. Grate a little nutmeg over the finished dish and serve warm plain, or with whipped cream or your favorite topping.

Note: my oven may be a little slow. Despite the timing in the original old recipe, mine needed to be stirred again, and then put in the oven for another ten minutes at 350 degrees to get it to set as much as I wanted. Use your judgment and know your oven!

Refrigerate the leftovers. When you'd like some more, scoop it into a bowl and microwave it, then add some cream or whipped cream . . . yum!

This is a great dessert for that Sunday when the family is gathered and you need something easy and pleasing for every taste. It's ideal for that still-cold late winter/early spring weather when you need something warm and nourishing for the body and soul.

Let me know how you and your friends and family enjoyed this delish treat!

✄ About the Author ✄

Victoria Hamilton is the pseudonym of nationally bestselling romance author Donna Lea Simpson. Victoria is the bestselling author of three mystery series, the Lady Anne Addison Mysteries, the Vintage Kitchen Mysteries, and the Merry Muffin Mysteries.

Victoria loves to read, especially mystery novels, and enjoys good tea and cheap wine, the company of friends, and has a newfound appreciation for opera. She enjoys crocheting and beading, but a good book can tempt her away from almost anything . . . except writing!

Visit Victoria at www.victoriahamiltonmysteries.com.

Made in United States
North Haven, CT
10 March 2025

66601342R00138